THE
THIRTEENTH
CIRCLE

THE
THIRTEENTH
CIRCLE

MARCYKATE CONNOLLY
AND KATHRYN HOLMES

Feiwel and Friends
New York

A Feiwel and Friends Book
An imprint of Macmillan Publishing Group, LLC
120 Broadway, New York, NY 10271 · mackids.com

Our books may be purchased in bulk for promotional, educational, or
business use. Please contact your local bookseller or the Macmillan Corporate
and Premium Sales Department at (800) 221-7945 ext. 5442 or by email at
MacmillanSpecialMarkets@macmillan.com.

Library of Congress Cataloging-in-Publication Data
Names: Connolly, MarcyKate, author. | Holmes, Kathryn, author.
Title: The thirteenth circle / MarcyKate Connolly and Kathryn Holmes.
Other titles: 13th circle
Description: First edition. | New York : Feiwel and Friends, 2024. | Audience:
    Ages 9–12. | Audience: Grades 4–6. | Summary: Seventh-grader Cat partners with
    Dani to study crop circles, but Dani secretly aims to disprove Cat's theory, and
    during their investigations they discover a dangerous rival also seeking answers who
    will stop at nothing to achieve their goal.
Identifiers: LCCN 2023028867 | ISBN 9781250891594 (hardcover)
Subjects: CYAC: Friendship—Fiction. | Extraterrestrial beings—Fiction. | Science—
    Fiction. | LCGFT: Novels.
Classification: LCC PZ7.1.C64685 Th 2024 | DDC [Fic]—dc23
LC record available at https://lccn.loc.gov/2023028867

First edition, 2024
Book design by L. Whitt and Maria W. Jenson
Feiwel and Friends logo designed by Filomena Tuosto
Printed in the United States of America by Lakeside Book Company,
Harrisonburg, Virginia

ISBN 978-1-250-89159-4 (hardcover)
ISBN 978-1-250-89161-7 (paperback)
10 9 8 7 6 5 4 3 2 1

To Gillian Anderson and David Duchovny—
for making us want to believe

DANI

THERE WAS AN ALIEN in Cat Mulvaney's bedroom.

That's what Dani thought in the split second before she realized that the alien was *Cat*. The other girl was wearing enormous safety goggles that magnified her eyes, making her look like an insect. She had a striped scarf covering her nose and mouth, but it had slipped down just enough for the pale freckled skin on the bridge of her nose to peek out. Her hair was tucked up under a ratty gray knit cap, but some frizzy blond strands had escaped to stick out sideways. Her hands were encased in yellow rubber gloves, and she wore a coat that was olive green, puffy, and about four sizes too big.

Cat caught Dani staring and pulled the scarf away from her face. "You're here! Welcome!"

Dani entered Cat's attic lair. That was really the only way to describe it: Her bedroom was like a mad scientist, a conspiracy theorist, and a detective had opened an interior-decorating business. One wall was papered with pictures of UFOs and imaginary creatures, like the Loch Ness Monster. Another had a giant map of the United States, dotted with pushpins and crisscrossed with multicolored strings. The ceiling was painted black, with tons of those stick-on glow-in-the-dark stars arranged into patterns that looked, to Dani's somewhat-knowledgeable eyes, astronomically accurate. There was an overflowing bookshelf, a desk with some lab equipment Dani didn't know seventh graders could even have at home, and a fancy telescope poking out of one window.

"Cool, right?" Cat beamed at the way Dani's eyes jumped from one strange thing to the next. "I moved up here a couple of years ago. It's still a work in progress. My mom doesn't care what I do with the space, as long as I don't burn down the house."

"Oh," Dani said. Her bedroom had a quaint seaside sunrise theme. Dani's mom was an artist and had picked out bedding, curtains, a rug, and lampshades to match two of her own paintings. The only thing in the room that felt like *Dani*—besides the science texts piled around the desk—was the periodic table of the elements Dani had found at Goodwill last year. Since it was done in watercolors and complemented the overall color scheme, her mom had let her put it up.

"Is that my doorknob?" Cat asked, pointing.

Dani looked down at her hand. "Yeah. It, um . . . came off?"

"It does that." Cat turned back to her desk, where a brown goo was bubbling in a glass beaker over a gas flame. She used a pipette to squeeze a drop of blue liquid into the mixture and then jotted something down on a notepad.

Dani still couldn't believe she was in Cat Mulvaney's house. Cat was the designated school weirdo. She seemed nice enough, but she and Dani were not friends. They were partners—by default. Dani and Cat were the only two kids in their middle school who had applied to compete for this year's McMurray Youth Science Award. Dani had tried to convince each of her best friends to join her, but they'd all said no . . . and so here she was.

As she watched Cat conduct her experiment, Dani felt her heart begin to rise. Cat clearly knew her way around a Bunsen burner.

Then the other girl said, "I suspect a haunting."

"A haunting?" Dani repeated faintly.

"The doorknob," Cat explained. "My tests have all come back negative, but that doesn't mean there isn't a paranormal presence here. I mean, this house is two hundred years old."

Dani's heart fell back down to the pit of her stomach. "You believe in ghosts?"

"Of course. There's a lot of evidence that supports—Ack!" The gooey substance in the glass beaker had begun to smoke. Cat rushed to put out the flame. "You jinxed me!" she joked. "I said that thing about Mom not wanting me to burn down the house and then . . . well, look."

While Cat fanned gross-smelling plumes out the open window, Dani took a closer look at the map on the wall. Each pushpin had a date written next to it, plus some letters and symbols. Dani had no clue what any of it meant.

When the air had cleared, Cat pushed her safety goggles up onto her forehead. The thick plastic had left a deep red groove around both eyes and across her nose. "Anyway, thanks for coming over to talk about our project," she said, rubbing furiously at her face.

"Thanks for inviting me," Dani said. "I brought a list of ideas. You have our registration packet, right?" Dani had been home sick all of last week, but she'd made sure to check in with Ms. Blanks, their science teacher and contest sponsor. The McMurray Competition was too important to not have all their ducks in a row.

"Ms. Blanks gave me our packet, yes . . . ," Cat said slowly.

Dani pulled a piece of paper from her bag and unfolded it, smoothing out the creases. "We could test for contaminants in the reservoir. Like, is there runoff from the Bug-Be-Gone plant that's affecting the water quality? I also thought a plant study in the Hill-dale Marsh could be—"

"Actually," Cat interrupted, "we're all set."

"All set?" Dani's pulse sputtered. "What do you mean?"

"I already submitted our proposal. Don't worry. You're gonna love it." Cat peeled off her rubber gloves and shrugged out of her coat. Underneath, she wore faded jeans and a tie-dyed T-shirt with a picture of a space alien wearing aviator shades. She started doing a drumroll on her desk. "For the tenth annual McMurray Youth Science Competition, we will be investigating . . ."

Not ghosts, Dani thought desperately. *Anything but ghosts!*

"The Weston Farm Circles!" Cat finished, making jazz hands for emphasis.

If Dani's heart had been in her stomach before, now it was in her feet. "No," she said.

"Yes," Cat said back.

To be fair to Cat, it was exactly the kind of thing Dani had expected her partner to propose. Cat had an alien on her T-shirt, aliens on her bedroom walls, and a bumper sticker on her door that read, "Aliens are real—just ask Bigfoot!" Little green men were her thing. Thus: designated school weirdo. But that's why Dani had come up with a list of awesome project ideas herself. Every one of her proposals was a potential winner.

And the Weston Farm Circles?

Every thirteen years, their tiny town became a tiny bit famous. What happened at Weston Farm was the reason why. "Everyone knows the circles are fake," Dani said. "There's nothing to investigate. Anyway, the McMurray is a *science* award."

Cat looked wounded. "Confirming the existence of extraterrestrial life is scientific. It's my life's work."

What was Dani supposed to say to a girl who genuinely believed aliens visited their small town every thirteen years to leave fancy patterns in a field?

Maybe Ms. Blanks could petition the McMurray committee to let Dani enter the competition on her own, even though the projects were supposed to be done in pairs. Dani knew she was one of Ms. Blanks's favorite students. Science was her best subject. And winning this award . . . well, it would mean everything.

Along with the trophy, McMurray winners received a full scholarship to a six-week summer science camp, ScienceU, held at one of the state's top universities. Dani was desperate to attend ScienceU. But her parents ran an arts day camp here in town, and every time she asked to do something else, they pointed out that the best—and cheapest—option was right here. If Dani won a full scholarship to ScienceU, they couldn't say it was too expensive. They would have to let her go.

She would be the best student ScienceU had ever seen. They'd offer her a full scholarship for the next summer and the next. And then nothing like the Dance of Doom would ever happen again.

The lights flickered.

Cat squealed with excitement. "It's beginning!" She lowered her voice so it was deep and serious. "There are signs before the circles. Power surges. Strange lights in the sky. Other unexplainable phenomena."

Dani scoffed. "There are plenty of explanations for lights flickering. You said your house is two hundred years old. I bet you blow fuses constantly."

"Nope," Cat said. "Dad paid to have an electrician update everything a few years ago."

The lights flickered again.

And again.

And again, four more times.

"Explain *that*," Cat said triumphantly.

"Um." To be honest, Dani was out of theories. Electrical stuff wasn't her area of expertise.

But she knew it wasn't aliens.

"It's a sign." Cat pulled out an oversize desk calendar and drew a big red X beside today's date. "The first sign. There's more coming. Just you wait."

"Well, it's getting late," Dani said, backing toward the stairs. "I should probably—"

"No way." Cat spun around. "We're going on a field trip."

"My parents want me home for dinner—"

"This won't take long. I have to show you something."

Dani sighed. "What is it?"

"A surprise." Cat wiggled her eyebrows.

"I have a lot of homework . . . ," Dani tried.

"This has to do with our project. It counts as homework." Cat thrust a heavy backpack into Dani's arms. "You rode your bike, right? Can you carry this? We aren't going far." She slung a second backpack over her own shoulders and headed for the stairs.

Dani hesitated, looking again at the UFO photos on the wall and the stars on the ceiling. Arguing with Cat felt like being blown along by a gust of wind.

"Fine," she finally said. "But only this once."

2

CAT

DANI WILLIAMS WAS NOT what Cat had expected. She didn't know her very well, of course, but in class she'd always seemed to be a hardworking student, genuinely interested in science.

Turned out, she was also kind of a complainer.

They were only riding their bikes a little less than a mile from Cat's house. And Dani wasn't even carrying the heaviest equipment.

Some people just didn't have the drive to go the extra mile for research.

But Cat wasn't about to let that get her down. If her calculations were correct—and they almost always were—she had quite the surprise in store for Dani.

"Where are we going again?" Dani asked for the third time. Cat sighed and brushed away the hair that kept slipping out from under her knit cap.

"The power substation. It's just up this hill." The road began to take a steep incline.

Dani groaned. "Why is it so important we go there *now*? My parents won't be thrilled that I'm out here alone, now that it's getting dark." She eyed the woods on either side of the road.

"Well, you're not alone. I'm here, too, and I know this path like the back of my hand. It's a safe neighborhood. My mom can vouch for that." Cat smiled. "As for why . . . you'll see. Five minutes after we get there, give or take. We'll have just enough time to set up the equipment."

They rode up the hill, Cat's adrenaline pumping. She was beyond excited to be participating in the McMurray Youth Science Competition for the first time. It was only open to grades seven through twelve, and each school in the state could send two projects per grade level. The contest was sponsored by the McMurray Corporation, which did pharmaceutical research, and the judges were always leaders in their various scientific fields.

No seventh-grade team had ever won the Grades Seven to Nine category. Cat planned to be the first.

But to Cat, this project was about so much more than just a science fair or even a scholarship to science camp. She *knew* aliens existed, and she wanted to prove it. Her dad was a scientist at NASA, and he lived for his work. Which was why he didn't live with them anymore. He had the coolest job in the world. For her tenth birthday, he had taken Cat to the NASA facility where the Apollo 11 mission control had been. She'd even had the chance to say a very nervous hello to one of the astronauts on the International Space Station. It was the best birthday ever.

Of course, that was before he moved to Houston permanently. Now he seemed to have trouble remembering her birthday at all. Cat wasn't sure he'd remember Christmas if it weren't for all the carols and trees and twinkly lights. That would change if she could discover something meaningful. Her dad had once told her that it wasn't a question of whether aliens existed—it was a question of when humans would make contact.

She'd made that her mantra: not *if* but *when*.

Her dad had given her all the tools she needed. When he lived here, he'd shown her how to use a microscope and how to run an experiment properly, with control samples that remained the same so they could be compared to test samples. He'd taught her algebra long before it was in the school curriculum. She'd loved it then and she loved it now. That's why she sometimes liked to wear his old coat while she worked in her lab. It reminded her of what she was fighting for.

She and Dani reached the top of the hill. They were greeted by an electrical substation. Power lines fed into the transformers inside the gated-off area.

Dani placed her bag of equipment on the ground. She looked uneasy.

Cat laughed. "We're not breaking in, if that's what you're worried about." She began unzipping bags and setting up the equipment with gusto. She'd brought along her handheld oscilloscope—a device that could measure electrical voltages—as well as recording equipment and a camera with a tripod that she'd rigged to shoot every three seconds. If something interesting appeared in addition to what she was expecting, she wanted to be ready.

"What is all this stuff?"

"The oscilloscope will detect any power spikes or other electrical anomalies," she said as she connected the device. "This baby over here will record the data we're collecting, and I always bring a camera. And binoculars." Cat patted the ones hanging around her neck. "I like to be prepared."

"Where did you get it all?" Dani asked—with a hint of jealousy.

"My dad." Cat began to unpack the tripod and checked her watch. Two minutes to showtime. "He works at NASA."

Now Dani looked *really* jealous.

Cat clicked the camera on, then brushed off the grass clinging to her knees. From where they stood on the hill, they could see the entire town spread out before them. The streetlamps glowed at regular intervals. The electrical lines crisscrossed the roads and lawns. Above them, the stars and moon shone clearly in the quickly darkening sky. Cat's heart raced. She couldn't have asked for a more perfect night.

"Ready?"

"For what?" Dani folded her arms across her chest.

Cat didn't need to answer.

Dani gaped as a black wave descended on the town. One by one, the lights went out, the darkness racing toward the hill where Cat and Dani stood. Behind them, something snapped, and sparks flew from the transformer. Both girls yelped and jumped sideways a couple of feet.

Then Cat pumped her fist in the air. "Yes! I knew it!"

Dani seemed a little shaken but also like she was trying to play it cool. "What's so special about a power outage?"

"For one, you're forgetting to ask the most important question." Cat tilted her head to the sky, binoculars glued to her face. "How did I know *when* it would happen?"

"How *did* you know?" Dani asked a little reluctantly.

"I've studied the previous Weston Farm Circle occurrences, of course. The first circles always show up in October. Before the circles, there's a series of lights that appear over the mountains on the horizon. Then, one hundred and thirteen hours after the last orbs disappear, plus or minus a couple of minutes . . . voilà!" Cat gestured grandly at the darkness that had fallen over their town. "The flickering you saw earlier was just a warm-up. This is the real deal."

"So whoever is behind the hoax has a pattern?" Dani asked.

Cat groaned. "It's not a hoax. The same thing happens every thirteen years like clockwork. Anyway, this substation and the one on the other side of town are both blown out right now, thanks to a power surge." She lowered her voice and looked away from her binoculars for a moment. "Between you and me, I suspect it's caused by the presence of alien ships disrupting the atmosphere, but I'm still working on proving that part."

Dani blinked. "Are we done here?"

"Not yet! I'm still collecting data. Plus, this is a great opportunity to watch the skies for any anomalies without the extra light pollution—"

Cat cut herself off as the sound of men's voices echoed behind them and the glint of flashlights bounced off the substation.

"Shoot!" Cat hissed. "Help me pack this up!"

They put away Cat's equipment, much faster than she'd taken it out to set up. Cat hoped nothing got damaged—but better damaged than confiscated.

They hopped on their bikes and were careering down the

hill as the people behind the lights appeared. They yelled after them, but Cat and Dani didn't stop until they reached Cat's house, breathless. Cat was laughing from the exhilaration.

Dani was not.

"We're not allowed to be up there, are we?"

Cat shrugged. "It's no big deal. I do it all the time."

"So the KEEP OUT sign was just a suggestion?"

"More of a guideline, really. We were just outside the station on the hill. It's fair use, I swear!"

Dani gave Cat a skeptical look as she gently set the equipment bag on the driveway. "I really do have to get home now. Sorry."

Dani seemed a lot more relieved than sorry to Cat, but that was all right. Cat had expected some resistance. It only made her more determined to convince her classmate that the crop circles were the real deal.

This was Cat's specialty and her life's work. She was up to the challenge.

3

DANI

"THERE YOU ARE!" DANI'S mom was waiting outside when Dani rode up. "I was worried! Did your cell phone stop working when the power went out?"

Dani got off her bike and removed her helmet, wiping sweat from her forehead. "I didn't check my phone," she admitted. "I was pretty focused on getting home for dinner."

The ride back from Cat's house had been eerie. Normally, the streetlamps would've been on. Normally, the houses would've been lit up. Instead, Dani had seen flickering candles in windows and wavy flashlight beams in yards as her eyes adjusted to the growing dusk.

"Speaking of dinner," Dani's mom said, holding the front door open, "I'd just put the baked ziti in the oven when we lost power. So we're having Leftover Surprise instead."

Leftover Surprise, aka eat whatever you can find in the fridge before it goes bad. Dani tried to remember what had been in there when she left for school this morning: some fruit and yogurt, fried rice from when they'd ordered Chinese takeout two nights ago, the heel ends of a loaf of sandwich bread . . . hmm.

None of it sounded appetizing. What *did* sound appetizing was baked ziti.

She wondered how long the blackout would last. If Cat really had predicted the timing, could she also have predicted the duration? Dani supposed she could text the other girl to ask . . . but what if Cat took the text message as confirmation that Dani had decided to work together?

No, better to limit contact until after Dani had asked Ms. Blanks about doing a solo project.

And as for the teensy-weensy inkling of curiosity Dani felt about Cat's methods, well, that would go away once Dani had a project of her own to tackle.

A proper project. An *award-winning* project.

Ten minutes later, as she sat down at the candlelit dining room table with her parents, the lights came back on.

"Hooray!" her mom cheered, raising her turkey-and-cheese sandwich into the air.

Dani's dad tapped the sandwich with his Tupperware of cold fried rice, like they were making a toast. "Now I can get back to my keyboard." Dani's dad was in a band, The Pop Rocks. All the members were dads who used to be in rock bands before they had kids and settled down.

He started to stand up.

"Not so fast," Dani's mom said. "Let's at least spend a few minutes together as a family. Dani, how was school today?"

"Fine." Dani took a bite of yogurt and strawberries, wishing it was cheesy, tomatoey pasta.

"You can do better than 'fine,'" her mom said.

"Um. It was interesting?" Dani tried.

"Interesting how?" her dad asked.

"Well, in science, Ms. Blanks's Fact of the Day was about roof gardens. Did you know that green roofs can increase biodiversity in urban areas by providing habitats for wildlife? And a green roof collects stormwater. Also, there's this thing called carbon sequestration—"

"We're not putting a garden on the roof, sweetheart," Dani's dad said.

"Though it would be pretty," her mom mused.

"I wasn't talking about *our* roof," Dani said testily, and her mom gave her a look. "Sorry, but you asked what was interesting about my day, and it was roof gardens."

It wasn't a surprise to Dani that her parents couldn't see what was so cool about Ms. Blanks's Fact of the Day. Her family wasn't made up of *facts* people. They were *feelings* people. Artists. Her mom was a painter. Her dad was a musician. Her older sister, Mallory, was a dance major in college.

Then there was Dani, who wanted to be a scientist.

No one in her family got it.

But there was one grown-up in her life who did: Dani's science teacher.

Ms. Blanks had shown up three-quarters of the way through the last school year, after moving to their area from Michigan or Minnesota or Mississippi or some other state that began with *M*. She wasn't one of the cool teachers. She dressed in khaki pants and solid pastel button-down shirts. The only accessories she wore were silky scarves, always in a muted color that went with her blouse. She was white, with grayish-brownish shoulder-length hair and grayish-brownish eyes. On the surface, there was nothing remarkable about her.

But when she talked about science, she came alive. Her voice rang with passion and authority during lectures about cell structure. She glowed when explaining natural selection. During the first week of school, she'd gotten so worked up about a pair of symbiotic insects that had recently been discovered in the Brazilian rain forest that she'd started crying.

Science made Dani come alive, too. Science made the world make sense. At the same time, it made everything feel even more mysterious and wondrous. When Ms. Blanks had wept about symbiotic insects, Dani had been a little embarrassed for her, sure—but she'd also felt understood.

Dani was good at science. She was *great* at it.

If she wanted to win the McMurray Award and get the scholarship to ScienceU, a research project on the Weston Farm Circles wasn't going to cut it. It was that simple.

"I didn't know you were interested in gardening," Dani's mom said.

"That's not—"

"It's good to hear you thinking about extracurriculars. Your father and I actually wanted to talk to you about something."

Dani groaned. "Not again."

"I know camp was a little rough this year—"

"A little rough?" Dani yelped.

"But the show must go on," her mom continued.

"That's right," her dad chimed in. "You'll find your niche. We believe in you."

"I have found my niche," Dani said. "That's why I entered the McMurray Competition."

Her mom blinked. "The what?"

"The McMurray Youth Science Competition."

"McMurdo?" her dad said.

"*McMurray*," Dani stressed. "Though you're kind of close. McMurdo is a scientific research facility in Antarctica." Just last week, Ms. Blanks had been telling their class about the experiments scientists from around the world were running down there, at the very bottom of the globe. Stuff like analyzing ice-core samples and measuring snowmelt and tagging penguins.

Her dad furrowed his eyebrows. "I showed a house to a client last month, and the seller's last name was McMurdo. Or Murdoch?"

Dani bit her tongue and forged ahead. "The science fair is on November eleventh. I already put it in your calendars."

"Well, you know we'll be there," Dani's mom said, "but that doesn't mean you can slack off in other areas." She switched to her lecturing voice. "Creativity is a muscle. Just as exercise is good for the body, creative pursuits keep the brain and the soul healthy."

"Blah, blah, blah," Dani muttered, her mind filling with images she'd rather forget.

As a little kid, she'd loved her parents' camp, ArtistiKids. There were sing-alongs and crafts and, best of all, no pressure. But as she'd gotten older, she'd sensed her parents—and their artsy friends—watching her. Waiting. Wondering.

Unlike her mom, Dani wasn't a gifted painter. Unlike her dad, she couldn't carry a tune. Unlike her older sister, she had two left feet.

The camp's offerings had expanded as her parents tried to figure out what Dani *was* good at. This past summer, they'd tried set design. Her parents had hired the high school drama teacher to stage a short original musical, bringing together the actors, the musicians, the dancers, the visual artists . . . and Dani. They'd told Dani she would be a "theatrical engineer."

Yes, this showed that they'd been listening when she'd begged to go to ScienceU. And yes, there did turn out to be a little bit of math involved. But mostly she'd spent the summer hammering nails and carrying props. It was boring, but it could've been worse.

Then the Dance of Doom happened.

If Dani hadn't been wearing a fuzzy bear costume at the time, complete with oversize cartoon head that hid her identity, she might never have lived it down.

Even so, she was never, *ever* doing anything like that again.

"What do you think?" her mom asked, bringing her back to the present.

"About what?"

Her mom sighed, exasperated. "Pay attention, sweetie. Ballroom dance lessons."

Dani set down her spoon and pushed her bowl away. "No."

"I know that tap and ballet didn't work out, but I have a good feeling about ballroom. It's a six-week introductory session. If you like it, we can sign up for more—" Her mom's phone buzzed.

She checked the message. "Oooh!" She beamed. "Mallory sent along some photos from her latest performance. Take a look, Rourke."

Dani's dad scrolled through the photos, making appreciative noises. "Look at the expression on Mallory's face in this one! She's really feeling the music." He showed Dani the screen.

"Nice," Dani mumbled.

As her parents kept going on about Mallory's gorgeous photos, Dani thought about the McMurray Award. If she was named one of the best science students her age in the entire state, her parents couldn't deny that this was her talent. Her *thing*. They'd have to let her pursue her dreams.

ScienceU—and all the doors it would open for her—would be within her grasp.

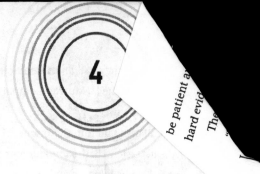

4

CAT

FIFTEEN MINUTES BEFORE THE first-period bell on Tuesday, Cat passed Ms. Blanks's half-open classroom door and noticed the teacher standing by the windows, talking on her cell phone— and Dani seated at a desk close to the door.

Cat slipped through the doorway and slid into the chair next to her project partner. "Dani!" Cat whispered. "I was hoping to run into you!"

Dani flinched. "Cat! Hi!"

"We have so much to talk about—"

"Hush," Dani admonished. "Ms. Blanks is on the phone."

Cat bit her tongue, but her knee bounced under the table with excitement. Last night's success with predicting the blackout had her anxious for the circles to begin appearing so she could prove more of her theories. She'd even worn her favorite denim overalls and a long-sleeve black shirt spotted with green alien heads to celebrate.

Not that she'd tell anyone yet about what she'd discovered— except Dani, of course. She'd read about too many investigations getting shut down just as they got close to the truth. No, she'd

nd wait until they had an undeniable mountain of
en...e to unveil at the McMurray Competition.

n vict...ory would be sweet.

Trust me," Ms. Blanks said into the phone. "I've got every—understand_—" A beat. "Listen, I have some students here." Another beat. "I'll be in touch." She hung up and tucked her phone into her pants pocket, grabbing her coffee mug from her desk as she walked over. "Danielle, Catrina. What can I do for you?"

"I just saw Dani and wanted to chat!" Cat chirped before Dani could respond. Then she frowned. "Why *are* you here, anyway?" she asked her partner.

Dani shot Cat a look that was half-embarrassed, half-apologetic. "Ms. Blanks, I wanted to talk to you because . . . I can't research the Weston Farm Circles. I just can't. So we either need to change our project proposal or else . . ." She cleared her throat, still looking uncomfortable. "I need to work alone."

"What?" Cat yelped.

Ms. Blanks's eyebrows went up. "Oh my. What brought this on, Danielle?"

"Well, first of all, I didn't have any say in picking the topic. If we're supposed to be a team, why did Cat submit a proposal by herself, without even running it by me?"

"Because it's the perfect project," Cat said immediately. "And because you weren't here. I didn't know when you'd be back, so I went ahead and sent in our materials."

Dani looked confused. "But . . . I thought the deadline to get proposals approved was today. That's why I went over to your house last night."

"The forms had to be postmarked by Friday in order to get there by today," Cat explained. "I didn't want to risk being late and having *no* McMurray project!" Just the thought of missing out on her first shot at the McMurray Competition in the same year as the Weston Farm Circles was enough to make Cat shudder.

Ms. Blanks held up a hand. "Catrina, I gave you the participant packet for your team last Monday morning, and we discussed your idea about Weston Farm after class that day. When exactly did you mail in the proposal?"

Cat squirmed. This must be what an amoeba under a microscope felt like. "Last Monday afternoon," she muttered.

"What? You could have called or emailed me any time last week!" Dani griped. "We could have talked all our ideas out and made a decision together!"

Cat felt her face flush hot. Maybe she *could* have gotten in touch with Dani to talk about the project. And maybe she *hadn't* done that because she'd been afraid Dani would say no.

"How would you feel, Catrina, if the shoe were on the other foot?" Ms. Blanks asked.

"Not great," Cat admitted. "I'm sorry, Dani. I should have made more of an effort to reach out. It's just that this is an opportunity I've been waiting for my whole life. I really wanted to be sure we got it in on time and that no one else took our project idea first." Cat scuffed her boot on the floor under the table. "I guess I got carried away."

"Thanks for the apology," Dani said. "But it doesn't matter. I still can't do this project."

"Why not?"

"Because the circles are a big joke! Nobody believes they're real—"

"I believe they're real and so do a lot of people!" Cat said indignantly.

Dani crossed her arms in front of her chest. "They're not worth studying."

"They are!" Cat insisted.

"I know Cat already mailed in the proposal," Dani said to their teacher, "but surely there's some wiggle room—"

"I'll stop you there," Ms. Blanks said. "I received an email from the McMurray committee this morning that your proposal has been approved. Once that happens, you're locked in. So you either study the Weston Farm Circles or you wait until next year's competition."

"Okay," Dani said, her face bleak but determined, "then Cat can investigate crop circles, and I'll do a different project on my own. I'll fill out the forms right now. There's such a thing as same-day shipping, right? I still have a chance!"

Cat's heart sank. After last night's huge success with the blackout, she'd been looking forward to having a partner to work with. Especially someone who loved science as much as she did.

"I'm afraid the projects must be done in teams," Ms. Blanks emphasized. "You're meant to demonstrate collaboration."

"But—"

"Danielle, if you drop out," Ms. Blanks said, "Catrina will also be out of the competition."

Cat gasped. "No! The circles won't return for another thirteen years! This is our one shot to study them. We'll never have another opportunity like this!" It was suddenly difficult for Cat to breathe. Her chest grew tight and itchy, and her eyes began to burn. It felt like her life's work was slipping away.

"Oh," Dani said softly. Her eyes met Cat's and quickly darted to the floor instead. "I guess I wouldn't want to do that to Cat."

"Thank you," Cat said.

"But . . . I still don't think this is the right project for me."

"Well, I approved Catrina's idea for a reason and so did the McMurray committee," their teacher said. "Though I didn't know Catrina hadn't told you about it before sending it in. She omitted that bit." Ms. Blanks raised her eyebrows at Cat, who sank back into her chair. "Still, I think you two can do something very interesting with the topic. Science has always been about making the unknown known." Her voice warmed. "Scientists are explorers. Once upon a time, much of what we now take for granted was considered to be a myth or a fantasy. Think about the things humans once believed! The earth was flat. Illnesses were caused by an imbalance of humors in the body. Metal could be turned into gold. What better unknown is there," Ms. Blanks said, lifting her coffee high, "than a phenomenon, like crop circles, that has yet to be explained?" She glanced at Cat. "Right, Catrina?"

"Right!" Cat grinned, partly from relief that their project would go on and partly in gratitude that she had a teacher like Ms. Blanks, who really understood the important things, like scientific discovery.

"The Weston Farm Circles aren't real," Dani tried again.

"Some think so." Ms. Blanks's eyes sparkled. "Others believe there's more to the story."

Dani groaned and put her face in her hands.

"Danielle, I want you to keep an open mind," Ms. Blanks said. "You two are among my most promising students. I want you to succeed. You said in your initial application that you hope to attend ScienceU and you need the scholarship to do that. I want to help make that happen. That means having a project that stands out—and this one will."

"Not in a good way." Dani looked up. "Crop circles aren't supernatural. It would be one thing if we were trying to figure out where they actually came from—"

"Aliens!" Cat squealed. "They come from aliens!"

"You *are* trying to figure out their origins," Ms. Blanks said patiently. "Whatever those might be. Natural or . . . supernatural."

Dani got a thoughtful look on her face.

Cat's spirits lifted. Dani was coming around. She had to be.

"Come on, Dani. This will be awesome. I've already started a list of experiments we can run!" It occurred to Cat that part of Dani's resistance might stem from the fact that she clearly didn't know much about crop circles, let alone UFOs and aliens.

Now *that* was something Cat could help with.

"This afternoon, why don't you and I go over the history of crop circles? I can make sure we're both up to speed on the currently available evidence."

Dani was quiet for a long moment. Then, to Cat's surprise, she said, "Sure."

"Awesome!" Cat beamed. "Meet me in the library media room after school?"

"See you there," Dani replied. "I just . . ." She glanced at Ms. Blanks. "Can I ask you one more thing? It's, um, private." She gave Cat that semi-apologetic look again.

Cat brushed it off.

Their project was going to be a blast. It would totally impress the judges on the McMurray committee.

And this afternoon, Cat would have a captive audience and a real opportunity to convert a nonbeliever. This was a moment she had been waiting for all her life.

5

DANI

WHEN MS. BLANKS HAD said, "Natural or . . . supernatural," a light bulb had turned on inside Dani's mind. As soon as she was sure Cat was out of earshot, Dani asked, "Do Cat and I have to work on the same hypothesis?"

Ms. Blanks blinked. "What do you mean?"

"What if she tries to prove the existence of aliens or whatever, while I look for the true explanation? Same project, different conclusions. Would that be allowed?"

"I don't think there's anything in the McMurray rule book that forbids—"

"Then that's what I'll do. She'll try to prove her theory, and I'll try to prove mine."

Her teacher looked skeptical. "You are supposed to be working as a team . . ."

"We'll be gathering evidence together. Testing it together. Just . . . with different goals."

"Hmm. I do feel bad that I didn't realize Catrina hadn't told you about her proposal . . ."

"Please," Dani begged. She might not be able to stop her mom from signing her up for ballroom dance lessons, but this felt like a battle she could win. "Please say yes."

After a beat, Ms. Blanks said, "All right."

Dani let out a little squeak of triumph. "Really? Thank you!"

"Why don't you check in with me on Monday mornings so I can make sure everything's going smoothly? Of course, you can also come to me anytime you need extra guidance. That's what I'm here for as your adviser. I can be your sounding board."

"Absolutely." Dani turned to leave.

Ms. Blanks stopped her with a hand on her shoulder. "One last thing. What if Catrina doesn't agree to this new angle?"

"I won't tell her," Dani said impulsively. "At least, not until I have a real theory and hard evidence to back it up."

"That might not be—" The teacher was interrupted by the warning bell.

"Thank you, Ms. Blanks!" Dani ran out the door.

"YOU *HAVE* TO WORK with Cat Mulvaney?" Dani's friend Nora asked as they approached the library after school. "I thought you got to pick your partner for this thing."

"Yeah." Their friend Laurel tilted her head. "You asked all of us. Why was Cat Mulvaney your next choice?"

"She wasn't," Dani said. "No one else applied."

The fourth member of their BFF group, Jane, squealed with

delight. "Dani! You're one of the top two nerds in the whole seventh grade! Congrats!"

"Ha-ha," Dani fake laughed.

"I wouldn't call Cat a nerd," Laurel said thoughtfully. "Isn't it 'geek' when someone's into sci-fi stuff? Like your brother, Jane."

"Yeah, Hayden's a geek for sure," Jane replied, "but Cat believes aliens are real, and she wants to study them. I think that makes her a nerd. Anyway, it's more about, like, the energy you give off. Dani—you know I love you—but you are *such* a nerd."

Dani had been friends with Jane, Laurel, and Nora since first grade. Jane was petite and delicate-featured, with pale skin and shiny dark hair. She was the most popular out of their crew— and the only one who'd been on a date. Nora was tanned, tall, and strong, a star on both the softball and soccer teams. Laurel was Black with long curly hair. She played three musical instruments and wore cool vintage outfits. Dani was white with brown hair that fell flat when she wanted it to curl and went wavy when she tried to make it straight and . . . well, her friends were right. She was a nerd.

Most of the time, she was fine with that. They all had different strengths. But ever since the Dance of Doom, she'd been plagued by a secret, nagging worry: If their foursome ever became a trio, Dani was pretty sure she'd be the odd girl out. She didn't have any evidence to support her theory. It was just how she felt.

"Have fun!" Jane held open the library door. "Don't do anything we wouldn't do!"

Nora snorted. "What, like, an extracurricular science fair project? Too late."

Dani watched the three of them head off down the hall, arms linked.

Then she squared her shoulders and went to meet Cat.

She entered the media room to find the other girl pacing and munching from a snack bag of popcorn. Behind Cat, the SMART Board was lit up with the words "A History of Crop Circles" in bright green letters.

"Hi!" Cat exclaimed when she saw Dani. "Popcorn?"

"Um, sure." Dani took a bag and opened it as she sat down in the chair Cat had set up directly across from the SMART Board.

"Make yourself comfortable, and I'll show you why I believe crop circles are real." Cat dimmed the lights and clicked to the first slide, a picture of the Weston Farm crop circles from thirteen years ago. "These are the circles we know and love," she began, "but making gigantic geometric shapes like this has a longer history than you might think. Crop circles date back to—"

"The nineteen seventies," Dani finished.

Cat made a face. "Where'd you hear that?"

"I did some preliminary research during lunch." Getting Ms. Blanks's permission to pursue an opposing hypothesis had been step one toward winning the McMurray Award. Now Dani knew she had to hit the ground running. "The guys who started making crop circles in the seventies admitted to it years ago. The rest are copycats, including the ones on Weston Farm."

"Au contraire!" Cat exclaimed. "The hoaxers were copying the real thing. The first legitimate report of a crop circle happened back in the seventeenth century in Hartfordshire, England. They called it the Mowing-Devil. Granted, the stalks were cut instead of burned or flattened like they are now, but I'm pretty sure your seventies hoaxers weren't alive four hundred years ago."

Dani studied the slide showing an old pamphlet about the Mowing-Devil. "What does this have to do with Weston Farm and our project?"

"Everything!" Cat inhaled a handful of popcorn, then clicked to a slide that showed a fractal shape stamped into a field. "This is a crop circle near Stonehenge in 1996."

"1996," Dani observed, "which is *after* the nineteen seventies."

Cat ignored the commentary. "This formation appeared on a sunny day during a forty-five-minute window and was first spotted by a pilot from the air. Other witnesses all independently confirm that timeline. Even the best hoaxers could never create something this complex that fast. Known hoaxers always need the entire night to complete their circles, and that's cutting it close. Which leaves us with supernatural explanations."

"I don't see any reason to jump to it being supernatural," Dani argued. "I mean, humans built the pyramids."

Cat held up both hands. "Don't even get me started on the pyramids! That's another whole slideshow."

"Oh-kay," Dani said slowly, not wanting to get off track. "Well, the witnesses are either lying or they missed seeing the crop circle earlier in the day."

"But there were eyewitnesses to the actual formation! They reported seeing a spinning mist a few feet off the ground. Below it, they could see the circles forming. The local police department got a ton of calls about cars pulled off the road because of it."

Dani let herself imagine seeing what Cat was describing. It sounded . . . incredible. And implausible. "If that's true, why hasn't everyone heard of it?"

"Because people hear 'crop circles' and 'aliens' and immediately write it off!" Cat was practically jumping around the room now. She took a swig of Mountain Dew from a can on the side table—which Dani now realized was next to a second, empty can.

"How many of those have you had?" she asked, a little alarmed.

"Did you know that up until a few years ago, there was a secret Pentagon initiative called the Advanced Aerospace Threat Identification Program?" Cat yelped. "It was supported by real US senators. There was even an article in the *New York Times* about it! Not to mention the Department of Defense released a whole report with video footage confirming actual encounters with unidentified objects in 2021! People refuse to believe in the extraordinary because they fear what they can't explain. Or rather, they fear the explanation!"

The media room door opened. "Everything okay in here?" the librarian asked.

Dani quickly tucked her popcorn bag out of sight. "All good! Just . . . excited. About science."

The librarian raised an eyebrow. "Keep it to a dull roar, please." She left.

When the door shut, Cat took a deep breath. "Sorry. Where was I?"

"Stonehenge."

"Right. So why would anyone make a design that can only be fully seen and appreciated from above?"

Dani shrugged. "Because it looks cool?"

"There are two possible reasons," Cat lectured. "One, crop circles are a message, a way of communicating something like, *We come in peace*. Or two, they're made by aliens as a sign to other aliens that this planet is taken. Sort of like how we stuck the American flag on the moon."

"At least you don't think the moon landing is a conspiracy," Dani said dryly.

"Of course not. I told you, my dad works at NASA."

Dani remembered that detail from last night. What must it be like to have a parent in the sciences? Someone who *understood* . . . The envy itched like a splinter under her skin.

Dani needed to hold on to that splinter feeling.

She needed to let it push her to be the best.

Cat flipped through a few slides showing other crop circles, stopping when she reached a picture of Weston Farm. "Our crop circles have been appearing every thirteen years since 1984. These were the first five."

Dani thought about what she'd read at lunchtime. "But there were six circles the first year."

"Aha!" Cat clicked, and another picture appeared on the slide. "I don't believe they were all real. The first five appeared within a forty-eight-hour span. Two the first day, then three the next. The sixth circle didn't appear for four more days. The second time, in 1997, seven crop circles appeared within the first five days, then two more later on. The third time, in 2010, eleven circles formed in seven days and then five others followed."

She paused, like she was waiting for Dani to fill in the blanks.

Dani leaned forward. She squinted. Then she saw what Cat was getting at. "Prime numbers."

"Bingo! Two, three, five, seven, eleven—all prime numbers. The extra crop circles don't match the sequence."

"Or," Dani said, "the total number of crop circles really *was* six, nine, and sixteen, and the number of days it took for them to be created was just . . . how long it took to do the hoax."

"No way!" Cat shot back. "One hundred and thirteen hours between the last orb appearance and the blackout! That's a prime number! And thirteen years between crop circle appearances—another prime number! The pattern is real!" She grinned triumphantly. "That brings me to our project hypothesis. This year, there should be thirteen circles in succession in the first few days—and it will be a prime number of days, by the way—with an unknown number of circles later on from copycats. When we test the real crop circles and the ones I believe to be hoaxes, we should find substantial, quantifiable differences."

"That's your hypothesis?" Dani asked, just to be clear. "The real circles and the fake ones"—she made herself resist putting air quotes around "real" and "fake"—"won't be the same? Which will prove that the real ones are real?"

Cat nodded. "What do you think?"

Dani thought it made a strange kind of sense . . . *if* you were someone who believed in aliens.

Which she wasn't.

But looking for quantifiable differences between crop circles would mean running tests.

Lots and lots of tests.

Tests Dani could use to look for clues to come up with a hypothesis of her own.

6

CAT

AS CAT POINTED HER clicker at the projector to move to the final slide—the one that summed everything up—Dani's phone rang.

"Sorry, one sec." Dani dug it out of her backpack and answered. "Hi, Mom. What's up?"

Cat bounced on her heels as Dani listened.

"I had something to do for my McMurray project," Dani said. "I forgot to let you know I'd be staying after school."

She frowned at whatever her mom was saying.

"I know. Sorry. I'll be right out." Dani hung up and looked at Cat. "I have to go."

"But I didn't show you the best—"

Dani slid off her chair. "I'll catch you later, okay?"

"Sure." Cat tried not to sound too disappointed. "Let's talk tomorrow."

"Mm-hmm," Dani said distractedly as she gathered her things and tossed her popcorn bag in the trash. "Have a good afternoon."

"You too."

When Dani was gone, Cat clicked forward to the last slide in her presentation, the one with all the numbers and patterns displayed on one screen. The evidence was overwhelming. And at the bottom: the number thirteen. Thirteen years between phenomena. Thirteen authentic circles due to appear this year. The double thirteens meant something. Cat was sure of it.

There was one other thing Cat hadn't told Dani: Cat knew *she* was meant to unravel the mystery behind the circles. Her birthday was coming up. She'd been born during the last occurrence thirteen years ago. This was her destiny.

Was Cat going to allow her partner's skepticism to get in the way? Not a chance.

Dani had started to do a little research on her own. That was a good sign. But unfortunately, she didn't seem at all interested in opening her mind. If Cat wanted to convince Dani that there was more going on at Weston Farm than a clever hoax, she had to make this project the best it could be in every way. She needed the best evidence, the most conclusive data.

Cat had her work cut out for her.

She packed up her laptop and slung her backpack over her shoulder, then turned off all the equipment in the media room. She gave the librarian an enthusiastic wave as she left the school.

When Cat reached the bike rack, she saw that she had a missed call and message from her dad. She eagerly pressed "Play."

Hey, sweetheart, it's your dad. Look, I got your email about the science fair and it sounds great, but I'm not going to be able to get away from work that weekend. I'm sorry. I promise I'll make it up to you. Need a new mini centrifuge? Or a new set of flasks? Send me some ideas and I'll get something fun in the mail. Talk more later. Love you.

She quietly tucked her phone away. Her dad had promised—promised!—that he'd come see the McMurray exhibition. He knew how important this science fair was to her. She'd been talking about it all summer, long before she'd teamed up with Dani. She'd known from the get-go what her topic would be. It was no coincidence that the Weston Farm Circles were expected to appear during the McMurray Competition. It was a sign.

Cat felt another twinge of guilt for submitting the project proposal without talking to Dani, but she shook it off. She *had* to prove the crop circles were real. She had no other choice, especially now. The only way she'd get NASA to send her dad back to his hometown was to discover something of major scientific importance.

That was exactly what she was going to do.

At the top of her list of evidence to acquire: eyewitness testimony. She knew just where to find it. As Cat rode her bike across town, she mulled over the problem currently troubling her. She hadn't yet figured out where on Weston Farm this year's batch of crop circles would appear. She had a few educated guesses, of course, but they lacked the neat pattern of the years and number of circles.

In 1984, the first-ever Weston Farm Circles had manifested the day after the power outage. In 1997, the circles showed up two days after the blackout. In 2010, the interval was three days. Five was the next prime number. Thus, Cat felt confident that the first circles would appear on Saturday.

But Weston Farm covered nearly a thousand acres of land. If she guessed the wrong location, she might not know the circles had shown up until the news hit the airwaves.

It was frustrating, to say the least.

The interview she was about to do might shed a little light on the matter.

Robbie Colton, the only person to ever witness one of the Weston Farm Circles being created, lived in a run-down old house on the far side of town. Cat had heard his story on the news and knew the gist but had never gotten up the nerve to actually talk to the man.

Cat had seen his house before. Little kids would dare each other to knock on the door on Halloween and then run away before Robbie could answer. People acted like he was a fool just because he was a believer. Well, Cat was a believer, too, and she definitely wasn't foolish, so she didn't see any reason why he should be, either. When a little garage with a half-collapsed roof came into view, followed by the house itself, she turned up the dirt drive, then parked her bike against the more stable-looking side of the garage. She shouldered her backpack, took a deep breath, marched onto the porch, and knocked.

The porch creaked under her feet. An old porch swing swayed in the breeze, looking like it was holding on by a thread. When the door opened suddenly, Cat jumped, even though she'd been expecting it.

"Who are you?" The man behind the screen door was probably younger than her dad, but he was rough enough around the edges that he appeared much older. His expression made it clear that he wasn't thrilled about having a visitor.

"My name is Cat Mulvaney. I'm doing a research project for school on the Weston Farm crop circles. Since you're the only eyewitness, I was hoping I could interview you?"

Robbie rubbed his eyes, almost like he thought he was dreaming. "You want to interview me?"

Cat nodded and pulled out her phone. "Mind if I record our conversation?"

Robbie shrugged and opened the door wide, still regarding Cat warily. He led her into a living room with a ratty plaid couch and chair and a TV blaring the local news. He turned down the TV and settled into the chair. Cat took a seat opposite him on the couch, fidgeting with her phone until she got the recorder app working.

"First, tell me about your encounter. And please don't skimp on the details."

Robbie chuckled. "You know this was thirteen years ago, right?"

Cat frowned. "Obviously."

"Well, it was dark, and I was walking beside the fields. I knew the circles were going to appear that night—"

"Because of the prime number pattern, right?" Cat interrupted.

Robbie looked surprised. "Yeah, yeah, that's right." Now he studied her with a little more respect. "So I was ready with my camera. Great camera, too. Brand-new. Spent a big chunk of my savings on it. Well, just when I thought I had to be in the

41

wrong place, a light appeared in the field. It was deep in the thick crop, and boy, it was moving real fast. I chased it, of course. Got all sorts of scratches from those wheat stalks. As I got closer to the glow, it turned this unearthly green. And that sound! Never forget it. It was high-pitched and wavering. I'd thought I was alone, but voices started calling from all sides. By the time I got to it, the light was gone, and all that was left was the circle. It was perfect. The crop was flat as a pancake. It was dead silent again. Heck, I was almost too scared to breathe."

Robbie took off his hat, wiped some sweat from his forehead, and placed it back on.

"I heard footsteps. Real fast ones. I couldn't tell where they were coming from, so I just started clicking my camera in all directions. Then someone . . . or some*thing* . . . came up behind me and knocked me right out. Took my camera, too. I was out two grand and seeing stars for days."

"And you confirmed there weren't circles in that field before that evening?"

"Sure did. Buddy of mine back then had a plane he used for crop-dusting. Let me ride with him before and after the circle got there."

Cat raised an eyebrow. That was a great idea—if she could find someone with a plane. "What brought you to that particular section of the fields that night?" she asked.

Robbie smiled. "Ah, you want to know all my secrets, huh?" He shifted in his chair and popped open the can of soda that sat next to him on a table. "Well, I tell ya, it came to me in a dream."

Cat's enthusiasm faltered. "A dream?" She couldn't exactly test dreams for a science fair.

"I was there in that field, marking landmarks. I could see the farmhouse from where I stood and what looked like the edge of the field," Robbie said. "When I woke up, I wrote down everything I could remember. Two days later, I went to the farm and . . ." He grinned wide and took a big swig of his drink. "Well, you know the rest."

"Have you had any dreams or visions like that recently?" Cat asked.

"Nah, I don't usually get that kind of thing." His face took on a wistful expression. "That year was special. The aliens had something important they wanted to share. But then someone had to go and intervene." He leaned forward and whispered, "It was the government. They don't want the truth to get out. But people like us, we have to wake everyone else up to what's going on, don't we?"

Cat nodded. While she believed Robbie's story about being there when the crop circle formed, she wasn't so sure about his methods. It wasn't like she could make herself have dreams or visions as part of her project. As much as she hated to admit it, it *was* possible he'd just gotten lucky thirteen years ago. She put her phone away and stood, but before she could leave, Robbie sat bolt upright and cranked the volume on the TV.

". . . reports coming in from around the region tonight of appliances and other electronics malfunctioning . . ."

"Happened last time, too," Robbie said with a knowing glance at Cat. "Microwaves, older TVs, all on the fritz. It's a sign. The aliens, they're trying to communicate, but they don't speak our language, see? They communicate through electromagnetic frequencies."

Cat glanced toward Robbie's grimy kitchen. "Do you have a microwave we could try?"

Robbie got shifty eyed. "I most certainly do not. That's how they get you!"

Cat wondered which "they" he was referring to but decided not to ask. She could read more about the microwave theory when she got home. "Thank you very much for your time, Mr. Colton. This was very helpful, and I really appreciate it." She shook his hand and turned toward the door.

Robbie made no move to get out of his chair. "All right, glad to help. Cat, right?"

"Yes, sir."

"I don't get many visitors. People tend to steer clear of me. We need more folks like you, who take the important things seriously. Stop by anytime you want to talk about . . . them." He raised his can in a salute-like gesture, which Cat attempted to return.

"Will do," she said.

7

DANI

AFTER CAT'S SLIDESHOW ON Tuesday, Dani had set herself two main goals for the week:

1. Research past crop circle hoaxes—who did it and how.
2. Read more about the circles at Weston Farm in 1984, 1997, and 2010.

She'd actually learned a lot. Like, the most popular method of creating crop circles involved stomping on a piece of wood to flatten the stalks. By slowly shuffling forward, moving the board a few feet at a time, hoaxers created elaborate designs that usually weren't noticed until morning.

Sometimes, the hoaxers later came forward and confessed. Occasionally, people were caught in the act. But neither of those two things was true for the Weston Farm Circles. No one had ever claimed responsibility. Meanwhile, people had camped out all around the farm, trying to catch the culprits, to no avail. The circles never appeared in the same spot twice.

Which was . . . interesting.

But not helpful.

Dani now knew more about crop circle hoaxes than she'd ever

imagined she would, but she felt completely stuck. She didn't have a concrete theory about who was behind the ones at Weston Farm. She didn't have anything *close* to a theory.

Her partner, on the other hand, seemed to have nothing *but* theories.

Since their meeting with Ms. Blanks, Cat had been blowing up Dani's phone. Dani hadn't responded to a single message. She wasn't proud to be ignoring Cat's communications, but . . . the other girl could be *a lot.*

It wasn't just a phone thing. This whole week, Cat had been outfitted with binoculars around her neck. Every time she was in a room with a window, she'd been sneaking glances at the sky. Yesterday, Dani had watched Cat jump to her feet in the middle of Ms. Blanks's class, staring intently at the clouds like a cartoon hunting dog. "Dani!" she'd shouted. "Check it out!"

Dani hadn't seen anything in the clouds. What she *had* seen was her classmates staring at the two of them. She'd pretended not to have heard Cat . . . and today, she'd been ducking around corners and avoiding eye contact.

Cat was strange. Dani had known that when they'd teamed up.

Having Cat's strangeness aimed in Dani's general direction was unsettling.

But the worst part was still the fact that Cat had a ton of leads, while Dani had nothing.

Never mind that Dani still felt a little guilty about not having told her partner about her new research angle—and that she was still mad about having this project submitted without her input.

Basically, there were a lot of feelings. Too many feelings.

All the more reason to come up with a viable opposing hypothesis—and fast.

DANI'S BRAIN WAS STILL in hypothesis mode when she showed up at Jane's for their weekly Friday-night sleepover. She followed Jane upstairs on autopilot and dropped her duffel bag in the corner before plopping down on the bed between Nora and Laurel.

"Good. You're here." Laurel handed Dani one of her Pixy Stix. "Give us an update on the Cat Mulvaney situation."

"Have you been able to prove that aliens exist?" Nora asked, lips twitching.

"*Cat* is trying to prove aliens exist," Dani said quickly, tearing open the straw and pouring a stream of pink sugar into her mouth. "*I'm* looking for the truth about the crop circles—where they really come from."

"Ooh, a competition," Nora said approvingly.

"You'll definitely win," Jane chimed in, and Laurel nodded in agreement.

Dani wasn't so sure about that.

"I'm honestly having a little trouble coming up with—"

Her phone buzzed.

"Ooh, is that Cat?" Nora asked. "What does she want?" She grabbed the phone before Dani could and read aloud:

CAT: Come over? I have something to show you. 👽

"Huh," Laurel said. "I was expecting something a bit more . . . cosmic."

"Should I answer?" Nora asked.

"Nope!" Dani snatched her phone back and tucked it away without responding. "I'm good, everything's good, the project's going to be amazing, can we talk about something else now?" Wow, the sugar had hit her brain fast.

"Okay, let's talk about the festival," Laurel said.

Dani stifled her groan. The mayor had declared on Wednesday that there was going to be a multiday festival near Weston Farm in honor of the crop circles. A festival to celebrate what was shaping up to be just about the worst thing that had ever happened to Dani—aside from the Dance of Doom, of course.

"We found out today that the middle school jazz band is going to play on the main stage one night," Laurel announced, "and I got a solo!"

"Yes!" Jane squealed, throwing her arms around Laurel. "Congrats! Which instrument?"

Before Laurel could answer, Jane's brother, Hayden, called from downstairs, "Pizza!"

"I'll go," Dani said, jumping to her feet. Maybe her friends would finish discussing the festival while she was gone, and she wouldn't have to think about crop circles or her sorry excuse for a McMurray project for the rest of the sleepover. "Be right back."

Hayden was on the phone when Dani entered the kitchen. ". . . collecting visual evidence," he said, pointing at the pizza that had just come out of the oven. "We'll need multiple cameras, in case there're any orbs we can capture."

Orbs . . .

Just like that, Dani was back on the crop circle train.

On Tuesday, outside the school library, Nora had joked about Hayden being a sci-fi geek. What if he knew something that could help Dani come up with a hypothesis? She busied herself with putting slices of piping-hot pepperoni pizza on plates, trying not to seem like she was eavesdropping. Even though she totally was.

"There've been reports of strange lights all over town the past few days." Hayden paused. "Of course I've thought about the possibility of electrical surges making the cameras malfunction. What kind of cereologist do you think I am?"

Jackpot! *Cereologist* was a word Dani had encountered in her research. Cereologists studied crop circles. They used the word *cereal* because crop circles happened in grain fields—not because they were particularly fond of Cheerios.

Hayden laughed into his phone. "Yeah, yeah," he said. "I know nothing's actually going to happen. It'll be a fun night out anyway, right?"

Dani cleared her throat and waved in Hayden's direction to get his attention. "Are you talking about the Weston Farm Circles?"

Hayden grunted. "Why do you care?"

"I'm, um. I'm interested. In the circles. How they're formed. I mean, I know they're fake. I don't believe in aliens or anything."

"Oh-kay . . ."

"Do you believe the circles are real?"

Hayden tilted his head. "Did my sister put you up to this?"

"No!" Dani said too loudly. "This is for school."

"Sure it is." Hayden sighed. "Hang on," he said into the phone and then turned back to Dani. "Do I believe in the possibility that there's intelligent life elsewhere in the universe? Yes. Do I think that intelligent life visits good ol' Hilldale every thirteen years, just to say hello by making cool patterns in a field? I wish. But no."

"Where do you think our circles come from, then?"

"Honestly? It's probably a prank. There're some guys on the football team this year—" Whoever was on the phone laughed and said something incredulous-sounding. "It's on the Internet," Hayden told the other person. "Anyone can replicate a crop circle."

"Who do you think might be in charge of a prank like that?" Dani asked urgently.

Hayden frowned, thinking. "Scott Crawley. If it's local kids, he'll be the ringleader."

Dani filed the name away, unable to stop a smile from spreading across her face. *Finally! A lead!* She'd never talked to a high school football player before, but there was a first time for everything.

"Thanks," she said as Jane's brother left the kitchen. He grunted in response.

As she headed back upstairs, carefully balancing four plates on her arms, Dani felt like a weight had been lifted from her shoulders. It didn't matter that Cat had a million ideas for their project. (Dani felt her phone buzz in her back pocket; if that was Cat again, the idea tally had probably just risen to a million and one.) Dani didn't need a partner to figure out who was responsible for the Weston Farm Circles.

She could do this all on her own.

8

CAT

CAT CONSIDERED HERSELF A patient person. Any good ufologist had to be. There were no shortcuts to the truth. But by Saturday, her patience with Dani had worn paper-thin.

Cat set her phone aside after the gazillionth text to Dani and focused once again on the map of Weston Farm. She leaned forward in her chair and considered the expanse of fields. It covered nearly a thousand acres and grew wheat, corn, and vegetables. Thus far, the circles had appeared only in the tall crops like corn and wheat. Which of course were the largest fields. But at least it narrowed down the possibilities. She'd marked the crop locations and the approximate acreage on the map.

In past years, circles had appeared in every quadrant of the fields. Sometimes, they'd shown up close to the road. Other times, they'd been deep within the crop. They'd never appeared in exactly the same spot twice, but the ones in the western and northwestern fields hadn't been too far apart last time. Cat had been poring over this map for days, and as far as she could tell, there was no clear pattern. The only thing she was sure about was that the first circle would be a big one. It always was. And it seemed to her that the most likely spot for a really big circle to appear would be in the cornfields in the eastern section. Or else smack-dab in the middle of the farm, where the wheat grew.

She'd tried to share this with Dani, but she couldn't get the other girl to listen to her. And the crop circles were going to start appearing tonight! Really, there was only one reasonable thing left for Cat to do.

She folded up the map and tucked it in her backpack, which was full to bursting with flashlights, snacks, two compasses, and smaller parts of the equipment she needed to bring. She slung it over her shoulder and headed downstairs. But before she reached the door, her mom's voice stopped her.

"Cat?" her mom said, perplexed. "It's eight o'clock. Where are you going?"

"I need to meet my McMurray project partner at Weston Farm." She paused, then added, "The owner of the farm will be there, so we won't be alone or anything."

Her mother sighed. "All right, but make sure you have your cell phone. And don't go out of cell range!"

"Sure thing—don't wait up!" As Cat left, she saw the smile edging her mom's lips. Her mom was happy because Cat had told her she was meeting someone. She worried about Cat's social life far more than Cat did. She just hoped what she'd said wouldn't turn out to be a lie.

CAT STOPPED HER BIKE in front of the unassuming two-story Colonial house and walked it up the short drive. Her palms were sweatier than she wanted to admit, but she was nothing if not determined. She knocked and held her breath.

The door was opened by a woman with a distracted air and paint smudged across her nose.

"Can I help you?" Dani's mom asked.

"Hi, Mrs. Williams. I'm Cat, Dani's partner on the McMurray project? I'm here to pick her up. We have research to do tonight at Weston Farm."

The woman blinked and glanced at her watch. "Research?"

Cat nodded.

"Dani didn't mention going out tonight."

"Well, it's Saturday, and the crop circles are going to appear soon, so it's really important—"

"Crop circles?"

"Cat!" Dani appeared in the doorway. "I didn't know you were here. Thanks, Mom, I got it." She tried to usher her mom down the hallway, but her mom didn't budge.

"Wait a minute, Dani. What's this about you going to Weston Farm?"

Dani winced as her dad appeared behind them, too, holding a piece of toast and looking puzzled. "You remember the competition I'm doing for the McMurray Youth Science Award?" When her parents nodded, Dani went on. "This is my partner, Cat Mulvaney."

"Nice to meet you, Cat," Dani's mom said.

Dani's dad swallowed a bite of the toast he'd been chewing. "What's your project about, exactly?"

Before Cat could say a word, Dani blurted, "We're investigating a periodic local phenomenon that affects wheat and cornfields. We're looking for . . . causality. Who or what is responsible for the crop damage? Can future occurrences be predicted? Is there anything our farmers can do to avoid being victimized?"

Dani's mom and dad exchanged a look; then her mom said, "Well. That sounds . . . fascinating." Her tone of voice said otherwise. "I suppose it's all right. But be back by ten. And—"

"Ten?" Cat interrupted, dismayed. "But the circles won't—"

"The *phenomenon* we're studying won't be evident until . . ." Dani faded off, staring at Cat with her eyebrows raised.

Cat didn't want to admit that she wasn't sure what time the circles were supposed to appear. "What if you spent the night at my house?" she asked Dani.

"Uh, okay. I guess." Cat could tell Dani was making a serious effort not to seem ticked off in front of her parents. But at least she was agreeing to Cat's suggestion.

"Great!" Cat nearly shrieked. "Mr. and Mrs. Williams?"

"Fine," Dani's mom said with a sigh. "Call me tomorrow when you're ready to be picked up, Dani. And don't think we're done talking about you signing up for that ballroom dance class—"

"Absolutely, Mom. Thanks." Dani closed the door, then whirled on Cat. "What were you thinking, coming here?"

Cat shrugged, but a small smile snuck out. "I'm thinking it worked. Why don't you want your parents to know we're doing our project on the Weston Farm Circles?"

"I want them to take me seriously."

That stung a little, but Cat tried to shrug it off. Dani's parents definitely didn't seem to be the science-loving types. They seemed . . . well, bored by it, almost. "They will when we win the McMurray Award."

"Fine, but did you have to come to my house?"

"You've been avoiding me. You stopped answering my texts. You left me no choice." Cat pointed at Dani's front door. "Get your overnight bag. And something to take notes with. Maybe a coat. I have everything else we'll need."

Dani groaned. "Give me a second." She went back inside and returned a few minutes later with a bag and a fall jacket. "Let's go."

WHEN CAT AND DANI reached Weston Farm, the moon was high and bright, illuminating the fields and energizing Cat.

This was it. The first crop circle would appear tonight, and here she was, ready to capture it all on camera, video, and Gauss meter.

Cat pulled out the map she'd marked up and showed it to Dani with her flashlight. "This summer, I mapped out all the fields and surrounding landmarks, so we won't get lost. Here's the farmhouse, and the main entrance, and the side entrance . . ." She tapped each location on the page. "Do you have a compass?"

Dani shook her head.

"No problem! I brought an extra." Cat grabbed the two compasses from her bag. "If you get turned around, head south. When you come out of the field, you'll hit the main road."

"Okay," Dani said, taking the compass.

"I think tonight's circle will appear on the eastern side in the cornfields, but it might also be in the wheat fields toward the middle." Cat waited for some kind of excited response from Dani, but the other girl was still considering Cat's map. "This week, I interviewed an eyewitness to the last appearance, and I've been trying to triangulate where the circles should appear. What have you been up to?"

"Research," Dani said after a beat.

"What *kind* of research?" Cat prompted.

"About crop circles," Dani said, not meeting Cat's gaze. "And the people who make them."

"People?" Cat repeated. She was starting to get an odd feeling. "But—"

"I have it on good authority that this year's circles might be a prank courtesy of the high school football team."

"That doesn't account for any of the pre-circle phenomena that've been happening all week. The power surges and blackouts, the orbs . . ." Cat patted her binoculars. "Why do you think I've had these with me at all times?"

"I guess Jane's brother did say something about orbs . . ." Dani trailed off.

"And the appliances malfunctioning?"

Dani frowned. "What? Everything's working fine at our house . . ."

Cat stared at Dani as the odd feeling turned into a solid shade of disappointment. "You're not taking this seriously, are you? I thought you really wanted to win the McMurray Award."

Dani's eyes snapped up to Cat's. "I do. I just—" She huffed out a frustrated breath. "You know way more than I do about crop circles, okay?"

Oh. Dani felt out of her depth. Cat could help with that. She straightened her spine and smiled. "I get it. You don't know where to start. Well, I already have some experiments in mind for tonight. Do you want to help me get some control samples?"

Dani bit her lip in silence for a second, then said, "Sure."

They hurried across the cornfield and stopped where Cat was hoping the first circle would appear. "Here." She handed Dani a pair of shears, a Sharpie, and plastic baggies. "We'll get some of the cornstalks now and maybe some wheat a little later. We need a few stalks from the midpoint down for testing and comparisons. Make sure to space out the samples so we know we're getting a good look at the field as a whole. Mark approximately where each sample came from on this diagram." She gave Dani a sheet of graph paper that represented this field, with the surrounding paths marked for reference.

"Got it," Dani said, tucking the paper into her pocket. "Just the stalks? Nothing else?"

"We should get some soil samples, too," Cat said. "But the stalks will make the best experiment, so let's focus on those first."

Dani got to work. She was quiet. A little too quiet. When Cat had imagined having a research partner, what she'd pictured hadn't been quite so . . . silent. Maybe it had something to do with her parents.

"So, ballroom dance . . . ?" Cat finally said.

"Ugh. You heard that?"

"I gotta say, you don't strike me as a sequin-and-feather kind of girl."

"It's my mom. She's an artist, and she wants me to be one, too. She doesn't understand that—"

"Science is an art," Cat finished.

Dani looked at Cat like she was seeing her in a new light. "Yeah," she said. Then her face fell. "Try telling my parents that. They run this arts camp—"

"ArtistiKids!" Cat exclaimed.

"That's the one," Dani said softly.

"I did that a couple of summers when I was little," Cat said. "I thought your mom looked kind of familiar— Whoa. Do you hear that?"

Dani glanced around. "Hear what?"

"That trilling!" Cat's voice quivered with excitement. "I've heard that it often starts just before a circle forms." She craned her neck, hoping to see stalks of corn rippling or white lights in the sky—anything to prove she was right. But the corn was too tall.

"Whatever it is, it sounds kind of far away . . . ," Dani said.

"Shoot. You're right. Hurry!" Cat grabbed her gear and ran headlong into the corn. Stalks whipped past her face as she ducked and wove. By the time Cat hit the wheat field, her chest burned. Her legs turned to rubber beneath her, and she stumbled to her knees. When she tried to push herself back up, she realized her hands were touching flattened stems.

Shocked joy electrified her. She leaped up and whirled around, taking it all in. It was perfect.

"Dani!" she shouted triumphantly. "It's here!"

9

DANI

DANI STUMBLED OUT OF the tall wheat. "Cat!" she gasped. "Don't run off like that . . . Oh."

Her mom kept a small zen garden in her art studio. That's what the crop circle looked like. It was as though someone—someone *big*—had drawn a perfect circle in the wheat with a gigantic rake. Each stalk was folded down sharply, a few inches from the earth. They all pointed in the same direction, spiraling out from the center of the circle.

"Oh my gosh, oh my gosh, oh my gosh!" Cat was dancing around like her feet were on fire. "I can't believe this! It's exactly like I imagined! Isn't it the coolest thing you've ever seen?"

Dani shifted her weight. It felt a little like she was standing on a lush, crackly wheat carpet. "It is pretty cool." This had clearly taken a lot of planning and work. These hoaxers, whoever they were, knew what they were doing.

It would almost be a shame to expose them. But if that's what it took for Dani to win the McMurray Award . . .

Cat set her backpack on the ground and started pulling out equipment. "This"—she waved around a metal piece that looked kind of like an old MP3 player Dani's dad still had, but bigger—

"is a Geiger counter. I'll use it to scan for radioactive particles the alien tech may have left behind." She frowned. "It won't detect any microwaves that might have impacted the stalks, of course, but who knows what the UFOs run on? Always good to check for all kinds of anomalies."

"Okay," Dani said, ignoring the part about alien technology. "What am I going to do?"

Cat handed Dani a clean pair of shears and another handful of Ziploc baggies. "The same thing you were doing before. Get a few stalk samples from the very center of the formation and then a few from halfway across the diameter, all around the circle, and then one last batch from around the circle's edge. Here's the diagram for this field." She passed over another piece of graph paper. "You can sketch the circle in."

"Okay."

"Be really careful to label these as the crop circle samples," Cat warned. "We don't want to get them mixed up with the controls!"

Dani huffed, a little insulted. "I didn't walk into a lab for the first time yesterday." She looked at her clippers. "How come you get to use the cool equipment and I'm stuck snipping wheat?"

"Because *someone* ignored me all week." Cat raised her eyebrows at Dani. "I don't have time to explain all of this to you right now. We have to get our samples while the circle is fresh. Before anyone else shows up and contaminates the scene . . . or worse." She lowered her voice. "There are probably government agents on their way right now to start the cover-up!"

Dani sighed. "Whatever you say, Cat."

She started clipping, bagging, and labeling samples while her partner waved the Geiger counter around in each quadrant of the circle. It didn't take long for Dani to get into a good rhythm. Despite feeling a bit sidelined, she had to admit that she wasn't unhappy. Being in this circle was pretty cool. Gathering evidence was part of the scientific process. So was testing and analyzing it. Plus, there could be something on these plants—dirt or some other material that didn't belong on this land—that might give Dani a clue as to who was responsible.

If she wanted to make a strong case for the McMurray judges, she needed a hypothesis *soon*.

CAT UNLOCKED HER HOME'S back door at 1:47 A.M. "I'll get us some caffeine," she said, darting inside. She returned with two sixteen-ounce Mountain Dews. She shoved one into Dani's hands and then launched up the stairs to the second floor and up the extra flight to her attic lair. "I'll set up the specimen slides while you separate out the samples," she said as she flipped on the lights. "Then we'll run our experiment."

Dani took a swig of her soda and began pulling out the snipped stalks. "What kind of experiment is it?"

Cat grinned mischievously. "You'll see." She bounced over to the lab area on the far side of her room, where she put on the enormous olive-green puffy coat she'd been wearing when Dani first came here.

"What's with the coat?" Dani asked, watching her partner roll up the too-long sleeves.

"Inspiration," Cat said without elaborating.

Dani shrugged. She was honestly more interested in the other girl's lab. Cat's microscope was much nicer than the ones they had at school. Cat had other pieces of equipment Dani had never even seen before, much less learned how to use. Basically, it was a science kid's dream. Dani supposed that's what happened when you had a parent who worked at NASA. They actually understood and supported the things you loved.

Dani's eyes prickled. She rubbed them, chugged the rest of her soda, and got to work.

When Cat had the microscope set up, she asked, "Are the wheat samples ready?"

"Yep," Dani said. "The controls are on the right, and the crop circle samples are on the left."

"Great. See these nodes?" Cat pointed to a bumpy spot on one of the stalks where leaves sprouted out. "That's what we want to examine. You can prep a control-sample slide and I'll get one from the circles."

Dani felt the thrill of a new experiment run through her. Now that the controls and samples were side by side, she couldn't help but notice that the crop circle ones did look different from the controls, like Cat had hypothesized. The crop circle stalk nodes seemed . . . stretched out.

Cat had clearly noticed the difference as well. She vibrated with barely contained excitement until the slides were safely under the microscope. Then she let loose. She grabbed one of the crop circle samples and waved it around. "Check out these nodes! This is classic crop circle phenomena!"

"Maybe they just grew differently?" Dani suggested.

Cat shook her head. "Let's look at the slides." She peered into the microscope, adjusting the scope, while Dani hovered over her shoulder.

Curiosity tickled the back of Dani's brain. Her partner's enthusiasm was definitely catching.

"Yes!" Cat shrieked and practically shoved the microscope under Dani's nose. Dani looked . . . and almost gasped. While the two nodes had appeared different to the naked eye, under the slide, it became clearer why. On the crop circle slide, the node showed evidence of fraying and possibly even burning. It was clear that it had not grown that way.

"Tell me a team of guys with flattening boards did *that*," Cat said, a gleam in her eye.

"You're right," Dani said reluctantly. "That does look—"

"Microwave radiation!" Cat leaped to her feet and did a booty-shaking victory dance. "Personally, I think the balls of light that are often reported just before crop circles appear involve some sort of heat laser. That's what makes the nodes explode."

Dani laughed. And then she couldn't stop laughing. It was so late, and she'd had so much Mountain Dew, and her lab partner was talking about heat lasers contained in floating balls of light . . . "You're ridiculous," she said between giggles.

Cat didn't look insulted. "I'll prove I'm right. Come on!" She grabbed one of each of the samples and dashed down the stairs, shouting over her shoulder, "Thank goodness our microwave made it through the week in one piece!"

Dani tiptoed after her, arriving in the kitchen just as Cat was closing the microwave door. "What are you doing?" Dani asked, though she already had an inkling. She was starting to understand how Cat's brain worked. She wasn't sure if that was a good thing.

Cat hit the "Popcorn" button. "Wait for it . . ." The microwave began to whir, and an odd smell filled the kitchen.

They waited. The silence began to get awkward. So Dani did what she often did when she felt uncomfortable: She blurted out a science fact. "Did you know microwaves don't actually cook things from the inside out?"

". . . from the inside out?" Cat finished in unison with her. "Yes! What they do is—"

"They excite the molecules throughout the food—"

"So it cooks more evenly. And did you know microwaves are used in radar, too?" When Dani nodded, Cat patted her appliance like it was an obedient puppy. "Microwaves are kind of awesome."

When the microwave dinged, Cat squealed with excitement. She proudly set the microwaved control sample next to the crop circle one on the counter. "Microwave radiation, baby."

Dani hissed in a surprised breath. "Huh. They really do look similar."

"See how each node got longer and bulged? The microwave radiation causes the liquid inside the plant to expand. The nodes may not have bent like the crop circle ones, but I expect a UFO would generate a much larger amount of microwave radiation than a household appliance." Cat scooped up the stalks. "Let's compare them under the microscope. I've done the microwave test on wheat and cornstalks before, just to see what would happen, so I knew that would work. But this is the first time I've had a real crop circle sample, obviously, to compare it with. This is so cool!"

"Have you ever tried another heat source?" Dani asked. "Like the oven? Or a grill?"

Dani wouldn't have thought it would be possible for Cat to look any more delighted—but she did. "You're right!" the other girl exclaimed. "We should test how the stalks react to other heat sources so we can demonstrate that the distinct, quantifiable differences in the crop circles could only be caused by microwave radiation." She clapped her hands. "Our project is going to be so awesome!"

Dani grinned. It was nice to know someone else her age who loved conducting experiments as much as she did. She and Cat might have different ideas about what was going on at Weston Farm, but they could still be sisters in science.

Except . . . Dani wasn't telling Cat everything.

She tried to ignore her sudden pang of guilt. If Dani wanted to win the McMurray Award, she had to be willing to do whatever it took. She had to come up with a solid hypothesis for the circles' origins, and then she couldn't rest until her case was airtight. She and Cat might be partners, but when it came to proving aliens existed . . . Cat was on her own.

CAT

CAT WOKE UP TO an earthquake. At least, that's what it felt like.

She sat bolt upright, hair pointing every which way and eyes scanning for falling posters and samples. But all she saw was a sheepish-looking Dani next to her bed.

"Sorry, I hated to wake you, but I thought it was rude to leave without saying goodbye."

Cat swung her legs over the edge and slid off the bed. "You're leaving already? We still have more data to analyze. There's the Geiger counter readings and the Gauss meter—"

Dani grimaced. "It's already noon. My mom's waiting downstairs."

Cat rubbed her eyes and checked the clock to confirm. "Shoot. I don't even remember falling asleep." They'd been testing samples well into the wee hours of the morning. Cat remembered microwaving more wheat and cornstalks to confirm the experiment was replicable and uploading data from her equipment into her computer. She sort of remembered writing down Dani's ideas for more experiments they could run, but that was where things got a little fuzzy.

The night had actually been pretty great. Dani wasn't so bad away from school, now that they were both getting into the project. And Cat suspected Dani was starting to see that there was something not so natural about the crop circles after all.

"Did you go to sleep when I did?" Cat asked, realizing she was still dressed in the jeans and long-sleeve shirt she'd worn to Weston Farm. She was rumpled and grimy, while Dani looked rested and clean. "When did you wake up?"

"I went to bed when you passed out, and I got up when my mom called, about half an hour ago. You sleep really soundly, by the way." Dani half smiled as she admitted, "Last night was fun."

"Oh!" Cat ran over to her desk and began shuffling through papers. "There should be more circles tonight. Can you get away again? We're going to need a lot of additional stalk samples for all the heat experiments—"

Dani shook her head. "Sorry, I have a ton of homework to do before tomorrow. There's no way Mom is going to let me stay out late again on a school night."

Cat's shoulders slumped, but she wasn't surprised. "I understand. That's okay. I'll be out there. Hopefully I'll catch the aliens in the act this time." She patted her camera.

Dani snorted. "Good luck. See you tomorrow."

"Bye!" Cat waved as Dani headed down the stairs and then got straight to work. There was so much to do—probably more than she should be trying to do on her own—but Cat would take too much data over too little any day of the week. Especially when it came to aliens.

CAT YAWNED AS SHE wandered downstairs into the kitchen an hour later and poured herself a bowl of cereal. Her mother glanced up from the island, where she was dumping ingredients from a freezer bag into the slow cooker, no doubt for Cat to eat later while she was working second shift at the hospital. Cat's mom was a nurse, and before her dad left, she'd worked the day shift. But second shift paid better, so she'd made the switch.

"Finally awake?" Cat's mom ruffled her daughter's already mussed hair.

Cat shrugged. "Research."

"Your friend seems nice."

Cat stiffened automatically. "We're not exactly friends, more like . . . partners."

"Well, it's good to see you socializing with someone with a common interest."

"Yeah," Cat said. "Speaking of which, I'll need to go back to Weston Farm tonight. More data collection." She didn't mention that this time, Dani wouldn't be there.

Cat's mom waggled a spatula at her. "It's a school night. I trust you to be responsible. Don't stay out too late."

"I won't—I promise." Of course, Cat's idea of "late" and her mom's might not be the same . . . but her mom would never know. She slept like the dead. Cat and her mom had that in common.

"Are you sure the owner doesn't mind you hanging around?"

"Nope, he was totally fine with it." Cat had talked to Mr. Hepworth, the owner of Weston Farm, two weeks ago in preparation for the project. He'd granted her permission to come and go as she pleased, as long as she didn't do any permanent damage to the crops. He'd also spent a long time complaining about the "lookie-loos"—the crop circle fanatics and other curious people who showed up whenever something like this happened.

Cat suspected there were a lot of lookie-loos at the farm today. She'd done a quick scan of the various accounts she kept to monitor supernatural phenomena, and everyone was buzzing about last night. Only one crop circle had formed, and it was *enormous*. There were plenty of photos from inside the circle, which made Cat extra grateful she and Dani had somehow managed to get there first. But the best picture of all was an aerial one posted by the local news station. It showed that the formation was a perfect fractal, just as Cat had hoped.

Every piece of photographic evidence, plus the radiation readings from the Geiger counter and the magnetic field readings from the Gauss meter, indicated that something much more super than natural had flattened that wheat. Now they needed data that showed quantifiable differences between the real crop circles and the hoax circles she was certain would come later on. And if they happened upon a smoking gun proving the existence of extraterrestrial life . . . Cat's mind whirled from the possibilities. Her knee bounced while she crunched the last of her cereal and drained the milk from the bowl.

Her mom laughed when she looked up from her recipe book. "Dear, your chin."

Cat grinned and wiped the milk off her face. She stayed with her mom as she finished packing up for work. When Cat's dad had lived here, she'd seen her mom all the time. Now, with her new job and second-shift schedule, sometimes days would go by with Cat seeing her mom only in passing, if at all. It was nice to have a couple of minutes to chat and catch up.

But as soon as her mom's car had pulled out of the driveway, Cat retreated to her loft to prepare for the evening's stakeout, head swirling with numbers and hope.

THAT NIGHT, CAT SETTLED in at Weston Farm—this time in a tree. There were already too many people crawling around in the fields, and she wanted a bird's-eye view anyway. Tonight, she wasn't going to miss a thing just because she was shorter than the tall crop stalks.

The trees that lined this field were the main reason she'd chosen this particular spot for her stakeout. Of the remaining parts of the farm that had never seen a crop circle, this was the one bordered by trees with branches low enough for Cat to climb. Although Cat had passed through a horde of eager ufologists on her way here, now she could see only one other crop circle hunter in the area. That was a very good sign . . . or she was way off on the location.

Either way, she'd crack the pattern sooner or later.

She scanned the horizon with her binoculars. Then she unzipped her backpack and pulled out a can of Mountain Dew and a few Starbursts. She popped the tab on her soda and waited for something to happen. So far, her equipment was quiet, and the camera she had set up on the branch above her head showed nothing unusual. But it was still early. The sun had barely set.

Cat waited. And waited. And waited.

Right around the time her butt began to ache from sitting awkwardly in a tree, she noticed something odd. It looked like smoke was drifting over from the next field. But there was no burning smell to go along with it, and there were no flames as far as she could see. There were no shouts of alarm or fire-engine sirens. In fact, there were no sounds at all.

And it wasn't smoke; it was fog.

The mist crept across the fields slowly at first, inching its way toward the line of trees. Then, suddenly, it was all around, thick enough that Cat could barely see the ground—or even her hand in front of her face. The same high-pitched trilling noise from last night began, and the Gauss meter beeped rapidly. Cat's heart leaped into her throat, and she peered through her binoculars. It was fog, fog, fog, as far as the eye could see.

The trilling stopped. The fog receded as quickly as it had appeared. When it was gone, Cat and the other crop circle hunter stared at each other from across the field—with a freshly formed circle between them.

11

DANI

"HOW'S YOUR RESEARCH COMING along?" Ms. Blanks asked Dani on Monday morning. "Tell me everything."

"I spent last week reading up on crop circles," Dani began. "Cat knows a lot more than I do."

"A wise researcher knows what she doesn't know."

"I learned a bunch about the way crop circles are faked. Did you know it's usually people with planks of wood?"

"I did know that," Ms. Blanks said, sounding amused. "So your working hypothesis is that the Weston Farm Circles are made using the plank method?"

Dani faltered. "Well . . . no. I mean, I'm not sure."

Ms. Blanks tilted her head but didn't say anything.

"I guess I don't really have a hypothesis yet," Dani admitted.

"Danielle, the science fair is less than three weeks away."

"I know."

"What's Catrina been up to?"

"A lot, actually," Dani said. "She took me to Weston Farm on Saturday. She knew the first circle was going to show up that night."

Ms. Blanks's eyebrows went up. "Catrina predicted the first appearance?"

"Yeah, and remember last Monday's blackout?" Dani asked. Ms. Blanks nodded. "Cat predicted that, too, based on a pattern she found from the previous Weston Farm Circle events."

"What was the pattern?"

"It had to do with prime numbers . . . ," Dani said uncertainly, wishing she'd paid more attention to her partner's excited rambling. "Anyway, Cat took me to the substation near her house to measure the power surge on this device she had—an oscilloscope?" Ms. Blanks made a noise like she knew what that was. "I guess the data she got from *that* confirmed when the first circles would show up. Or it was another prime number thing. I'm . . . not totally sure."

"What did the two of you do at Weston Farm?" Ms. Blanks asked.

"We took a bunch of stalk samples and went back to Cat's place to test them."

"What were you testing for?"

"Evidence of microwave radiation," Dani said, relieved to know the correct answer this time. "Cat put some control samples in her microwave, and they came out looking a lot like the ones from the crop circle."

"You looked at the samples under a microscope?"

"Yeah. We examined the nodes on the stalks. And Cat said—"

"Danielle," Ms. Blanks cut in gently, "this doesn't sound like a partnership of equals."

"What do you mean?" Dani squeaked.

"It sounds to me like you're sitting back and letting Catrina take the lead. I know this whole thing was her idea and that it's much more in her wheelhouse, so to speak, but . . ." The teacher pursed her lips, seeming to consider her next words very carefully. "If you want to win the McMurray Award, you're going to need to show more initiative."

Dani felt stung. "I can't help it that Cat knows more than I do or that she's the one who owns all the fancy lab equipment."

"True, but are you keeping an open mind?"

"I still don't believe in aliens, if that's what you're asking."

Ms. Blanks smiled. "That's not quite what I meant. What I'm trying to say is . . . are there angles of investigation you aren't considering?"

"Angles of investigation . . . ," Dani murmured, closing her eyes. Sometimes, shutting out visual distractions helped her think more clearly. "I was researching *proven* hoaxes, where people confessed how they did it," she said slowly. "Cat isn't focused on those hoaxes. She cares about the circles that *haven't* been explained."

"Go on," Ms. Blanks said.

"Obviously, all crop circles are fake," Dani continued, "but are they all fake in the same way? No one has ever been caught making the circles at Weston Farm. No one has ever taken credit for them. So . . . what if *this* hoax is different from the other hoaxes?"

There was a furrow between her teacher's eyebrows. "That," she said, "is a very interesting question. How might you go about answering it?"

Dani's phone buzzed. She glanced at the screen.

CAT: We have to talk!!!!!!!!!!

Ten exclamation points. Whoa. Well, whatever Cat was so worked up about could wait.

Despite wanting to consider other hypotheses, Dani didn't feel like she could just throw out the board-stomping method as an explanation. After all, it was the most common way to create crop circles—and the wheat in the circle she'd seen on Saturday had been folded down as if it had been stepped on. But wooden planks wouldn't create those burned-looking stalk nodes.

So what if . . .

What if heat were involved—perhaps to flatten the stalks more easily? But it would have to be a portable heat source and one that wouldn't set the field on fire. Like . . . a hair dryer? Or maybe a space heater?

Meanwhile, Jane's brother, Hayden, thought the high school football team was behind the whole thing. Dani supposed it *would* take a really big group to pull off a circle the size of the one she'd seen without getting caught. Would some guys be on board-stomping duty while others applied heat to the stalks?

Oh! Cat had wanted to take soil samples on Saturday night, but in all the fuss with finding the circle, they'd forgotten! What if some of the players had dirt from Weston Farm on their sneakers? Could she check the soil from the crop circle against a sample from Scott Crawley's shoes?

"You look like your wheels are turning," Ms. Blanks observed.

Dani nodded. "Thanks for the push," she said and ran off to first period.

CAT SLID INTO THE chair next to Dani in fifth-period science, even though Laurel always sat there. "How come you didn't answer my text? I thought we were past all that."

Dani blinked. She'd been thinking about whether or not splinters from the hoaxers' boards could get stuck in the wheat stalks. "Oh, sorry. I wasn't ignoring you on purpose. I've been coming up with experiments for us to do."

"Yeah?" Cat smiled as wide as the happy Swamp Thing on her T-shirt. Luckily, Cat's grin wasn't filled with slimy green algae and brown leaves. "Like what?"

"Like . . . if we're going to test other heat sources besides the microwave, we need to know at what temperature the damage to the stalk nodes occurs. My mom has an oven thermometer. I can borrow it and bring it to your house. Oh, and do you have a hair dryer?"

"A hair dryer?" Now Cat looked confused.

"In case the hoaxers brought one to the field to heat the stalks," Dani explained.

Cat snorted. "Did they also bring their super-duper-extra-long extension cord? And their backup generator?"

"I mean, maybe," Dani said. "Oh! That could've been the trilling sound you heard!"

"Speaking of trilling sounds . . ." Cat wiggled her eyebrows. "Last night, I was actually there when the circle was created! I was sitting in a tree right next to it when it appeared!"

Dani gasped. "Wait, you *saw* it happen?"

"Well . . . no. There was this really thick fog that rolled in out of nowhere, and—"

"So you didn't see anything." Dani was surprised at how let down she felt.

"The field was normal," Cat said, her voice taking on a story-telling quality. "Then the fog came up, and I heard the trilling sound. My equipment went haywire! When the fog disappeared, the circle was right below me! It was incredible, Dani. You should've been there."

"Your equipment," Dani said slowly. "Like, your camera?"

"Of course my camera! I mean . . . all it recorded was fog. But the Gauss meter—"

"How long did all this take?"

"It was so fast," Cat said. "Only a couple of minutes. There was no way hoaxers could—"

"Depends on *how many* hoaxers," Dani said, thinking again of the high school football team. "And maybe they play that trilling noise to cover the sound of their footsteps—"

A throat cleared behind them. "Um, this is my seat?"

Dani jolted. "Hi, Laurel! Cat and I were discussing our project. But we're done now. Talk to you after school, Cat?"

"Sure." Cat seemed dismayed, but she bounced back fast. "I love your dress, Laurel. It looks like the aurora borealis."

"Thanks . . . ?" Laurel said. "I like your . . . shoes."

Cat clicked the heels of her clunky Doc Martens, which were painted to look like the night sky. "Thank you! I bet they'd go great with your dress. You could do a whole astronomy-themed outfit. Want to borrow them?"

Laurel coughed, looking at her stylish ankle boots. "No, but thanks. Can I sit down now?"

"Oh. Yeah." Cat got to her feet. "Later, Dani!"

"Later."

Laurel waited until Cat had gone to her usual seat by the windows and then said quietly, "How's the research going?"

"Good. I think."

"You think?"

Before Dani could explain, Ms. Blanks called the class to order. As their teacher took roll, Dani studied her friend. Cat was right; the pattern on Laurel's dress *did* look like the aurora borealis. Laurel probably didn't even know what the aurora borealis was.

Which was fine. So Laurel wasn't a science person. So none of Dani's friends were into science the way she was—the way she and Cat both were. Friends could like different things.

Dani glanced over her shoulder at Cat. She was staring out the window, chin in hand. She looked far away, probably dreaming up experiments to do for their project. Dani was honestly kind of excited to learn what Cat had in mind next.

But first, it was time to run an experiment of her own.

12

CAT

"WHY ARE WE HERE?" Cat asked, puzzling at the locker room door.

"I'm following a lead." Dani pushed the door open. "Hello?" She flinched.

"What's— *Oh*." Cat was assaulted by a wall of thick, rancid air. The stench was so bad, she could still smell it after she pulled her Swamp Thing T-shirt up over her nose.

Dani had told her she needed to talk to someone at the high school for their project, but she hadn't told her anything else— such as who this mysterious source was. Cat loved the idea of having their very own Deep Throat!

But Cat wasn't sure what kind of source they'd meet in a locker room. And the smell. It was . . . bad. She'd botched a fermentation experiment in her lab once, and the stink had lingered for weeks. Amazingly, this was worse.

"Is anyone in here?" Dani asked as they rounded a corner. "I'm looking for . . ." She faded off, and Cat ran smack into her back.

They both stared.

High school boys. Shirtless. Some wearing nothing but towels wrapped around their waists.

One of the guys spotted them. "What the— Get those kids out of here!"

"Who're you calling a kid?" Cat retorted.

"Scott Crawley," Dani said, pink-cheeked. "We need to talk to Scott Crawley."

A white guy with blond hair stepped forward, pulling on his shirt. "I'm Scott. Do I know you?"

"No," Dani said. "But we're conducting some research you might be able to help us with."

"They have *research* they want you to *help them with*," another guy chimed in to laughter and catcalls from the rest of the football team.

"Shut up, Landon," Scott said. "Shut up, all of you."

Dani raised her voice. "I was told you might be the guy to talk to about this year's Weston Farm Circle hoax."

Cat groaned. "Dani—"

"Whoa, whoa, whoa. You think I'm the one making those weird circles?" Scott asked.

"That's what I was told," Dani said primly.

"Who said that?" Scott demanded. Cat wanted to know the answer to that, too.

"I can't tell you. Researcher-source privilege." She leaned in to whisper in Cat's ear, "Sample the dirt on Scott's sneakers. I'll keep him distracted."

"What?"

"Dirt. Shoes. Go."

Cat snapped into action. "Can I sit here?" she asked, walking over to the bench behind Scott. She sat without waiting for an answer. She surreptitiously pulled a plastic baggie from her pocket—she always carried sandwich bags with her just in case—and went to work on the shoes, angling her body to hide what she was doing.

Of course, the dirt on Scott's shoes wouldn't prove anything. Even if he had been at Weston Farm over the weekend, it didn't mean he'd made the circles. But if this was what it took to convince Dani to abandon her hoaxer theories, Cat would happily play along.

"Okay, 'fess up," Dani said loudly, pulling the room's focus.

Scott laughed. "I've got better things to do than draw pictures in a field."

"My source said it was a senior prank," Dani insisted, "and that I should look at the football team. Maybe someone here has a brother or cousin who was in high school thirteen years ago? Or it's a team tradition?"

"Guys!" Scott addressed his team. "Who here has a secret identity as a little green man?"

"*Your mom* is a little green man!"

Even Cat snorted at that one. Dani shot her a desperate look. Right on cue, Cat pried off a hunk of dried mud. She shoved it into the baggie and tucked the entire thing away in her jeans pocket.

"Thank you for your time," Dani said stiffly, and she and Cat ran for the door.

Out in the hallway, Dani leaned against the wall, catching her breath. "Thanks for the backup."

"Of course. We're partners." Cat paused. "But it would've helped to know what you were trying to do before we walked in."

Dani glanced at her. "I wasn't sure you'd come with me if you knew. I mean, Scott Crawley isn't an alien."

"That we know of . . ." Cat made a silly face, and Dani giggled. She grabbed Dani's arm. "Come on. We did your thing. Now it's my turn."

WESTON FARM WAS COMPLETE chaos. There were news vans and camera crews, vendors selling alien-themed merchandise, and a guy taking bets on where the next circles would appear. Across the street, a gigantic tent was going up for the festival that the town had planned for the next couple of nights. People with signs saying things like WE COME IN PEACE and THE TRUTH IS HERE lined the edges of the fields, singing and chanting and raising their hands to the sky.

Cat's chest filled with a strange emotion—part pride, because these were totally her people, but also a little embarrassment at what Dani might think.

She spied a man in a flannel shirt at the produce stand near the entrance. "Oh, hey! There's Mr. Hepworth. He's the owner." Cat dragged Dani toward him. "Mr. Hepworth, this is my lab partner, Dani Williams!"

"Hi," Dani said. "Thanks for letting us have access to your fields."

Mr. Hepworth grunted. "I trust you two are being careful, yeah?"

Cat and Dani both nodded. "Absolutely!" Cat said.

"Good, that's more than I can say for the rest of these folks," the farmer grumbled. "At least it's only every thirteen years. Have fun with your project, girls."

"Come on." Cat tugged on Dani's jacket sleeve. "Let's get to the fields. This place is crawling with ufologists and groupies, and I want to check something before it gets any more crowded."

"*More* crowded?" Dani blurted.

"It'll get worse when the sun goes down and people are waiting for the next circles to appear." Cat led Dani toward the field where she'd seen the second circle form. "Last night, while I was sampling the crop stalks, I was getting all kinds of weird readings on the compass," she explained. "I want to see if it's still wonky today." When they reached the cornfield by the tree line where Cat had perched for hours, waiting, Cat raced to the center of the crop circle and pulled out her compass.

Dani crouched and ran her fingers through the soil. "Hey, Cat, on Saturday, you mentioned getting soil samples. But we never got any."

Cat smacked her forehead with the palm of her hand. "You're right!" She dug through her bag and produced a trowel, a box of plastic bags, a Sharpie, and yet another graph paper diagram. "Here."

Dani took the supplies, walked to the very center of the circle, and began to dig. "You know," she said slowly, "since you've been doing so much work already on the stalk nodes and on the readings from your equipment, why don't I take the lead on the soil samples?"

"So you can compare them with the dirt I pulled off Scott Crawley's shoe?" Cat smiled as Dani opened her mouth and closed it again. "Yeah, I figured it out. And I'm not mad. The more hoax explanations we can dismiss, the closer we'll get to the actual truth."

"Okay. Anyway, I'm sure there's a lot of other interesting stuff in this soil . . ." Dani faded off, intently studying the dirt in her trowel.

"Find something?" Cat asked.

Dani quickly bagged and labeled the pile of soil. "I don't know." She checked the time on her phone. "I'll bag some more samples while you collect your data. But my mom wants me home for dinner. She needs to talk to me about something."

Cat rolled her eyes. "She planning to force you to try basket weaving now?"

Dani gave a half-hearted laugh. "She's still stuck on the ball-room dancing idea."

"Oh! You said your mom's an artist, right? You know what you could do to show her that science is an art, too? Show her the crop circles—they're fractal patterns, and they're beautiful."

Dani squirmed, looking uncomfortable. "Honestly, I'm not sure it would help."

"Couldn't hurt, right?" Cat said.

The look on Dani's face suggested that yes, perhaps, it could. Cat opened her mouth to ask her partner what was wrong but then decided she should probably butt out. Dani clearly wasn't ready to open up about her parents. Still, Cat's scientist brain couldn't help wanting to solve a tricky problem.

While Dani kept collecting soil samples, moving methodically outward from the center of the circle, Cat walked to the far edge, eyes glued to her compass. The readings wavered the closer she got to the midpoint but calmed to normal as she reached the perimeter.

"Looks like there's still some residual magnetic polarization here!" Cat called to Dani.

"Um, Cat?"

Cat spun around. Dani was at the circle's southern edge, flanked by two white men in black suits. Cat's breath caught in her throat.

Men in Black. She'd never seen one in person. She certainly hadn't expected them to come to their little nowhere town, even for a paranormal event as exciting as the Weston Farm Circles.

"What do you think you're doing?" she cried, running toward them. Of course, she already knew the answer to that. They were doing what Men in Black did: stealing evidence and shutting down investigations. One of the men was already holding Dani's trowel and sample bags. "Those are ours!" Cat shouted.

The first man put out a hand to stop her. "This site is closed," he said in a low, gravelly voice. He flashed a badge, but so quickly that Cat couldn't tell what department he was with. "By order of the United States government."

He might as well have dumped cold water on Cat's head. She didn't want to get on the wrong side of the government, especially since her dad worked for NASA. She wanted him to come home for the right reasons—because he was proud of her, not because she'd royally screwed up.

"We're doing a science project. It's for school." Cat put on her best innocent face, but it had no effect. Between the two men, Dani stood perfectly still, white as a sheet.

"I don't care if aliens sold you this plot of land," said Man in Black Number One, who was tall, broad-shouldered, and wore a permanent scowl. "You can't be here."

"But we—"

"I don't want to hear it, kids. Get out of here." Man in Black Number Two, a short, stocky guy wearing wire-frame glasses, shoved Dani forward. She grabbed Cat, tugging her away before she could object.

When they reached the next field, Dani slowed her pace and released her grip on Cat's arm. "Sorry," she said, "but those guys were serious."

"And kind of scary."

"Very."

They walked back toward the farm entrance, which was now deserted. The Men in Black must have chased away all the revelers and news crews.

"I can't believe they took my trowel! And the soil samples!" Cat stomped in frustration.

To her surprise, Dani smiled. "Well, they may have missed some." She opened her backpack and moved her sweater aside. Cat peeked in: Several filled sample bags sat neatly at the bottom.

She grinned and high-fived her partner. "I would never have pegged you as one to smuggle material out of a 'government site.'"

Dani shook her head, but her smile widened. "Neither would I."

13

DANI

DANI STARED AT THE row of jars on Cat's workstation. Each one contained a generous scoop of soil from Weston Farm. Of the five samples she'd saved from the circle Cat swore had appeared out of the fog, three were from the midpoint and two were from the outer edge. It wasn't much, especially without control samples for comparison—but it was a start.

She also had the crusty piece of mud from Scott Crawley's sneaker in a jar, ready to be analyzed. But it was pretty obvious even to the naked eye that the dirt wasn't the same. Scott's sneaker mud was orangey brown. The soil from the farm was a deeper, richer brown. And then there were those little black specks . . .

Dani picked up one of the canisters of Weston Farm soil and peered through the glass. The sample was filled with tiny black dots. There were no dark specks in the hunk of crusty dirt from Scott Crawley's shoe, which meant her first and only lead . . . was a bust.

Why wasn't she more upset?

Because this project had just gotten exponentially more interesting.

Why would there be government agents at Weston Farm? Did they believe this alien nonsense, too? Or was there something else going on? The question she'd asked Ms. Blanks floated through her mind: *What if this hoax is different from the other hoaxes?*

The agents hadn't wanted Dani and Cat to sample the soil. That had to mean there was something worth investigating. If there *was* evidence in the soil . . . Dani had to find it before Cat did.

"All set over there?" Cat called from her bed. She was buried in a thick book on crop circles, rereading everything about how microwave radiation affected cereal stalks.

"I'm good," Dani said. "Thanks."

She grabbed her notebook and started preparing slides so she could examine the soil under the microscope. It was engrossing work, and she lost track of time. She'd just finished lining up her samples in the slide holder when Cat said, "Are you going to answer that?"

"Answer what?"

"Your phone. It's rung four times already."

Dani dug her phone out of her bag. "It's my mom. Ugh. I'm late for dinner."

Cat unfolded herself from the bed. "I can finish prepping the samples if you need to go."

"No!" Dani slammed her notebook closed. The quick motion rattled the slides in their box, and she winced. She had to be more careful—and less jumpy. She didn't want Cat to get suspicious. The other girl *was* looking at her curiously, so Dani said, in a calmer voice, "I guess I'm done for today. How about you?"

"I have some reading to do for English and a math worksheet to finish. But after that, I thought I'd take another look at the nodes from last night's circle. I wish I'd gotten some samples from before the fog . . ."

"Next time," Dani said, trying to be encouraging.

Cat moaned. "There won't *be* a next time, remember? Those Men in Black locked down the whole field."

Dani blinked. "Wait. Men in Black? Like the movies? There's no such thing."

"Dani." Cat spoke slowly and carefully. "Two men in black suits, who said they work for the government, just shut down a crop circle site. They were absolutely Men in Black."

"But—"

"You're right about one thing, though: There should be more circles coming. Eleven more, to be precise. *Those* we can try to sample more comprehensively."

"Sure," Dani said. She looked at her soil samples. "Can I, um, come back tomorrow? I didn't get a chance to use the microscope. It's so much better than the ones at school . . ."

Cat frowned. "You're only being nice to me because of my lab equipment, aren't you?"

"What? No!"

"Relax," Cat said, laughing now. "I'm teasing. Please come over tomorrow." She cleared her throat. "This is going okay. Isn't it? Us working together?"

"Yeah." To Dani's surprise, it wasn't entirely a lie. "Thanks for letting me be in charge of the soil testing."

Her partner beamed. "Are you kidding? I'm glad you want to."

"In fact," Dani went on, hoping she wasn't pushing her luck, "why don't we divide and conquer? We can check each other's work later." This was the problem with their research lab doubling as Cat's bedroom. Unless Dani wanted to carry all those jars of dirt home every night—which would be *really* suspicious, not to mention potentially messy—she had no way of keeping Cat away from her work.

"Divide and conquer?" Cat repeated.

"Just for now," Dani said quickly. "The circles are only here for a short time, and we only have a couple of weeks until the science fair. We'll cover more ground if we take separate jobs. You'll do the stalks, and I'll do the soil."

Cat still looked a little doubtful. "I guess. But you'll tell me if you find anything good? Or if you have any questions?"

"Of course. You're still our UFO expert."

Cat's face broke into a wide smile. "Sure am."

"Then I'll pick up where I left off tomorrow, and you can fill me in on anything new you find tonight." Dani held out her hand.

Cat shook. "Deal."

AFTER DINNER, DANI SAT at her computer and googled "black specks in crop circle soil." A few clicks later, she stumbled upon a treasure trove of information. "Iron microspheres," she read aloud.

Some cereologists believed that during the creation of a crop circle, particles of magnetic material were brought down from space. The heat from the spaceship, and from all that radiation Cat kept going on about, fused that material together into tiny globs of metal. This was supposedly one way to tell a "true" crop circle from a hoax: Iron microspheres in the soil meant aliens had visited.

Dani didn't believe that for a second.

But she couldn't deny that the iron microspheres were *there*.

She was suddenly extra glad she'd asked Cat to let her handle the soil samples. If Cat spotted the iron microspheres, she'd get the wrong idea. She'd call it hard proof, instead of seeing it for what it was: another variable to explore.

And oh, it was an *interesting* variable.

If iron microspheres were common enough in crop circle stories to have a supernatural explanation, they also had to have a non-supernatural explanation—a scientific explanation. Dani could try to figure out where they really came from and whether they were part of the hoax.

Cat's excited face flashed in her mind. How would Dani's partner feel when she found out Dani hadn't told her about a key piece of evidence?

Well, it wasn't like Dani was going to hide the iron microspheres forever. Just until she had a firm hypothesis about their origins. Once Dani knew exactly what she was going to present to the McMurray committee, she'd tell her partner the truth.

And anyway, scientists did this all the time. They challenged each other to be more rigorous. This was how breakthroughs happened. There was nothing wrong with a little competition.

Except that this particular competition was one-sided. Dani knew. Cat didn't.

With a sigh, Dani refined her Google search. Querying "iron deposits in soil" got a lot of hits about soil composition and gardening. She scrolled and skimmed until something jumped out at her.

Whoa. Iron could be used as a natural weed killer? There was a word Dani didn't recognize, describing the form the iron had to take: *chelated*. Feeling the helium-balloon giddiness of a developing hypothesis, Dani typed "chelated iron herbicide" into her search engine. Right away, she struck gold. The local Bug-Be-Gone pesticide factory was about to release a new herbicide, Weed-Be-Gone.

What was one of the product's primary ingredients? *Chelated iron.*

And where was the factory located? *Three miles from Weston Farm.*

Dani heard her parents come upstairs. Luckily, they went straight down the hall to their room. Thank goodness. Dani wasn't in the mood for another tense discussion about ballroom dance lessons.

Thinking about strutting around in sequins and feathers reminded Dani of Cat's suggestion that she show her mom the art hidden in the crop circles. Obviously, she wasn't going to do that . . . but it was a nice idea. Cat was pretty thoughtful. Why was it that the only person who seemed to really understand Dani's passion was the person whose research she was essentially hijacking?

Dani puffed out a frustrated breath and got back to reading. She couldn't afford to feel guilty now. She was only doing this because Cat had submitted the project proposal without her. Dani was fighting an uphill battle to win the McMurray Award.

She had to become an expert on chelated iron herbicides ASAP.

It was going to be a long night.

14

CAT

"HI!" CAT SET HER green alien-head lunch box on Dani's desk in fifth-period science. "I have news."

"Cat! Hello!" Dani eyed the lunch box. "What's up?"

"Please don't let me intrude," Dani's friend Laurel said from the next seat over. She turned to talk to the girl on her other side, and Cat watched as a look of raw vulnerability flickered across Dani's face.

Then Dani shook herself and faced Cat. "What's up?" she asked again.

"You're coming over to work on the project after school, right?" Cat bounced on her toes.

"Of course."

"Perfect. Bring a hat and a windbreaker."

Dani raised an eyebrow. "Why would I need a hat and a jacket to test soil samples?"

Cat grinned. "We'll continue our experiments *after* we take a little ride."

Dani sat up straighter. "What are you talking about?"

Before Cat could spill her secret, Billy Baker and Shawn Lee sauntered up to Dani's desk, smirking at each other. "Oh, look!" Billy said loudly. "It's Science and Strange."

"Wh-what?" Dani stammered.

"Hey, so," Shawn said, "I've got this problem at my house? The toilet keeps overflowing, and I think it's a poltergeist."

"A poltergeist?" Cat repeated. "What makes you say—"

"Call a plumber," Dani cut in.

"Aw, c'mon." Billy made a pleading face. "Don't you wanna come over and test the bathroom for ectoplasm or whatever?"

Cat's eyebrows went up. "Wait, did you seriously find signs of—"

"Cat, they're making fun of us," Dani said through gritted teeth.

On cue, both boys burst into laughter. So did everyone else who was within earshot. Everyone except Laurel.

"Ha-ha, show's over," Laurel said dryly, scooting her desk closer and turning her back on the boys. "You okay?" she asked.

Dani nodded, and Laurel's eyes angled up to Cat. "All good," she said. She'd been made fun of before, and she would be again. It was the cost of being a visionary. And if Shawn's bathroom *had* had a poltergeist, she might've been able to do something about it, so the joke was on them, really.

At the front of the room, Ms. Blanks was writing something on the board. Class was about to start. Cat wasn't sure she could keep her secret inside for the entirety of fifth period.

"Dani!" She bent down and lowered her voice, since her partner still seemed shaken. "My dad has a friend here in town who does crop-dusting. Since he's feeling super guilty for not being able to make it back for the science fair, Dad pulled some strings: His friend's going to take us for a ride over Weston Farm!" Cat hugged her lunch box to her chest. "We're going to see the crop circles from above! And not just on TV! For *real*!"

Dani's eyes widened. "Wow, that's . . . wow. What about the Men in—the government agents?"

"You can say it: Men in Black. We won't be anywhere near the perimeter they set up," Cat said matter-of-factly, "because we won't be on the ground."

WHEN THEY GOT TO Weston Farm after school let out, they found a small Cessna plane waiting for them on the far side of the fields, where there was a long, wide grassy strip used for landing and takeoff. Cat had only ever flown twice before, to visit her dad in Texas, but that had been in a commercial aircraft.

This was different. It looked . . . rickety.

But it would be worth it, of that she was sure.

Dani, however, was looking a little green around the gills. "You're *sure* this is safe?"

"Flying is totally safe. Safer than driving to the mall. My dad says Mike is a great pilot."

"And your mom's fine with this?" Dani asked.

"Let's just say what my mom doesn't know can't hurt her. Besides, my dad thinks it's fine. Otherwise, he wouldn't have set this up. Did *you* tell your parents what we were doing?"

Dani flinched. "Not . . . entirely."

"They would've said no, huh."

That earned Cat a sharp laugh from her partner. "Yes, they would've said no."

Cat waved to Mike as they walked toward the plane. He looked familiar. She must've met him before when she was younger and her dad was still around. He wasn't quite how Cat had pictured a pilot, with a funny hat or at least some aviator goggles. Instead, Mike looked like he could have just as easily been running out to the store.

"You must be Cat," he said when they reached him. "Your dad tells me you're interested in this year's crop circles?"

Cat nodded vigorously as she shook his hand. "We can't wait to see them from the air."

"Get on in. You two ever flown in a plane like this before?" He patted the side of his Cessna.

"Nope," Cat and Dani said at the same time.

Mike laughed. "Then brace yourselves." He helped them settle into the passenger seats and buckle in securely. Then he hopped into the cockpit and began fiddling with all kinds of buttons and knobs. Cat was fascinated. She leaned forward to get a closer look as the propeller began to spin. It wasn't long before they were bumping down the grass strip. Dani clung to her seat with white knuckles, and Cat grinned in her partner's direction.

"Hold on!" Mike called back as the plane picked up speed. Cat's stomach hit her knees as they lifted into the air.

She pressed her face to the window to get a better look. The fields passed beneath them in green-and-yellow waves. She pulled out her camera and her map so she could flag the circles on it more accurately.

When they reached the fields with the circles, Cat's breath caught in her throat.

They were perfect. The most exquisite things she'd ever seen.

TV and the computer screen didn't do them justice. How anyone could believe these were man-made was beyond her. She quickly checked the orientation on the map and made a couple of adjustments. Then her camera clicked nonstop.

The circles weren't just circles. They were sweeping swirls and concentric rings. The first fractal looked like a snail shell, while last night's formation was more like a starfish. As Cat had expected, each formation adhered to the golden ratio. She'd always been fascinated by the Fibonacci sequence, where each number was the sum of the two before it, and she loved how the golden ratio expressed that in beautiful things in nature, like sunflowers and seashells. But seeing it in her hometown crop circles took her breath away.

And there was something else . . .

Excitement swept over her as an idea began to form. Seeing the three designs from above, all together, felt different than studying individual photographs. There was something about where the formations were placed that was more geometric than she'd realized.

Cat was so absorbed, she nearly forgot about Dani. It wasn't until they were headed back to the landing strip that Cat looked over at her partner. Dani was scribbling something in that notebook of hers. Her face was flushed. Cat hoped it was with excitement and not terror.

The descent was as bumpy as the takeoff. Cat had to admit she was relieved to be back on land, despite the thrill of flying over the circles. She and Dani got out of the plane on wobbly legs.

"So, what did you think?" Mike said, grinning.

"A-MA-ZING!" Cat whooped, then steadied herself on the side of the plane.

"They sure are something, real or not," Mike said.

Dani stepped forward. "Do you actually dust these fields for Weston Farm?"

"Usually, yeah. Not this year, though. Some newcomer outbid me."

"Do you work for a specific company or for the farmer?"

"Whoever will hire me. It's seasonal work and extra cash. My day job is actually at Computech. This is a little more fun."

"How much do you know about the pesticides and herbicides they use on Weston Farm?" Dani demanded.

Mike shrugged. "Not much. I just use what they give me to load up on the plane."

"Not even the brand?"

Mike considered, squinting in thought. "They've used different brands over the years, but this year I hear they're testing out some new weed killer. Not on the market yet. From that factory near here . . ."

"Was it Weed-Be-Gone?" Dani asked quickly.

"Might have been," Mike answered with a shrug. "Like I said, I didn't get the job."

Cat listened, frowning. This line of questioning had nothing to do with UFOs or crop circles, so she didn't understand why Dani was so interested. Maybe she had a secret horticultural hobby?

"Anyway," Mike said, "I gotta get going."

"Thank you so much!" Cat shook his hand. "It was so cool."

"I hope you found what you were looking for," Mike said.

Dani grinned—the first genuine smile Cat had seen from her all day. "Thank you. Yes, I believe we did."

DANI

FROM THE SKY, THE circles had looked like they'd been stamped into the earth. Smaller circles spiraled out from the big ones in patterns that were meant to be mathematically perfect. They were beautiful. If Dani hadn't been certain that crop circles weren't the least bit extraterrestrial, she might've gotten swept up in the wonder of it all, just like Cat.

But Dani was a realist. She believed in what she could prove.

She was . . .

She was *Science*, and Cat was *Strange*.

Dani's classmates' laughter echoed in her memory. It wasn't that she was embarrassed about being a nerd. She loved science, and there was nothing wrong with that.

No, the part that bothered her was that she preferred to fly under the radar. Being teamed up with Cat, who wore her nerdiness on her sleeve (and her lunch box, and her overalls, and her backpack . . .), was making the radar zoom in on her. Dani didn't want to be a target—even if the nickname "Science" felt kind of like a badge of honor.

It was confusing.

Dani tried to focus on the aerial photo of Weston Farm on Cat's bedroom wall. The quick interview with Mike after the flight had thrown her herbicide hypothesis for a loop—in a good way. Her plan had been to look up the relative elevations of Weston Farm and the Bug-Be-Gone factory, to see if the iron-filled weed killer was seeping downhill to the affected fields in the groundwater.

Not anymore. According to Mike, Weston Farm was a test site for Weed-Be-Gone. So that solved that mystery.

What Dani still didn't know was:

1. Were there iron microspheres in the soil outside the crop circle formations?
2. Did the iron in her crop circle soil samples even match the chelated iron in the herbicide?

To answer the first question, she needed control samples. Unfortunately, thanks to the government agents prowling around Weston Farm, getting her hands on those controls was going to be difficult.

To answer the second question, Dani needed a sample of Weed-Be-Gone. She'd looked up "chelated," and while she didn't understand all the complex chemistry terminology, it seemed to mean that the iron had been bonded to another compound, which would help it absorb into the soil. Would that look like the tiny black dots she saw in her soil jars? She had no idea.

What if it didn't? How, then, would she know if the iron in the soil came from the herbicide?

What if this was another variable that had to do with heat? What if the same heat source that had caused the damage to the stalk nodes also affected the chelated iron? If she heated up the weed killer, would it—

"You look like you're calculating the probability of the existence of a multiverse."

Dani startled. "What?"

"You're thinking really hard." Cat walked over to stare at the aerial photo from Dani's vantage point. "Clue me in?"

"Um. Not yet."

"Talking it out can help," Cat said, bumping Dani's shoulder.

"Soon," Dani said. "I promise."

Her partner shrugged. "Sure. But remember, we're in this together. And like you said, I'm the UFO expert."

"I remember," Dani said as the guilt over keeping secrets from Cat crept back in.

"DO YOU HAVE A pH testing kit?" Dani asked Cat an hour later.

"As a matter of fact, I do!" Cat swung open her closet door and began to rummage around. "A few years ago, I thought our garden was being attacked by fairies. When I told my dad, he advised me to run some tests. I used my allowance on this pH kit." She started tossing things over her shoulder: a stuffed bear with oversize Bigfoot feet, a black knit ski mask, a camouflage makeup set, a life jacket. "It's designed for little kids, not real scientists, but it should do the trick."

"Fairies?" Dani stepped out of the way as a hot-pink whistle flew past her head.

"I was eight," Cat said from inside the closet.

Dani snorted. Cat believed in aliens and ghosts, but apparently fairies were a step too far. "How about potassium permanganate?" she asked. "And a colorimeter?"

"A color-what-now?" Cat emerged from the closet with a dusty box in her hands and an intrigued look on her face.

"A colorimeter. I read about them online. I want to do an active-carbon test on this crop circle soil. You mix a purple liquid—a solution of potassium permanganate—with the soil sample. If the liquid becomes less purple, the soil is healthy."

"And if it stays purple?" Cat asked.

"Then the soil is dead. I think the colorimeter tells you *how* dead."

"By 'dead,' you mean things can't grow in it?"

"Healthy soil is packed with microorganisms like bacteria and fungi," Dani explained, glancing at her notes. "Those organisms, along with bigger ones like bugs and worms, break down organic matter, providing the nutrients that help plants grow. Dead soil won't support life."

Cat nodded thoughtfully. "I see where you're going with this. The microwave radiation from the spaceships probably would affect the health of the soil. What does pH have to do with it?"

"I want to see if the soil in the crop circles is more acidic or alkaline than the control soil." As usual, Dani ignored the part of Cat's statement that mentioned spaceships. What was important was determining whether the soil was quantifiably different within versus outside the circles—and then figuring out what Weed-Be-Gone had to do with it.

"If you write down what you need, I can get my dad to buy it," Cat said. "He'll ship express if I tell him it's for the McMurray Competition."

"That's amazing!"

"Yeah," Cat said, but with about half her usual enthusiasm. "My dad's really supportive."

"Obviously." Dani gestured at the lab. "He got you all this equipment, right?"

"Sure did." Cat looked away.

Cat's lackluster response made Dani feel that splinter feeling again. "All my parents ever get me is paintbrushes and tap shoes," she said, her voice coming out sharper than she intended.

A beat passed before Cat muttered, "At least both your parents are here."

Dani didn't know what to say. She didn't want to put her foot in her mouth, so she busied herself with unboxing the pH testing kit. Across the room, Cat shoved junk back into her closet.

After a couple of minutes of heavy silence, Cat asked, "Do you want to stay for dinner? My mom left a lasagna in the fridge. We can heat it up anytime."

"Sounds great," Dani said, relieved the awkward moment had passed. "I'll text my mom."

"I'll go preheat the oven." Cat headed for the stairs but paused at the top. "We can cook some crop stalks once the lasagna's done! Did you bring the oven thermometer?"

Dani pulled it from her backpack and handed it over with a flourish. "Ta-da!"

Cat grinned at her, and Dani grinned right back.

THE NEXT MORNING, WHILE Dani was in the kitchen pouring herself a bowl of Cheerios, she heard something that stopped her in her tracks:

We interrupt this broadcast with breaking news from Weston Farm, where local farmer Frank Hepworth has just claimed responsibility for this year's crop circles.

Dani dropped the cereal box and sprinted for the living room.

"Well," the farmer drawled on the TV as Dani threw herself onto the sofa. "My boys and I—"

"These are your sons, here with you today?" interrupted the reporter, a pretty brunette named Selina Diaz.

"Yes, ma'am. This is Bart, my oldest, and Leo, my youngest. And my nephews, Stan and Joe."

"The five of you worked together to create the crop circle designs?"

"Oh, you're awake," Dani's dad said from the recliner. He reached for the remote.

"Don't!" Dani yelped as her dad's finger hovered over the "Mute" button. "I'm supposed to do a report on the news. For school."

Her dad raised his eyebrows at her but left the TV alone.

"—this very plank," Mr. Hepworth was saying on-screen. He held up a board with a length of rope attached and demonstrated how he could shuffle forward, flattening a stalk of wheat at the edge of the field. "And that's how it's done."

"Weston Farm has been family-owned for generations," commented the reporter. "You married into the family twenty-five years ago and took over business operations in 2011. Were the Westons and the Hepworths also responsible for the previous crop circle phenomena?"

Mr. Hepworth got a mischievous look on his face. "I'm afraid I can't tell you anything more. This is a highly classified operation. I've already said too much."

"Then why are you talking about it on live TV?" Dani muttered.

"What's that?" her dad asked, going for the remote again.

"Nothing!" Dani said just as Selina echoed her confusion:

"What made you come forward?"

"Well, Selina, things have been a little different this year than they were in the past. There're all these people traipsing around, destroying the rest of my crops—I started to think, maybe the publicity's not worth it anymore." The farmer paused dramatically. "But that doesn't mean I'm going to reveal all our family secrets."

Selina flashed her white teeth flirtatiously. "Can't you give us anything, Frank?"

The old man chuckled. "I'll tell you this: The key to a good crop circle—besides ol' Betsy here"—he held up his plank of wood—"is making a good map and carrying a strong length of twine. If you don't plan out your design and measure everything just right, you won't get those beautiful pictures." He pulled a folded piece of paper from his pocket, spread it out, and showed it to the camera. It was a scale drawing of one of the circles Dani and Cat had seen from the crop-dusting plane yesterday. "I must say, it was a pleasure to make these five circles the past few days. I've always had a bit of the artist in me."

"And are you really done?" Selina asked. "Have you created your last crop circle?"

Mr. Hepworth made a show of tapping at his chin. "Well . . . you'll just have to wait and see."

The reporter faced the camera. "You heard it here, folks. The famed Weston Farm Circles have finally been explained. Up next, we're going live to Hilldale High, where the new sports training complex is almost complete."

Dani sank back into the cushions, reeling. Could it really be that easy? What about all the work she and Cat had already put into their project? It was too late to start something new; the science fair was in two and a half weeks. How were they supposed to win the McMurray Award now?

And how was Cat going to handle the news?

16

CAT

CAT HID UNDER HER covers. She had no interest in leaving her safe, warm cocoon. Because outside was a world where aliens didn't exist.

Or at least, that's what everyone else in town now believed, thanks to Mr. Hepworth.

Every Wednesday morning, Cat's mom did meal prep. She kept the news on in the background while she chopped and boiled, mixed and baked. This morning, when Cat had wandered downstairs, groggy and crusty-eyed, she'd been met with a nasty surprise.

Cat knew—knew!—Mr. Hepworth was lying. She'd been there in that field the other night. She'd witnessed the second circle forming in mere minutes. There had definitely not been anyone stomping around the fields with a plank. She would have noticed.

The MIBs must have forced the farmer to come forward. Mr. Hepworth's story was part of their cover-up. But Cat had no idea how to prove it. The fog had made the video she'd taken that night useless. Meanwhile, her project with Dani was ruined. No

McMurray Award, no NASA sending her dad back to his hometown, no convincing Dani aliens were the real deal.

She'd watched to the end of the segment and then had turned around and gone back to bed.

Now she reluctantly pushed back the covers. As much as she hated to admit it, she needed to go to school. Her mom would be disappointed in her if she skipped classes today, and her dad even more so. The last thing she wanted was for her dad to think she wasn't trying hard enough.

She pulled on the first shirt and jeans she found without even glancing in the mirror. She didn't bother brushing her hair, just pulled it back into pigtail braids. She grabbed her favorite lunch box, even though she never actually kept *lunch* in it, and headed out the door . . . into the pouring rain. By the time Cat got to school, she was drenched.

It was official: The universe was conspiring against her.

Her shoes squelched as she shuffled into the school, with its treacherous linoleum floors. Cat barely made it to first period on time, since she had to walk slower than usual so she wouldn't slip. When she slid—literally—into her chair, the girls around her laughed.

Cat ignored them. She pulled out her soggy social studies textbook and hid behind it for the rest of the period.

When lunch rolled around, Cat was starving. She'd forgotten about breakfast. Her stomach rumbled in the lunch line, earning more snickers. Usually she was able to let the laughter roll right off her. Not today.

Cat slopped chicken nuggets and two servings of french fries onto her tray. When she keyed in her account code at the checkout, the lunch lady looked at her a little funny. Cat tried to brush it off. People always looked at her funny. It was so normal, she rarely even noticed it. But today was . . . different. It was almost like everyone could sense what a failure she was.

As Cat crossed the cafeteria with her lunch tray, the strange looks swelled like a wave, carrying her with it. One table of girls Cat had never liked was quivering with laughter—and their giggles were clearly aimed in Cat's direction.

How did everyone know that her life's work was a bust?

Cat's shoulders slumped. It was time to have the conversation she'd been dreading. She needed to talk to Dani. Would her partner be thrilled that Cat had been proven wrong? Or would she still want to work together and find evidence that the hoax was, well, a hoax? Cat scanned the room and saw Dani sitting with her friends. Great. More people to witness her failure.

She looked longingly at an empty table in the corner and then turned back toward Dani's group. As she approached, she heard Laurel saying something about Halloween next week. As if a little holiday mattered in the slightest when *the truth about the universe* was on the line! Cat's thirteenth birthday was on November 2, and she barely cared about *that*, aside from how it related to the Weston Farm Circles.

Dani was nodding absently as her friend talked, her brain clearly somewhere else. Then she glanced up and saw Cat approaching.

"Hey, Dani," Cat said, trying and failing to make her voice upbeat.

Laurel, Jane, and Nora cracked up. But Dani stood, frowning at them. "Guys, it's just a math joke. It's not that funny. Be nice." Dani pulled Cat away. "Come on. Let's find somewhere to talk."

"What do you mean, 'just a math joke'?" Cat said, completely confused. "What's going on?"

Dani pointed to Cat's shirt—and Cat's stomach turned over.

In her funk, she'd grabbed a shirt from the pile of clothes she'd been meaning to give to Goodwill. This one was a Christmas shirt that said, in bright red and green letters: HO^3

Dani was right; it was a math joke. Ho, Ho, Ho, otherwise known as Ho cubed. The shirt had been sent to Cat a couple of Christmases ago by her clueless great-aunt. Cat had never worn it and had never intended to. So, of course, she'd picked today for its debut.

Universe: infinity. Cat: zero.

With a groan, Cat sank into a seat at an empty table, resting her head on her crossed arms.

Dani put a tentative hand on her shoulder. "You didn't even realize you were wearing that shirt, did you?"

"Nope. I thought everyone was laughing because I believed in the crop circles and now the owner of Weston Farm is on TV claiming he did it."

"I saw that," Dani said quietly. "I texted you to see if you wanted to talk about it, but you didn't answer . . ."

"I forgot my phone at home," Cat said. She could picture it, plugged in and sitting on her workstation between her computer and her microscope.

"I—" Dani was interrupted by two of the girls from the lunch table Cat had tried to avoid.

"Hi, Science. Hi, Strange," one of them, a cheerleader named Melody, said sweetly. "See any spaceships lately?"

"I think Cat let the aliens take her shopping," snickered the other girl, Ariana, who was captain of the middle school dance team. "How else can one person own so many awful outfits?"

"I thought everyone wore silver unitards in space. Are you saving your unitard for a special occasion?" Melody asked Cat, smirking like she'd made a real zinger.

Cat did, in fact, own a shiny silver unitard. And she *was* saving it for the right moment. But she wasn't about to give Melody and Ariana the satisfaction of knowing they were right.

"We get it—you're cool and we're not," Dani snapped. "Can we get on with our conversation?"

"Go right ahead," Ariana said after a beat, like she wanted to get the last word. But Dani had already turned her attention back to Cat.

"Look, I'm sorry about the hoax," Dani said as the other two girls stalked off. "I can't fix that, but I do have an extra T-shirt from gym class if you want it?" She dug around in her backpack and pulled out a plain black shirt.

Cat took it gratefully and pulled it on over her other shirt.

"I'm also sorry about my friends laughing at you." A wrinkle appeared between Dani's eyebrows. "I'll tell them not to do that again."

"Thanks," Cat said, even though Dani's friends were the

least of her worries. "But the crop circles aren't a hoax. There's no way that circle the other night could've appeared that fast with just five guys and a wooden plank. I'm not upset because I believe Mr. Hepworth—it's that now, no one's going to believe me. I mean, *us*. No one is going to believe *us*. That's what's so horrible." She paused. "Maybe this is what I get for not telling you about my project proposal. Did I say I was sorry for that? I really am."

"Thanks. And for the record, this isn't the universe, like, paying you back. I don't believe in karma."

"Of course you don't." Cat sank deeper into her chair. Her mind was a blank. She'd spent so much time preparing for the circles to appear, but she hadn't prepared for *this*.

Everything had gone so wrong so quickly. This was the worst day ever.

Then Dani actually smiled. "I have an idea."

17

DANI

"BUMPER CARS?" CAT EXCLAIMED. "*This* is your big idea to fix all our problems?"

Dani shook her head. "I told you, I can't make the hoax not be a hoax anymore."

"Gamez and Carz," Cat read from the lopsided sign over the main entrance. "Nope and nope."

"This will help take your mind off everything," Dani said patiently.

"It won't work," Cat grumbled.

"Try it." Dani dug around in her pocket and pulled out a couple of dollars. "My treat."

Cat scowled as they waited in the short line for the bumper cars, surrounded by hyperactive kids. She scowled as Dani paid the fee. Her scowl grew and grew until she was strapped inside a bright yellow car, facing Dani's red car head-on.

The second the starting buzzer went off, Dani drove at Cat and slammed into her.

Cat's jaw dropped. "Hey, I—"

Dani backed up and plowed into her again. "Fight back!" She reversed and drove in a tight circle, waiting for Cat to take the bait. "Come and— Oof!" One of the littler kids crashed into her side and drove off, squealing with glee. Dani raised her eyebrows at Cat. "Are you just gonna sit there?"

Cat let out a heavy sigh. "Fine." She gunned it forward and hit Dani so hard, Dani's car slid back a few feet. Then she reluctantly said, "That did feel kind of good, I guess."

"Again," Dani urged. She braced herself for the jolt. But before Cat could reach her, two boys drove between them at top speed. One of them sent the other spinning, hitting Cat, who knocked into another girl. After that, everything was chaos. When the session ended and the power went off, Dani's face hurt from smiling so much.

She *loved* bumper cars.

This used to be something she did with Jane, Laurel, and Nora. Then things had changed. Dani's friends had moved on. The last time Dani had suggested Gamez & Carz, about a year ago, Nora had said bumper cars were for babies. Dani hadn't mentioned it again.

But she still came here, every once in a while, by herself. When she was feeling stressed about school or her parents and their ridiculous artistic expectations. A couple of rounds of smashing into things always made her feel better. She hoped it had done the same for Cat.

"Well?" she asked her partner when they were stretching their legs outside the arena.

Cat grinned. It wasn't her full-power *aliens are real and let me tell you everything there is to know about them* smile, but it was much better than the face she'd been making all day. "Yeah, yeah," Cat said, ducking her head. "I had fun."

"I thought this would cheer you up," Dani said, satisfied. "It worked on me after—" She clamped her mouth shut.

"After what?"

"Nothing," Dani said quickly.

"My life's work went up in smoke today," Cat said. "Whatever it is can't be worse than that."

Dani sighed. She looked at her partner . . . and decided to trust her. "Did you hear about what happened at ArtistiKids this summer?"

"No . . ." Cat pursed her lips. "Wait. Maybe I did. A set fell down during one of the shows?"

"It didn't fall down," Dani said quietly. "It was knocked over."

"Potato, po-tah-toe—"

"I'm the one who knocked it over," Dani said.

Cat blinked at her. "On purpose?"

"Of course not!"

"Then what happened?"

"I was the theatrical engineer," Dani began slowly. "Basically, I did all the calculations to make sure the set was sturdy and safe. Maybe I got something wrong— No," she corrected herself. "I quadruple-checked the math. The set wasn't the problem." She gnawed on her lip for a second before admitting, "The problem was *me*."

She sat down heavily on a bench, resting her elbows on her knees. Cat sat beside her. "And?" she prompted.

"Jayla Spenser sprained her ankle."

Cat winced. "When the set fell on her?"

"No, the day before the show. Jayla was the dancing bear. She didn't have an understudy, because no one else could do the fouettés. My parents—" Dani could barely hold back a hysterical laugh, even now. "They decided I would go on in her place. With modified choreography, obviously. Mom pitched it as a reward for my hard work backstage. I didn't want to do it, but Mom said . . . she said they needed me. She said I would save the show. Instead, I ruined it."

She dropped her head into her hands.

"I barely knew the steps. The costume was too big. I couldn't see a thing. I tripped over my feet and fell into the wall. My safety calculations didn't account for impact. The set came down on top of me. And . . . and I . . ." Dani scrunched up her face as she looked at her partner. "I split my pants, so everyone saw my underwear."

Cat barked out a surprised laugh and then clapped her hand over her mouth. "Sorry! Sorry. That's awful. But . . . why isn't everyone at school talking about this?"

"The bear head," Dani explained. "Jayla was in the audience, and there was no understudy listed in the program, so Mom and Dad were able to keep my identity quiet."

"Was anyone hurt?"

"No, thank goodness." Dani was mortified enough without having gotten her parents sued. "But now Mom and Dad are talking about ballroom dance lessons—as if the last time I tried to do choreography wasn't a complete disaster—and I—" She shrugged helplessly, trying not to cry.

Cat looked at her with soft eyes. "You know what you need?"

"What?" Dani asked, swallowing down the lump in her throat.

"A delicious, refreshing Mountain Dew," Cat declared. "Does this place have a snack bar?"

Dani nodded.

"My treat this time." Cat strode over to the door and ushered Dani inside.

The interior of Gamez & Carz was dark but filled with flashing neon lights from all the old-school video game consoles. The carpet was gray with yellow spots, and the walls were teal blue. By the entrance, there was a counter with a lit-up sign overhead that said: SNACKZ!

"Do you want any snackzzzzz?" Cat asked Dani, putting extra emphasis on all those Z's. "We could share a bag of chipzzzzz."

Dani snorted.

"Or look," Cat went on, pointing. "They have nachos and cheezzzzze sauce."

"No thankzzzzz," Dani answered. "Nacho cheezzzzze givezzzzz me zzzzzits."

Cat cracked up. That set Dani off. They spent the next couple of minutes making *zzzz* noises at each other and laughing hysterically. When Dani's giggles finally slowed down, it was only because she was wheezing too hard to continue.

"Okay, enough!" she said, wiping away tears. "I can't breathe!"

Out of nowhere, Cat wrapped Dani in a bear hug. "Thank you," she said quietly. "No one's ever—I mean, no one else at school would—" She stepped back. "This was just what I needed."

"Me too," Dani said, and meant it.

They each had a drink and a bag of chips, and then they hit the arcade. After scanning the room, Cat ran straight to an old game with black-and-white graphics and really basic controls.

"Asteroids?" As Dani walked up, a flying saucer danced across the screen.

"Asteroidzzzzz," Cat corrected her, already putting in her quarters. "I'll go first." She started shooting rocks on-screen, tongue poking out of her mouth as she concentrated. "It's too bad they don't— Yes!" she whooped as she destroyed a spaceship. "Too bad they don't have a crop circle game. I could blow up some of those right about now. Four of them, to be precise."

"Why only four?" If it were Dani whose life's work had been proven wrong, she'd want to destroy a lot more than four things.

"That's how many circles we've had at Weston Farm so far this year." Cat pumped her fists in the air as she destroyed another flying saucer.

"Oh, right," Dani said. Something was nagging at her. It was something Cat had said. But also something she'd heard someone else say.

"Aw, I died. Your turn."

Dani shook off her weird feeling and stepped up to the console. "Here goes," she said. "FYI, I'm not very good at these things."

"I believe in you!" Cat bumped her shoulder.

Dani had barely cleared Level One when it hit her: the thing that felt wrong.

"Um, Dani? You're supposed to *shoot at* the asteroids," Cat joked.

"There have been four crop circles so far . . . ," Dani said.

"Yeah. One per night. Which is unusual, by the way—every other year, the formations have been clustered together."

"On the news this morning, Mr. Hepworth said he'd made five."

Cat froze. "Really?"

"I'm pretty sure."

"How sure?"

"I mean, I didn't record the news or anything. But that's what I remember."

Cat let out a roar of triumph. "This is amazing!"

"It is?"

"Yes! This proves Mr. Hepworth's lying!"

Dani's heart leaped at the idea of relaunching her research, but she didn't want to count her chickens. "He might've said the wrong number by accident."

Her partner shook her head. "He's definitely lying." She headed for the door. "You coming?"

18

CAT

"WHAT WERE WE DOING when you went home last night?" Cat was so excited, she answered her own question. "Recording all the data from the oven tests, that's right. How awesome is it that not a single oven test gave us the same results as cooking those stalks in the microwave? They just burned all the way through, not focused around the nodes like the crop circles."

"Pretty awesome," Dani answered with a faint smile.

"*Incredibly* awesome," Cat corrected her, rolling her desk chair over to the computer. "Okay, do you want to keep doing your soil pH tests, or should we . . ." She faded off as a thought tickled the back of her brain.

"Should we what?" Dani asked.

Cat sat bolt upright as the tickle turned into a full-on brainstorm. She grabbed her crop circle map. She clicked on her mapping software and drummed her fingers on the desk impatiently while she waited for it to load. When it did, she got right to work. She began with the map of the first year of crop circles, then overlaid it with the second, and the third, and finally added the circles that had formed so far this year.

Dani watched silently from the chair beside her.

When every single circle was mapped, Cat grinned.

"I did it," she murmured. "I cracked the code!"

The circles formed a fractal. One huge fractal, spread out over Weston Farm.

"Tonight's circle will appear in the southwest quadrant of the cornfields!" she shouted, pumping her fists in the air.

"Here?" Dani pointed. "How can you tell?"

"Look at the circles and at the negative space around them." Cat talked her partner through the order in which the circles had shown up—how they spiraled around the farm just like the stalks spiraled around the midpoint of an individual circle. "It has to be one of these empty areas, and based on the existing pattern . . ."

"Southwest cornfields." Dani was nodding along.

"We have to get to the farm. Let's go!" Cat ran for the stairs.

"What about our tests?" Dani chased after her, pulling her jacket on as she went. "What about the Men in Black? What about my parents—"

"Where are you two going in such a hurry?" Cat's mom appeared in the kitchen doorway as they raced by.

"Weston Farm. I've got my phone." Cat swung open the back door. "Love you—"

"Not so fast, sweetie." Cat's mom pushed the door closed. "I think you should stay in tonight. Catch up on some of your other schoolwork."

"But, Mom—"

"No buts. I understand you have an English paper due tomorrow?"

Cat waved her hand dismissively. "I'll get an extension."

Her mom raised an eyebrow. "Isn't this already an extended deadline?"

Out of the corner of her eye, Cat saw Dani shrink back, like she was trying to become invisible. Cat groaned. "They called you?"

"Your teacher wanted to make sure everything was okay at home." Cat's mom took her by the shoulders. "I know this science project is important to you, but you can't let your other assignments fall by the wayside."

It was one late book report. Okay, maybe there was also a math quiz Cat hadn't studied for. Who cared? English and math would still be there in a few weeks. The Weston Farm Circles would not.

"I have to get to work," her mom said. "I'm going to call the home phone every hour. I expect you to answer."

Cat let out a long-suffering sigh. "Sure, Mom."

"Have a good night. I love you." Cat's mom kissed the top of her head and turned to Dani. "Nice to see you again, Dani."

"You too, Mrs. Mulvaney," Dani said.

"Get home safe."

"Oh." Dani seemed to realize she was being dismissed. "Thanks. Um. Bye, Cat."

Cat raised a hand in a glum wave.

She tried to focus on her schoolwork the rest of the night. She really tried. But her eyes kept sneaking over to the composite image of the giant crop circle fractal. This was it. She could feel it in her bones. She was really on to something.

Her dad would have no choice but to notice her.

THE FIRST THING CAT did the next morning was check the local news. A bull's-eye-shaped circle had appeared in the southwest quadrant of the cornfields, just as she'd predicted. She added the new circle to the master map and calculated where the next circles would be. When she saw the answer, Cat grinned. She knew just where to go tonight at Weston Farm. That is, if those Men in Black weren't around to ruin the fun . . .

She pushed that thought away and hurried to school, completed book report in her bag.

When fifth-period science rolled around, Cat was the first to arrive. Not even Ms. Blanks was in the room when she walked in. On her way to her seat, she decided to drop off the homework she'd finished at lunch. She stepped up to her teacher's desk and set her worksheet down in the center. Then something caught her eye: The corner of a map peeked out from beneath some other papers. It looked a lot like the Weston Farm map Cat had spent the better part of the last two weeks staring at.

Cat leaned in close, her fingers itching to pull the map free and get a closer look. Why would Ms. Blanks have—

"Everything's on schedule." Ms. Blanks's voice echoed from the hallway. She swung the door open and startled to see Cat standing at her desk. "Catrina! You're here early."

"I just wanted to hand in my homework," Cat said. "And hopefully catch Dani early, too."

The teacher smiled, smoothing her blouse as she ended her

phone call. "I'm so glad that you and Danielle are working well together."

"Yeah, Dani's been a great partner. She's had some good ideas for research angles that will really flesh out our thesis." Cat glanced down at the desk, unable to contain her curiosity a moment longer. "Ms. Blanks, why do you have a map of Weston Farm?"

"Oh! Well, I . . ." Ms. Blanks's expression turned sheepish. "Honestly, I find the whole thing fascinating. I didn't grow up here in Hilldale. After you shared your project proposal, I started doing a little research of my own."

"Really?" Cat grinned. It sure was nice to have a McMurray adviser who was truly invested. "What have you learned?"

Ms. Blanks held up a finger. "Catrina, I don't want to influence *your* research. Ask me again after the science fair."

"I will."

Cat turned to go to her desk, but before she could walk away, Ms. Blanks said, "I actually wanted to touch base with you and Danielle—does the farmer having come forward as the hoaxer affect your hypothesis?"

"Not one bit," Cat said confidently. "Mr. Hepworth is *totally* lying."

The teacher tilted her head. "What makes you so sure?"

This time, Cat hesitated before answering. Ms. Blanks was their project adviser, so she should probably tell her . . . but the fact that the Men in Black had already locked down the site made Cat wary of telling anybody. If Ms. Blanks was doing her own research on Weston Farm, she might catch their attention, too. The bad kind of attention. And she definitely didn't look like the type who'd hold up well under an interrogation.

No, it was safest for everyone to keep her cards close to her vest for the time being.

Luckily, Dani appeared in the doorway just then, saving Cat from the conversation.

"Hey, Dani!" Cat waved enthusiastically as she ran to Dani and practically dragged her over to her desk by the windows.

"I saw the news this morning," Dani said. "You were right. Good job."

"We have to go to the fields tonight!" Cat stage-whispered. "Do you think your parents will let you? It's for science!"

Dani laughed. "I don't think *that* will convince them, but I'll see what I can do."

"The circles will show up on the western side of the cornfields. Meet me there at eight o'clock."

WHEN CAT ARRIVED AT Weston Farm that evening, Dani wasn't there yet, but someone else was: two more Men in Black (although technically, one of them was a woman). Cat spied them just as she passed the festival tent—which was still empty, due to a reported snafu with the permits. Yet another thing the MIBs had ruined.

Grumbling to herself, Cat backed up and stowed her bike in

a ditch by the edge of the road. Then she ducked behind a tree and texted Dani.

CAT: MIBs at the farm! I'll meet you before the driveway!

Dani didn't text back, but Cat supposed she wasn't the type to text and ride. She'd have to intercept her.

It wasn't long before Cat heard the familiar sound of bicycle tires on gravel. She leaped out from her hiding spot into the road, hissing, "Stop!"

Dani skidded to a halt so fast, she nearly fell off her bike. "Gah! Cat!"

"Shhhhhh!" Cat hushed. "The Men in Black are here. We have to be sneaky. The MIBs will want to keep a tight lid on any evidence of alien visitation getting out to the public." She showed Dani where to hide her bike. "Tonight's circles will be on the western side. Hopefully the fact that the MIBs are over here means they haven't figured out how to predict where the circles will appear. Then again, maybe the two agents we met the other day are waiting for us in the western fields . . ."

"I hope not," Dani said.

"Me too. Either way, if there's a chance we know something the MIBs don't . . ." Cat tapped her chin. "We should keep the mapping-software thing between us. Just in case."

"In case of what?"

"In case the Men in Black are listening!"

"Sure, Cat," Dani said. "Whatever you say."

Cat knew Dani was only humoring her. She also knew she was acting paranoid. But the MIBs had already kicked them off the farm once. It wasn't unreasonable to assume they'd do it again—especially if they found out she knew when and where the circles would appear next.

Cat led Dani to a path that was barely noticeable from the street. It circled around the other fields and eventually let them out near the western side, where all you could see was ears of corn for what felt like miles. It was dark, but the skies were clear, and no circles had appeared yet.

Not a single government agent in sight. Cat sighed with relief.

"Let's get to work." She opened her pack and handed Dani a trowel and a box of sample-collection baggies. They worked quickly, mindful to get control samples of the soil and stalks now so they could compare and reaffirm the results after the circle appeared.

When the samples were safely stored in her backpack, Cat ventured farther into the field to set up her equipment. Video camera? Check. Gauss meter? Check. Geiger counter? Check. Compass? Check. She even logged the air and ground temperatures.

"What time do you think the circles will appear?" Dani asked. She was crouched nearby, examining a handful of dirt with her flashlight. "Or the hoaxers," she added.

"Dani, we agreed Mr. Hepworth was lying."

"He probably was," Dani allowed, "but he could've been covering for whoever is really responsible. Either way, one human telling lies doesn't mean we jump straight to aliens."

"You'll see the truth soon enough," Cat promised. "Anyway,

I'm still not sure about timing. Hopefully soon?" She peered at the sky through her binoculars. "What did you tell your parents to convince them to let you out on a school night?"

Dani made a face. "You'll have to back me up on this one. I said you were into night photography. After this, we're going back to your house to, uh . . ." Dani waved her hands. "I used photography words. Aperture. Exposure. Framing."

Cat stared at her. "*That's* more believable than working on our science project?"

"In my house," Dani said bitterly, "in the battle of art versus science, art wins."

"Huh." Cat paused. "I know nothing about photography."

"It's fine; I'll just say I turned out to be terrible at it—"

A flash of something in the distance caught Cat's eye. "Dude! Do you see that?"

Dani stood and brushed the dirt from her hands. "See what?"

"Over there!" Lights hovered above the cornfield a little ways away. Actual floating lights! This was everything Cat had ever been waiting for!

She heard a slight trilling sound. It was gradually getting louder. This was really happening.

She ran.

19

DANI

ONE SECOND, DANI WAS chasing Cat through the fields. The next, she was flat on her face in the dirt. The fall knocked the wind out of her. She rolled over and looked up at the sky, trying to catch her breath. Her shoulder ached from where she'd hit the ground, and her palms were skinned.

She was alone.

"Cat?" she called out once she could speak again. "Cat! Wait for me!"

No response.

Dani pushed to her feet, looking in all directions. The other girl had vanished into the sea of corn. Dani strained to listen, hoping to hear Cat's feet pounding the ground or her body brushing past the stalks. Nothing, nothing, nothing.

She began to run. Dani had never been claustrophobic, but all of a sudden, it felt like the corn was closing in on her. The path in front of her was shrinking. If she didn't find her partner soon, she'd be trapped in this field forever.

"Cat!" she shrieked. She'd dropped her flashlight when she fell. And her compass. And then she'd run off without picking them up. How could she have been so thoughtless? "Cat! Help, I—"

Her path stopped abruptly. But not in a dead end. She was in one of the circles.

So was Cat. The other girl was waving around one of her fancy gadgets. She brushed it against the ground and pointed it at the sky. Then she spun, seeing Dani. "There you are!" she shouted. Cat's face was radiant in the moonlight.

"You left me," Dani said. She was beginning to realize that her feelings were as bruised as her hands. "You ran off and left me!" she said more forcefully.

"I was following the lights!" Cat exclaimed. "Weren't you?"

Dani walked toward Cat. "What lights?"

Cat fiddled with a gauge on her equipment. "Ha-ha-ha! 'What lights?' she says! Next you're going to say you didn't hear that trilling noise."

"I didn't see any lights," Dani insisted. "I heard a noise, but it could've been a lot of things."

Cat looked up. "Wait. Really?"

"Yes, really," Dani said. "It was dark, and I fell, and you left me. Not. Cool."

"Okay, I'm sorry," Cat said, not sounding *that* sorry, "but you have to look at this." She held out her camera. "Press 'Play.'"

"I know how to watch a video, thank you very much—" Dani broke off, staring at the black screen. "What am I supposed to be looking at?"

Cat snatched the camera back. She pressed a few buttons.

Nothing happened. She shook the camera, eyes wide. "No, no, no, no!"

"What—"

"It was there! I had actual, clear footage of extraterrestrial phenomena." Cat turned to Dani and growled, "There were glowing green lights hovering over the field. Then they zipped around, brushing the tops of the stalks."

"An airplane—" Dani started.

"It was way too low to be an aircraft. Even a crop duster. Besides, we would've felt the wind. We would've heard engines. But these lights, they just made this noise like . . ." She made a whistling, buzzing sound.

Dani suppressed a laugh. "That's what spaceships sound like?"

"This isn't funny!"

"Glowing green lights that go *bzzzz-whoooshh-phewww*?" Dani asked. "Come on."

"I can't believe my camera failed." Cat looked like she was about to burst into tears. "I did everything right. I read the instruction manual, like, a hundred times. *UFOlogy Weekly* recommends this model as the best for capturing verifiable footage. And—"

"*UFOlogy Weekly*?"

"Don't poke fun, Dani. Please don't."

Dani's burst of irritation and hurt feelings had faded. So had the urge to laugh at her partner. All she was left with was pity. "I'm sorry, Cat, but I didn't see a thing. And if you don't have any evidence . . ." She shrugged. "I don't know what to tell you."

Cat stared down at her equipment, shoulders slumped. "I missed it," she murmured.

"It's okay. We can try again. Now that you can predict the appearances, we'll know where to go tomorrow night, right?"

"I had it, and I lost it." Cat started walking back the way they'd come.

Dani chased after her. "Where are you going?"

"What were you carrying when you fell?" Cat asked in a tight voice without turning around.

"A flashlight, a compass, and— Oh." She'd also had the backpack with all their samples.

"Yeah. *Oh.*" Cat stomped out of the crop circle and into the upright rows of corn. "Know what else is in that pack? The rest of my equipment. My camera may not have recorded anything useful, but I can still test for alien substances in the area. And we can still gather samples from this circle to compare with our controls. Assuming you still care about the *science* here?"

"Of course I care about the science," Dani answered, stung. "That's why I'm here."

"You don't have any idea how important this is to me!" Cat yelled.

"*You* don't have any idea how important the McMurray Award is to *me!*" Dani yelled back.

"The award," Cat said. "Because that's all that matters to you."

Dani's irritation returned. "You know what? Yeah. Winning the McMurray Award matters to me. It matters a lot. It clearly doesn't matter to you, or else you would've chosen a real project topic. But I'm here—"

"Are you?" Cat shot back. "I'm not sure you've ever taken any of this seriously. I've shown you so much evidence, and you're just like, *It's all a hoax*." She said that last bit in a whiny falsetto. "And for your information, confirming the existence of extraterrestrial life *is* a real research topic. Plus, it'll make us stand out. No one else will be studying these circles."

Dani snorted. "There's a reason for that."

Cat scowled at her. "If you don't want to be here, why don't you go home?"

"Maybe I will," Dani said.

They stared at each other for a minute. Dani didn't want to be the first to break. It wasn't her fault she hadn't seen whatever it was Cat thought she'd seen. Honestly, if Cat had really wanted her to see those lights, she wouldn't have run off. She would've grabbed Dani's hand so they could chase the aliens together.

Cat finally spoke. "I have to find my backpack. And then I have to get to work. You know, before the Men in Black show up."

"There's no such thing as Men in Black," Dani said.

Cat's eyes narrowed. "If you're going to go, go."

"Fine," Dani said.

"Fine," Cat shot back. "FYI, south is that way." She pointed down a row of corn.

Dani spun on her heel and stomped off into the night.

20

CAT

CAT MARCHED THROUGH THE cornfield, batting away half-shed tears of frustration.

How could this have happened?

The lights—the perfect, beautiful orbs!—had been circling right over this field. Directly above the spot where the circle had formed. She'd seen it with her own eyes and then through the lens of the video camera. There was no question they'd caused the formation. None.

And that footage had been there. She'd seen it recording. But now, nada.

To make matters worse, Dani thought she was a lunatic.

Cat couldn't understand how Dani could have missed the lights. They were so bright! She must have been distracted by her soil samples. She'd been really focused on those lately.

Except, of course, for the part where she'd left them behind.

Cat shook her head and let out a growl. All she wanted was a partner who was as excited about their project as she was. And to make her dad proud. Was that too much to ask?

An ear of corn bonked her on the side of the head. When she

stopped to rub the bruise, she spied the backpack Dani had dropped. She scooped it up and dug through it. Fortunately, none of the equipment inside seemed damaged. She breathed a sigh of relief. It wouldn't be easy to replace. She looked closer at her video camera, frustration rising again. She pressed button after button, but nothing happened. It was like it had just run out of batteries, but she knew that wasn't the case. She'd put fresh ones in all her equipment before leaving home, specifically to avoid an issue like this. She just didn't understand—

Something crunched in the field not far away. Cat froze. Faint voices floated over to where she stood, hidden by the tall stalks of corn.

One voice was the first Man in Black they'd encountered last time. His voice was low, gravelly, and unmistakable. He muttered something that made Cat's heart nearly stop.

"Well, if anyone on the farm has a device . . . it's cooked now."

The voice that responded wasn't familiar, but it was clearer: "Why didn't she warn us?"

The gravelly-voiced man grunted in response.

Realization felt like ice water poured over Cat's head. Of course. It wasn't that she'd screwed up the camera. It was the MIBs. They'd probably set off a short-range EMP. Cat glanced around. Even the farmhouse lights were out, though she supposed Mr. Hepworth could've just gone to bed.

Cat balled her hands into fists. She'd been sabotaged!

She slunk quietly out of the cornfield in the opposite direction of the MIBs, fear churning in her gut. She'd now seen four government agents at Weston Farm. What if there were even more lurking nearby, ready to pounce? And if they were willing to set off an electromagnetic pulse to keep people like her from sharing the truth with the world . . . what would they do next?

21

DANI

DANI REPLAYED HER ARGUMENT with Cat the whole bike ride home, feeling worse and worse about the things she'd said. She'd grown to like Cat, even though she still thought the other girl was a kook. She could even see the two of them having fun together at ScienceU next summer. Also, Cat wasn't wrong: There was a mystery hidden in the circles. It just had nothing to do with aliens and everything to do with cold hard science.

Dani wanted to solve the mystery. When Cat had run off without her, she'd been examining the soil. She hadn't seen any iron deposits in the control field. She was willing to bet there *were* black specks in the fresh crop circle, though, which would add weight to her hypothesis that heat plus Weed-Be-Gone equaled iron microspheres. She wished she'd taken a moment to sample the soil in the newly formed circle. Instead, she'd let Cat goad her into an argument.

It was too late to go back. She was almost home, and her parents were waiting up to talk to her about her night photography lesson. All she could do was text her partner and hope for the best.

After Dani parked her bike by her garage, she dug around in

her bag for her phone. It wasn't there. Not in any of the pockets. Had she lost it in the fields? Or somewhere on her bike route? Dani ran up to her bedroom, holding her breath, and was incredibly relieved to see it sitting on her pillow, attached to its charger. She clutched the phone to her chest and then typed:

DANI: I'm really sorry about what happened. Can we talk tomorrow?
DANI: Also, can you sample the soil in the crop circle for me? Thank you!!!

No response.

With a sigh, Dani went back downstairs to talk to her parents. Even though the whole photography thing was made-up, she felt a familiar lurch of dread in her stomach. Without the McMurray Award, this would always be her life. She would keep moving from one artistic failure to the next.

Dani had to get Cat to talk to her again. Her partner had the soil and stalk samples. She had the state-of-the-art lab in her bedroom. She had the results of each of their experiments thus far documented on her computer. All Dani had was her notebook.

But she wasn't ready to let go of her dream.

22

CAT

WHEN CAT GOT HOME, her night went from bad to worse. As she unpacked her backpack, she checked the electronic devices she'd brought to the farm. Not a single piece still worked, not even her phone.

Her parents were not going to be happy.

While they'd probably replace her phone, they definitely weren't going to buy her another Gauss meter or Geiger counter—they'd only just given her those things as early birthday presents, after Cat had explained that she'd need them for her McMurray research. Plus, Cat's dad had already ordered the colorimeter and the potassium permanganate for Dani's active-carbon soil test. With those items in the mail, he'd be even less likely to replace the things the EMP had fried.

But the McMurray exhibition was in sixteen days.

And the Weston Farm Circles were happening *now*.

At least she still had her computer, research, and lab equipment. That was . . . something.

After sitting in sulky silence for several minutes, Cat got up and carefully stored away the soil and stalk samples she and Dani had collected. She wasn't in the mood to run the tests right now.

What she was in the mood to do was find out more about these MIBs who'd ruined her tech. She checked her favorite ufology forums, looking for any word on MIBs in the area or ones matching the description of those she'd seen at Weston Farm. At first, it was all the same: People often mistook cops—or anyone who didn't like them being on the land where the circles had appeared—for Men in Black. But finally, Cat stumbled upon a post from a researcher in Arizona that made her sit up straighter in her chair. The MIB in question had a gravelly voice.

Just like the agent at Weston Farm.

She quickly wrote to the researcher in Arizona, asking for more details of his encounter. She'd barely sent the message when she heard a knock on her loft door. A hard knot tightened in her gut. She braced herself as she went down the attic stairs and opened the door.

"Hi, honey," her mom said warmly. "I had an earlier shift tonight and thought I'd peek in, since you're still up." Her smile faltered when she saw the look on Cat's face. "What's wrong?" She craned her neck to see around Cat, who was still blocking the doorway.

Cat sighed, opening the door wider to let her mom follow her back upstairs. She was going to find out about her ruined equipment soon anyway. Why delay the inevitable?

"I had a bad night."

"What happened? I thought you were meeting up with Dani again."

Cat nodded. "I did. And we witnessed a crop circle appearing!"

Her mom frowned, puzzled. "Isn't that a good thing?"

Cat flopped back onto her bed. "It would be if my video camera hadn't stopped working."

Her mom's expression turned serious. "Cat, what happened to your camera?"

"Nothing! I didn't do anything. Someone set off an EMP—an electromagnetic pulse. These guys were talking about it in the fields. Now my phone is a brick, and my Geiger—"

"Your phone is a what?" Cat's mom held up her hands to stop Cat's verbal onslaught, her voice tinged with dismay.

"It's a brick. The EMP—"

"Cat. I know you love looking for aliens, and I support your interests in science and even the stranger avenues your hobby takes. But you can't blame the universe for everything."

"I'm not! There were Men in Black at Weston Farm tonight, I swear." Even as the words left Cat's mouth, she knew her mother would never believe her. Her mom had a relatively open mind, but she drew the line at conspiracy theories—and MIBs fell into that category.

"Honestly, Cat, maybe you shouldn't visit those conspiracy forums anymore. I think you're taking them too seriously."

Cat curled up into a ball on her bed. "They're not conspiracy forums; they're ufology forums."

"Call it whatever you want. The fact remains that if your phone broke, you're still responsible for it. I'll get you another one tomorrow, but don't expect it to be a nice iPhone. If you want something expensive, you'll have to save for it or wait for Christmas. We just don't have extra money lying around right now."

"What about my birthday next week? Can we—" Cat cut off at her mother's stern look.

"Some of that equipment *was* for your birthday." Her mother stood up and brushed off her pants. "Whatever you did to it, you should own up to it and tell your father. He might replace it eventually if you take responsibility."

"You're going to tell Dad?" Cat said meekly from her fetal position.

Her mom rested a hand on Cat's back. "I won't," she said, "as long as he hears about it from you." With that, she quietly left the room.

Tears welled in the corners of Cat's eyes. Her dad would be so disappointed that her new equipment was ruined, and since he worked for the government, he wouldn't be keen on believing MIBs did it, either. There'd be no hope of him coming home for the science fair.

Telling her dad was the literal last thing in the world she wanted to do.

23

DANI

CAT STILL HADN'T REPLIED to Dani's texts by the time Dani reached school on Friday morning, and Dani's feelings were a little hurt. She hadn't realized her partner was capable of holding grudges. All Dani had done was fail to witness something Cat was sure she'd seen.

Well, that wasn't *all* Dani had done. She was still lying to Cat about her project hypothesis, and she was withholding evidence. But Cat didn't know about either of those things.

Dani was definitely going to come clean soon.

Maybe not today. Not while Cat was upset about her camera malfunctioning.

And not when Dani was already in a terrible mood.

At breakfast, she'd been quietly eating her oatmeal when her mom had pushed a sheet of paper across the table. It was a flyer with a picture of a dancing couple at the top. Dani's appetite had instantly disappeared.

"What's this?" she'd asked.

"Your ballroom dance lessons!"

The bite of oatmeal in Dani's mouth had turned to cement. "No."

Her mom had ignored her. "You'll start the Monday after your science fair. Isn't that timing perfect?"

"You don't understand—" Dani had stopped herself. It wasn't just that her mom would *never* understand. It was also that there was no way she could explain the twists and turns her project with Cat had taken. Her parents didn't even know what they were actually researching . . . and they probably wouldn't care. "Fine," she'd muttered, and her mom had smiled and patted her hand.

Dani was imagining herself gloomily twirling in sequins when she spotted her partner turning a corner up ahead. She broke into a jog, calling, "Cat! Wait!"

Cat didn't. And judging by how she walked faster, Dani was pretty sure she'd heard her.

"Cat!" she tried once more, but the other girl had disappeared into a crowd.

"Hello? Dani?"

Dani spun to see Jane and Nora. It was Jane who'd spoken. Her friend tilted her head at her.

"We said your name three times."

"Oh. I was chasing Cat. We had an argument. She's not answering my texts."

"Science and Strange, broken up already?" Nora asked, raising an eyebrow.

Dani gave her friend a sideways look at the nicknames but said, "I hope not."

"I'm sure you'll figure it out," Jane said kindly.

"We have to," Dani said, wringing her hands with worry. "The science fair is really soon, and all our research is at Cat's house."

"Ooh, what's her house like, anyway?" Nora asked. "I've always imagined Cat living in, like, the creepy run-down house in the movies that turns out to be haunted."

"Yeah, does she have a ghost?" Jane asked, cracking up.

Dani jolted, remembering the very first time she'd been in Cat's room, when the other girl had talked so casually about her haunted doorknob.

"Cat's not into ghosts, remember?" Nora said to Jane. "It's all aliens all the time." Nora straightened her soccer jersey; their team was in uniform at school today in honor of their big game this weekend. "Or maybe she's into all the weird stuff? Aliens, ghosts, werewolves, vampires—"

Jane bounced on her heels. "Witches, things that go bump in the night—"

"Lions and tigers and bears, oh my!" Laurel walked up. "What are we talking about?"

"Nothing," Dani said, exactly as Jane said, "Cat Mulvaney."

Laurel looked interested. "What did Cat do now? Is it another fashion disaster? I don't see how she can possibly top that Ho shirt."

"She was having a bad day," Dani said, but her friends weren't listening. In fact, the three of them had started walking away. It was Dani's nightmare about being the odd one out come to life.

Except that Jane looked back. "Aren't you coming?"

Dani felt a rush of relief, even though it made perfect sense for Jane to ask. They all had first-period English together. It was the only class where their four schedules aligned.

She linked arms with Jane, grateful to find that they'd already changed the subject to Laurel's new maxi dress, which was an explosion of tropical color.

"It's like a bird-of-paradise," Dani said when it was her turn to compliment Laurel's look. "The flower, I mean. Not a member of the Paradisaeidae family."

"The who?" Nora asked.

"There are, like, forty-two species of birds of paradise," Dani explained. "Most of them live in Indonesia, Australia, and Papua New Guinea. It's mostly the males that have the elaborate plumage, but that's the case in a lot of the avian community."

After a beat, Laurel said, "Well, thanks."

Jane pulled Dani close. "You're such a nerd," she said affectionately. "Don't ever change."

Dani leaned into the hug, feeling a bubble of unease form in her chest.

The thing was, she *was* changing. How could she not after spending so much time with Cat? It was like Dani had opened a door she hadn't even known was there. She hadn't stepped all the way through it yet, but . . . maybe she wanted to. Maybe.

As they passed the hallway where she'd last seen Cat, Dani couldn't help checking over her shoulder. Her partner was nowhere in sight.

24

CAT

TODAY, CAT DID SOMETHING she'd never done before: She cut school. She knew her parents would be disappointed in her if she got caught. But after last night's debacle, she had to do something to clear her name.

Skipping school was easier than she'd expected. Now she was on a bus headed across town to the local hardware store. If Cat wanted anyone to believe her about the EMP, she needed proof. Whoever had made it had to have gotten the parts somewhere, and this was the likeliest place. Of course, for all she knew, the MIBs might carry special government-issue EMPs with them wherever they went—but at least this was something she could investigate and rule out.

Cat knew the hardware store owners well. She was there all the time getting odds and ends for her experiments.

But as soon as she walked through the door, she winced. Travis was at the register today. He'd never warmed up to her. She crossed her fingers that Sam and David were out back.

She sidled up to the register and cleared her throat. Travis, a college kid with red hair that was way too long, rolled his eyes.

"What do you need today, kid?"

He always called her "kid." She hated that.

Cat plastered a grin on her face anyway. "Hey, Travis. Are Sam and David around?"

"Nah, just me today. They won't be back until later in the week."

Cat decided not to see this as a setback. She'd just have to charm Travis to give her the information she needed instead.

"Darn. I was really hoping they could help me with something important."

Curiosity glinted in Travis's eyes. "What is it?"

Cat had no idea how to spin this into anything convincing. She decided to straight-up tell the truth and hope for the best. "You know the McMurray Youth Science Award?"

"I've heard of it, yeah."

"Well, my lab partner and I are investigating the Weston Farm Circles for it. Last night, an EMP was set off while we were recording some really great evidence. We want to know who did it. I'm hoping the EMP was homemade and that whoever it was came here for supplies."

"An EMP?"

"An electromagnetic pulse," Cat explained. "It's a burst of electromagnetic energy aimed at destroying electronic equipment—"

"I know what an EMP is, kid." Travis was clearly having a hard time stifling his laughter. "What I don't know is, what do you want me to do about it?"

"Can you see if the following items"—Cat slid a list across the counter—"were purchased here recently?" She grinned again, though it felt more like she was baring her teeth. "Please?"

"All this stuff at the same time?" He raised his eyebrows.

Cat nodded. "Yep."

This time, the laugh came out. But at least it was only a little one, Cat told herself. And Travis did start looking through the computer records.

"Why not?" he said, scrolling. "It's been a slow afternoon. But I'm not going to tell you who bought them without permission from Sam and David."

"I'm sure they wouldn't mind!" Cat squeaked, but Travis just gave her a look. "Thank you for whatever you can tell me."

She tapped her toes against the linoleum floor, scanning the sidewalks outside the store while she waited. There were a ton of alien-obsessed people wandering through the downtown area, though whether they were looking for extraterrestrial beings or lunch, Cat couldn't tell. But given the amount of alien-printed clothing they wore and the kitschy souvenirs in their hands, she knew they were her people. She'd have to interview some of them once she was done here.

"Huh," Travis said, brushing his hair out of his face. "You know what, we did get a big order for these items a couple of days ago."

Cat let out a whoop of triumph. Then she remembered Travis's terms. "You really can't tell me the name on the order?"

"Sorry. If you had a subpoena, sure, but I don't think you're that kind of investigator."

She sighed. "Fine." She supposed it wasn't the end of the world. The MIBs were probably using aliases anyway. Still, she wanted to tie up the loose end if she could. "I'll be back later to talk to Sam and David," she promised. "Could you flag that order to make it easier to find next time?"

Travis snorted. "Sure, kid."

Feeling equally frustrated and vindicated, Cat took to the streets of downtown. She began talking about Weston Farm to anyone wearing anything alien-related. Not everyone she interviewed had been at the farm last night, but of those who had, all but one reported issues with their technology today. Cat recorded their locations around the time of the EMP on a sketch of the farm, which revealed an approximate radius of the blast. She also used her old camera to take photos of several fried phones, a video camera that wouldn't turn on, and a car that had been towed to the local garage for repairs.

Between that evidence and the fact that someone had very recently bought the supplies necessary to make an EMP generator, Cat's confidence began to return. The broken equipment wasn't her fault, and she had almost everything she needed to prove it.

25

DANI

DANI WALKED INTO FIFTH-PERIOD science with her phone out. She hadn't caught another glimpse of Cat all day, and Cat still hadn't written her back. She was typing up one more text—

DANI: I really am sorry, and I want to talk. Please?

—when Ms. Blanks beckoned. "Danielle, can I speak to you?"

"Sure," Dani said, pressing "Send" and walking over.

"Were you and Catrina at Weston Farm last night?"

"How did you know?"

Ms. Blanks smiled. "I ran into an acquaintance this morning. She's on the Channel Four news crew. She mentioned that she'd seen two young girls poking around the circles. I suspected she was talking about my intrepid McMurray researchers."

"Yeah, that was probably us. We were collecting soil and stalk samples." Dani frowned as the emotions from her argument with Cat swept over her yet again. "Then Cat said she saw floating lights, but I didn't see them."

"That's too bad," Ms. Blanks said. "Was Catrina able to record anything?"

"Her camera malfunctioned." Dani shrugged. "I don't think

there was anything to see in the first place. We kind of . . . had a fight." She mumbled the last part, embarrassed to admit that they'd let their feelings get in the way of their research. She didn't think real scientists did that. "I haven't talked to her since."

"Chin up, Danielle." Ms. Blanks patted her shoulder. "Catrina will come around." She paused, looking toward the door. "I do have one more question for you, though. How did you end up so close to the circle as it formed? The farm's huge."

"Cat found some sort of pattern. She put all the circles from every year on top of one another and was able to predict where the next one was going to form."

Ms. Blanks's head shot back toward Dani. "That's fascinating."

"Cat's got it all mapped out on her computer. You should ask her about it."

"She has the equipment to do that?"

"Yeah, the setup in her bedroom is . . ." Dani sighed, trying not to seem too jealous. "It's almost a professional lab. It's amazing. Oh, but . . ." She couldn't believe she was about to say this. "Maybe don't tell anyone else about Cat's mapping software and that she can predict the circles. She wants to keep it all hush-hush for now."

Her teacher's lips twitched. "Really? Why's that?"

Dani definitely wasn't going to tell Ms. Blanks that Cat believed in Men in Black. "She's worried about science-fair sabotage," she said instead. "Like, one of the other teams might try to mess with us, to keep us from winning the award."

"Ah, well, in that case . . ." Ms. Blanks pretended to zip her lips.

"Thanks."

"Still, I can't wait to hear more about what you two have been up to," Ms. Blanks went on as the bell rang. "Let's conference again on Monday morning?"

"Definitely." Dani wasn't sure what more she'd have to share after the weekend, given where she and Cat had left things, but now she was even more determined to make up with her partner. Ms. Blanks was counting on her. Her approval made Dani feel like she was glowing all over.

"Take your seats, everyone!" Ms. Blanks announced. "I have an errand to run during my planning period, which means I'll be ducking out right at the bell, and I don't want to waste a minute of our valuable class time. If you'll turn to chapter eleven . . ."

Dani spent fifth period watching the door.

Cat never showed up.

26

CAT

WHEN CAT ARRIVED HOME around four that afternoon, something was off. She couldn't put her finger on what was wrong; it was just a feeling. She opened the front door half expecting someone to jump out at her from the darkened living room. But no one did. She poked around the ground floor of the house, and when everything seemed normal, she told herself she was just jumpy and headed upstairs to her room. She set her camera on her desk and slid into her chair—and almost slid right off again.

Her notebooks were gone. Every. Last. One.

She scrambled through her drawers to see if she'd tucked them away. They weren't there. Not under the bed, not in her bureau, and not even in the bathroom.

Cat was certain she'd left her notebooks on her desk. Last night, after she'd uncurled from the fetal position, she'd recorded what she remembered of the readouts from the equipment before it got fried. She'd read through her notes before heading off to school. She also remembered the notebooks being here when she came back this morning to pick up her camera.

Panic knotted in her stomach as she flicked on her computer. While she waited for it to boot up, she opened the mini fridge where she kept her lab experiments. Her hand froze on the handle.

The shelves were empty. All her experiments—from the microwaved and oven-baked stalk nodes to Dani's jars of soil to specimens that had nothing at all to do with the McMurray project—were gone.

Cat's knees went weak. She sank into her chair. When she glanced at her desktop computer, a cursor blinked back at her from a black screen.

```
Operating system not found.
```

Cat couldn't breathe. She put her head between her legs. She'd heard that should help, but it only made her feel dizzy.

All her research, all her files, even the work saved on her computer—had vanished.

No, it hadn't vanished. It had been *stolen*.

It had to be the Men in Black. But how did they even know who she was or what she had on the circles? It made no sense.

She grabbed the backpack she'd worn all day today and pulled out her laptop. Thank goodness she usually took this computer with her to school. The MIBs had only stolen her desktop hard drive. Of course, that was where all her experiment data had been stored. From now on, she was going to make multiple backups, just to be safe.

Still, there was no question she was being targeted. She had to talk to Dani—

The landline ringing snapped Cat out of her thoughts. She ran down one level and picked up the phone in the hall outside her mom's bedroom.

"Hello?"

"Cat? It's Dad."

Normally, Cat looked forward to calls from her dad. Not today. Not after the tragedy she'd discovered upstairs. But she tried to put on a cheery voice.

"Hey, Dad. How've you been?"

"Oh, I'm fine. Your mom mentioned you have something to tell me?"

Cat grimaced. *Thanks, Mom.* "Um. I guess I do."

Her dad gave her a moment and then said kindly, "Spit it out, kiddo."

"Well. I, um. I sort of need a new phone."

"What do you mean, 'sort of'?"

"My lab partner and I were doing research on the Weston Farm Circles, but some Men in Black were there, too, and they set off an EMP, and—"

"Whoa, whoa, slow down, honey. What are you saying?"

"An EMP ruined all my stuff. Including my phone."

"Even the very expensive video camera I got you last Christmas?"

She sighed. "Yeah."

There was a long silence on the other end of the phone.

"Cat . . . really? An EMP? Men in Black? What actually

happened to your equipment? Did you drop it in the pond on the outskirts of the farm?"

"No! I'm telling you the truth, I swear." Tears burned in the corners of her eyes.

"I don't know what's gotten into you," her dad said. Cat could practically hear him shaking his head with disappointment. "This isn't acceptable behavior. I trusted you to take good care of those things. I'm happy to buy you equipment when you need it, but I can't just replace items every time you break them. You're going to have to earn the money to replace those things yourself."

"But, Dad, I—"

"This isn't up for debate, Cat. Look, I have to get back to work. We'll talk more later."

"Okay. Bye, Dad."

Cat put the phone in the cradle. She stared at it, sniffling a little. Then she picked the phone back up. She might as well get all the unpleasant things over with at once. She dialed Dani's cell number, which she'd memorized as soon as they were partnered for the McMurray Competition, and bit her lip.

"Hello?"

"Hey, Dani. It's Cat."

"Cat? What number are you calling from? I've been trying to reach you all day."

"This is my home phone. My cell phone is fried."

"Fried? How?" Before Cat could answer, Dani went on. "We need to talk about our project."

"There's no point," Cat said bleakly.

"Oh. Are you . . ." Dani's voice went soft. "Are you really that mad at me?"

"It's not that."

"Then what is it?"

"Our research—it's been stolen."

27

DANI

DANI ASKED A MILLION questions. Cat had answers to all of them. Yes, she was sure the research had been on her desk when she left for school. No, she hadn't taken it with her and lost it on the bus. Yes, she was sure the desktop computer's hard drive was wiped. No, her mom wouldn't have cleaned out her specimen fridge without asking.

And on, and on, and on.

Eventually, Cat let out a frustrated "argh!" and hung up on Dani.

Then she called right back. "It's *my* turn to ask *you* some questions," she said.

"Okay," Dani said. "What do you want to know?"

"Who have you told about our investigation?" Cat demanded.

"Um . . . no one?"

"Your friends?"

"They know what we're researching," Dani said, "but I haven't really filled them in on the details." She imagined herself explaining soil sampling and stalk snipping to Laurel, Jane, and Nora and shook her head. "They really aren't interested in any of this."

"What about your parents?"

"They know I'm doing a project on crop damage," Dani said. "That's it."

"Crop damage . . . at Weston Farm. Surely they've put two and two together," Cat pressed. "Maybe they've talked to their friends, who talked to *their* friends, and somehow the information made its way to the Men in Black . . . ?"

"My mom and dad are definitely not out there bragging about my science project." Wow, that hurt to say out loud. But it was the truth. "I promise I haven't told anyone else. Only Ms. Blanks, and I told her to keep our research findings quiet for now."

"You did?" Cat sounded surprised. "When?"

"Today before class. She asked me for an update."

On the other end of the line, Cat was quiet for a moment. "Well, thanks," she finally said. "Can you meet me at Weston Farm tomorrow morning at six?"

"Six A.M.?" Dani yelped.

"Early bird catches the worm," Cat said and hung up.

Dani's gaze fell to the duffel bag by her feet, all packed for tonight's sleepover at Nora's house. If she had to be at Weston Farm by six . . . ugh. With a sigh, she texted her BFFs that she wasn't going to join them after all.

Instead, Dani went to bed early. But she didn't sleep well. Her restless thoughts cataloged the work she and Cat had put into the project thus far: the samples they'd collected that they'd have to collect again, the experiments they'd have to repeat, the valuable data that were lost.

Or, if Cat was to be believed . . . *stolen*.

Five thirty came far too soon. Dani dressed in silence, grabbed an apple for breakfast and chugged a soda for caffeine, left a note for her parents, and slipped out the door.

Cat was waiting for her at the spot by the farm where they'd been stashing their bikes. Dani's partner looked even worse than Dani felt. Her eyes were bloodshot, and her hair was matted. She was wearing the same outfit she'd had on at school yesterday, when Dani had called to her in the hall.

"Morning," Dani said cautiously.

Cat marched into the fields. "This way."

As usual, Dani found herself rushing to keep up. "Is this where the circle formed last night?"

"We're not going to the newest circle," Cat said without looking back. "We're going to the last place we ran into the Men in Black."

Dani groaned. "Cat. We need to get more samples—"

"We're going to find the Men in Black, and we're going to follow them, and we're going to get our research back." Cat shook her fist in the air. "No one steals from Catrina Mulvaney! Or Danielle Williams," she added a beat later.

Dani puffed out a frustrated breath. She was upset that their work had gotten lost on Cat's watch and even more upset that her partner was refusing to take responsibility. But Dani also still felt bad about the fight they'd had two nights ago. She'd said things she wished she could take back. She still wanted to work with Cat. Or work with her while working against her. Whatever.

But in order for there to *be* a project, much less an award, they had to collect samples and run tests—

"Shhh!" Cat hissed. She grabbed Dani's arm and pulled her into the tall grain.

"Did you hear something?" Dani murmured.

Cat jerked her head to the right. Dani strained to listen. Sure enough, there were footsteps crunching the leaves that had fallen from the dry stalks. Footsteps and voices.

Two people in black suits entered the crop circle. A man and a woman. He was Black, tall and wiry with a closely shaved head. She was Asian, of average height and sturdily built, with shiny black hair pulled into a tight ponytail.

The male agent carried—more like *wore*—a bizarre and expensive-looking piece of equipment. "That looks like a lidar device!" Cat breathed, awestruck. "That stands for 'Light Detection and Ranging.' It's used to survey the ground," she told Dani.

"It's . . . a backpack," Dani said. "With a robotic arm coming out of it?" It was definitely one of the strangest things she'd seen—and after hanging out with Cat for the last few weeks, that was saying a lot.

"It's so much more than a backpack! This model came out a few years ago. I read about it in my ufology forums. The Men in Black must be checking to see how the UFO impacted the landscape and whether it left anything behind."

Dani was more focused on the walkie-talkie in the female agent's hands. "The area is secure," the woman said into the speaker. There was a burst of static. "Repeat that?" The woman put the receiver to her ear. More loud static. "I can't understand you." She shook the device, looking disgusted. "She could've told us to clear out before she set off that thing the other night," she said to the man. "I was in the line of fire."

Cat nudged Dani so hard that Dani almost fell out of her crouch. "What?" Dani whispered.

Her partner mouthed something back.

Dani raised her eyebrows higher.

E. M. P! Cat enunciated silently.

"There's nothing here," the male agent said. "Let's go. There's a cinnamon roll at the continental breakfast with my name on it."

"That's if we even get to have breakfast," the woman said. "Guess who's in a terrible mood?"

"Again?"

"Always. Today, he needs a medic." The female agent rolled her eyes.

"That's what he gets for running through the fields in a suit in the dark," said her partner, shaking his head.

Cat stood, carefully and quietly, as the two agents left the circle. "I know where they're going," she said to Dani.

"Really?" Dani followed Cat back to their bikes, but not without a longing look over her shoulder at the soil she should be sampling. She really, really needed to figure out where those iron microspheres came from. "Where?"

"That Man in Black said 'continental breakfast.' They're staying at a hotel!"

Dani stopped in her tracks. "That's all you've got? There are dozens of hotels in town, and that's if they're even inside the city limits—"

"Which is why we have to move." Cat grabbed her bike from the bushes. She took a running start and hopped on, just as a black sedan pulled out of the main Weston Farm entrance up ahead. "Dani! Come on!"

Dani jumped on her own bike, stumbling a bit before finding a rhythm with her feet.

And then they were flying down the dirt road after the government agents' car. They were literally eating Man in Black dust. Dani had to admit, the chase was thrilling—even if she was sure they were chasing after nothing. She gripped her handlebars, ducked her head, and pedaled faster.

28

CAT

CAT DID HER BEST to keep the black sedan in sight until they reached the highway. Then the car sped up and away onto the on-ramp. Breathless, she stopped her bike and waited for Dani to catch up.

Dani skidded to a stop next to her. "Sorry, Cat. It was a good try."

"Sorry about what? I know exactly where they're going." Cat grinned at the surprise on Dani's face. "They went north. If they'd gone south, we'd be in trouble. But there's only one hotel on the north side of town. Come on, we can catch the bus on the corner near my house."

They hurried to Cat's house and left their bikes leaning against the garage. Without waiting for Dani, Cat broke into a run. "The next bus will be here any second!"

It pulled up to the curb just as they arrived, and they boarded swiftly. Cat slid into a seat, still grinning at Dani. "They're going to the Parisian Hotel on West Street. It's *got* to be that one." Cat frowned. "Unless they knew we were on to them and just wanted to lose us."

Dani was quiet for a moment. She was making her thinking-hard face. Cat had learned from experience that Dani tended to wear this face right before telling Cat exactly why her theories were wrong. Cat braced herself for the latest argument . . . and then was surprised when her partner said, "Hmm. I guess it's worth a shot."

"Did you hear them, though? They were talking about an EMP! The one that fried my equipment got that woman's equipment, too. I told you so." Cat felt flushed with the thrill of vindication, but Dani looked skeptical.

"I mean, she never said *EMP*. She could've been talking about something else."

Cat laughed and leaned back against the seat. "I'll convince you yet."

Dani laughed, too. It was nice to hear that laugh. After their fight the other night, Cat hadn't been sure they'd ever laugh together again.

When they reached their stop, just down the street from the hotel, they hopped off the bus. Cat immediately dragged Dani into the bushes lining the road.

"What are you doing?"

"They might have people posted out front," Cat whispered. "We need to be sneaky."

"Cat, it's a hotel. People go in and out of it all the time."

"Yeah, but we don't have any adults with us. We might attract attention." Cat was beginning to regret not changing out of her neon-green overalls for this, but she'd have to make do. "Can we please just do this my way?"

Dani held up her hands. "Fine. You're the boss."

"Thank you."

Right now, Cat was grateful Dani was going along with her at all. But next, she had to prove what she was certain was true: Their research was somewhere in that hotel. The building had one main entrance, as well as several side entrances from the parking lot that wrapped around the building. Cat gasped when she spied the sedan they'd been following parked in the back of the lot.

"Look," she whispered. "It's the agents' car! I memorized the license plate number. We're in the right place!"

Dani looked impressed. "Nice. Now what?"

Cat looked around. "That." She pointed to a school bus full of kids, no doubt here to see the crop circles. "It's the perfect cover."

Dani followed as Cat wove through the line of cars leading to the bus. When they reached the rear of the bus, Cat yanked Dani to her side as she flattened herself against the back door. "On the count of three, let's join the crowd, okay?"

Cat could've sworn she saw the beginnings of an eye roll before Dani nodded, but she decided to ignore it. Once they found what was left of their research, Dani wouldn't be able to deny these precautions were necessary.

"One . . . two . . . three!" They moved into the group of kids, garnering only a couple of strange looks from those around them. Cat's adrenaline spiked as they passed through the hotel doors without being stopped. She spied a couple of official-looking men in dark suits nearby—hotel security or MIBs, she couldn't be sure—but they didn't even notice her and Dani.

Sometimes, being a kid had its advantages.

The inside of the Parisian was chaos. Kids from the bus were everywhere, while their chaperones tried to get them under control and checked in. As soon as she felt safe to do so, Cat dragged Dani toward the elevator. They caught it as the door closed, which was lucky because a crowd of people would be getting on the next one, Cat was sure.

This one, though, was empty, which was just what they needed. Cat pressed the button for the lowest-sounding floor, labeled SB (hopefully for subbasement).

"Why are we going to the basement?" Dani whispered, even though they were alone.

"We need to find the incinerator."

"Do hotels still have incinerators? That sounds like something out of an old movie."

"If they don't, we'll head back upstairs. And if they do . . ." Cat let the sentence fade out into an ominous silence.

Dani folded her arms across her chest. "You think they burned our work?"

"Once they were done going through it, of course."

"Fine. Let's get this over with," Dani said as the elevator dinged and they exited. Despite the stern look on her face, she seemed a little nervous. To be honest, Cat was nervous, too, down here. Dark shadows hugged the corners of the basement hallway, and the only light came from the couple of bare bulbs dangling from the ceiling.

"Are you sure this is where the incinerator will be?" Dani took a tentative step forward.

Cat swallowed hard. "Not really. But it's the best guess I've got. Come on."

They quietly tiptoed down the corridor, hoping not to run into anyone. The hallway was dotted with locked doors. Dani checked each handle right after Cat did, which would have driven Cat bonkers if she hadn't been pleased her partner was being thorough. Dani also put her ear up against each door, listening intently for signs of life on the other side. "Nothing," she murmured. "No Men in Black here." Dani's eyes twinkled as she said that last part, but again, Cat didn't mind so much. Not when Dani was actually participating in their mission.

Finally, they reached the last door. Cat met Dani's eyes. "Here goes . . . ," she said and turned the knob. The door swung open to reveal a large room filled with pipes and boilers and storage boxes.

They crept forward. Above them, the pipes creaked. The plumbing and boxes cast weird shadows in the dim light, and Cat could feel a breeze coming from somewhere, tickling the back of her neck. She shivered, and then something caught her eye. It was a ripped piece of paper, stuck on the rusted edge of a low-hanging pipe.

The paper had writing on it. Cat squinted. She gasped. The handwriting was *hers*.

The gasp had made Dani jump about a foot. "What is it?"

Cat picked up the paper between two fingertips. "Proof," she said, both awed and scared. "It's proof."

29

DANI

DANI'S HEART WAS POUNDING as she took the scrap of paper from Cat's outstretched hand. She studied it for a second. "Is that . . . ?"

"Yeah. I wrote that."

"It says something about . . . magnetic polarization . . ." The words were smudged. So was a diagram of a circle, which featured a few spots marked with stars.

"Never mind what it says," Cat said. "It's from one of my notebooks! That means the Men in Black definitely brought our work down here! I bet they shredded it first, and this fell out on the way to the incinerator." Cat marched toward the far side of the basement.

Dani followed her and found the other girl struggling with the heavy metal door to the incinerator. There was a wheel and a few levers and latches to maneuver. Together, they figured out how to open it.

"Okay!" Cat exclaimed. "Let's see what . . . Oh."

Dani peered past her partner into the blackness of the incinerator. All she could see was a pile of ash. But maybe there was something buried deep in there, something that hadn't fully burned up. She spotted a metal poker leaning against a nearby wall. She used it to sift through the pile, pulling her shirt up over her nose and mouth so she wouldn't breathe in too much ash.

"I don't think there's anything left whole," she finally said, stepping back. "But it does look like this was burned pretty recently."

"How do you know?" Cat asked.

"The ash is still hot, for one thing." Dani paused. "Although ash can actually retain heat for a couple of days after the fire goes out."

Cat just looked at her.

"We have a firepit in my backyard," Dani explained. "One time, my sister, Mallory, messed with the ashes before they were cool, and Dad got really mad. He said she could've started a fire. My point is, if we're assuming our research was taken from your house yesterday before . . . what time?"

"Four P.M."

"Before four, and the ashes inside the incinerator are hot right now . . . we can make an educated guess that the burn took place either last night or this morning." Dani paused, thinking. "This morning seems more likely, if they needed time to read through it all first."

Cat groaned and put her face in her hands. "I still don't understand how they even knew about our investigation. Tell me again who you've talked to about the project?"

"Ms. Blanks. My parents, sort of. Jane, Laurel, and Nora." Dani ticked the names off on her fingers. "Does Scott Crawley count?"

Cat barked out a laugh. "Ha, no. I doubt he has any secret government contacts." Her smile dropped away. "So if the leak didn't come from you . . ."

Dani ignored the part about a leak and got back to business. "Did you bring any sample bags? Let's collect some of the ash."

"Middle pocket," Cat said. "No, wait. If the ash is still hot, the baggies could melt. I have my lunch box. Use that."

Dani set down the fire poker and went for her partner's backpack. "We can put some similar stuff in the firepit at my house—notebook paper, stalk and soil samples, whatever else was taken—and then compare it to this ash," she said. "I'll look up some tests we can run." *And come up with a story to tell my parents about why we're burning random stuff*, Dani added silently. "I'm sorry about the lost work. This really stinks."

"It does. But . . . wait." Cat's face lit up. "You said, 'whatever else was taken.' Does this mean you believe me?"

Dani paused, carefully considering what she was about to say. "I do."

Cat squealed and threw her arms around Dani. "I knew you'd come around!"

"Hold on." Dani pushed Cat off her. "I believe that your research was taken. The scrap of paper you're holding proves that at least part of what was in your bedroom made its way down here, and you weren't anywhere near this hotel yesterday. This pile of hot ash is pretty incriminating, too . . . especially if we're able to determine that these ashes contain corn and wheat stalks. That would be a pretty weird thing for a hotel to be burning."

Cat squealed again, and Dani held up a hand.

"*But*—that doesn't mean I believe these imaginary Men in Black are responsible."

"Imaginary?" Cat shrieked and then lowered her voice. "You saw them. We followed them here. They're completely, one hundred percent real."

"We followed two people here," Dani said patiently. "Two supposed government agents. But for all we know, they're from, like, the Department of Agriculture. There are tons of reasons the government might send people to look into crop circles."

Cat slowly shook her head. "You are impossible, Dani Williams."

"I'm a scientist," Dani said.

She wasn't sure she'd ever said it flat out like that before. Not that she'd be a scientist *one day*—that she was one already. Using that title felt so right. It fit like perfectly broken-in sneakers. She was a scientist, and that meant she couldn't operate based on wild hunches or random coincidences. She required evidence. Each hypothesis had to be proven or disproven before they could move on.

Who had taken Cat's work? That was less important than the question that was *in* the lost research: What was going on at Weston Farm? Where did the circles really come from?

Humans.

And herbicide.

And heat.

Dani was sure it was some combination of the three.

She sighed. It really was time to tell Cat about her hypothesis.

She could do it today. They could gather some new soil samples and then Dani could show Cat the iron microspheres . . .

"Come on." Dani held out her hand. "Let's get out of here. If we hurry back to the farm, we can spend the rest of the day re-doing our experiments. We can still win the McMurray Award—"

Cat was shaking her head.

"No, you don't want to finish our project? No, you don't want to win the award?" Dani hadn't thought Cat was the type to throw in the towel after a little setback.

Okay, having your hard work incinerated was actually kind of a big setback. But still.

"No, we can't leave yet." Cat grabbed the metal poker from where Dani had set it down, and she stuck it into the incinerator.

Dani was almost afraid to ask . . . but she did anyway. "Why?"

"Because there's something else in here." Cat put on an over-size protective glove that was hanging by the incinerator and then reached into the kiln and pulled something out. She blew off a cloud of ash to reveal a small, rectangular piece of metal.

"What's that?" Dani leaned in. It was about the size of an external hard drive but much thinner. She put on a protective glove of her own, and her partner dropped the metal piece into her hand. It was lighter than she'd expected it to be. It looked like iron or steel but felt like aluminum. Even stranger, despite having been in the incinerator, it was cool to the touch. After Dani held her other hand close and felt no radiant heat, she took a chance and poked it with a bare finger. "Did it come from your lab? Is it part of your equipment?"

"I don't recognize it," Cat said. "But if it was in the incinerator with my notebooks, that means they were trying to destroy it. Except . . ." She took the object back from Dani and studied it from all angles. "It's not burned. It doesn't even look singed. Oh! Maybe there's evidence left on it!"

"Evidence of what?"

"We'll find out." Cat wrapped the metal rectangle in one of her sample baggies and then tucked it away in her backpack. "I'll run some tests at home."

"Right. At least you've still got your lab. Let's go." Dani tugged on Cat's arm and began to sneak through the basement to the exit.

A *ding* sounded, somewhere not so far away. The elevator. Dani heard the doors clank open and then hushed voices arguing.

"Hide!" Cat tugged her behind a stack of boxes. They crouched down, trying not to give away their location with their stuttering breaths. They waited.

The hushed voices and footsteps drew closer.

30

CAT

"THIS IS NOT MY fault," said a woman.

"It's not mine, either, so you can stop blaming me," said a man.

Cat peeked over the pipe and glimpsed the pair of agents they'd followed to the Parisian, both wearing dark suits and dour expressions. She ducked down quickly.

"I'm not blaming you," the woman said. It sounded like she was almost on top of Cat and Dani now. Cat held her breath and motioned for Dani to do the same. "I'm saying," the woman went on, "we can't be careless. Our jobs are on the line."

"Let's just get rid of this, all right?" her partner said.

Cat risked another quick glance outside their hiding place. The MIBs were beelining for the incinerator. They were carrying something rolled up in a sheet. They had to be destroying evidence.

But evidence of what?

Aliens, obviously. No matter what Dani said, Cat was positive these two had nothing to do with the Department of Agriculture.

She nudged Dani. The other girl rose up out of her crouch to see what was happening. They watched the agents toss the sheet-wrapped whatever-it-was into the incinerator and turn on the machine. It roared to life, immediately making the basement about twenty degrees hotter. When both agents turned and hurried toward the elevator, Cat and Dani dropped to the floor.

The moment they were gone, Cat dashed out from behind the pipes toward the incinerator. She looked through the glass window, but all she could see was the burning sheet. It had to be more than just soiled bedclothes, but she wasn't about to open the incinerator to find out. She'd have to come back later to see if anything had survived.

Dani came up behind her. "That was weird," she admitted, peering into the flames.

Cat let out a frustrated growl. "We've got to find the agents' hotel rooms. Something strange is going on, and we have to figure out what it is."

Dani opened her mouth to argue, and Cat narrowed her eyes. If her partner said one more thing about that blasted award, she didn't know what she'd do. Couldn't Dani see the situation had changed? They'd stumbled onto something so much bigger than a science fair.

But again, her partner surprised her. "If there really is something going on," Dani said slowly, "they'll have guards. We'll never make it into their rooms undetected. Also, we don't know what floor they're on."

"We'll check every floor," Cat said.

"And if we get caught?"

"We'll play the *stupid kids* card."

"The what?" Dani squinted at Cat.

"The *stupid kids* card. You know, we act like we don't know where we are or can't find our parents. That kind of thing."

"Oh. That might work. Except—"

"No more excuses or what-ifs," Cat said firmly. "Let's just try. I'm the boss, remember?"

This time, Dani did roll her eyes. It was epic, like she'd been holding the urge in all day.

They searched the hotel floor by floor. The first eight levels produced nothing but grumbling from Dani. But Cat wasn't discouraged. They still had the ninth floor, which was divided into two penthouse suites.

Cat's fingers began to tingle the moment the elevator bell dinged. She poked her head out into the hallway. "All clear," she whispered.

No sooner had the words left her mouth—and the elevator doors shut behind them—than one of the two penthouse doors opened. Cat and Dani froze as a woman in a bathrobe snuck out, holding an ice bucket. She raised her eyebrows at the two of them but said nothing as she passed them on her way to the ice machine, got her ice, and went back into her room.

"I guess the MIBs are in that one," Cat murmured, nodding toward the opposite suite.

Dani swallowed hard. She'd been looking more and more uncomfortable the closer they'd gotten to the penthouse floor.

"Are you okay?" Cat asked.

"I don't want to get arrested for trespassing."

"That's what the *stupid kids* card is for," Cat reminded her. "And I don't think we'll get arrested. At worst . . . yelled at."

Dani nodded but still looked queasy. Giving her partner what she hoped was an encouraging smile, Cat tiptoed to the left-side penthouse door. It was locked, of course, but—

Voices on the other side of the door made her pause. She waited another second and then ducked behind the nearby ice machine, dragging Dani with her, just as the penthouse door opened. Two MIBs walked out: the stocky white guy in glasses and the Asian woman. They walked toward the elevator and pressed the call button. When the elevator doors opened, they stepped inside.

Cat watched, breathless, as the penthouse door slowly swung closed.

The second the elevator was in motion, taking the MIBs with it, she lunged. By some miracle, she managed to slip her fingers into the gap in between the door and the jamb. It pinched, but she wasn't about to complain about injuries received while pursuing the truth.

Cat cracked the door open an inch. She could hear voices farther back in the suite, but no one was in the entryway. She stepped inside and held the door for Dani.

Her partner hesitated. "I don't know about this . . ."

"Come on—it's for science." That was the one thing Cat could think of that might convince Dani to join her. Although, if she were being honest, she didn't really want to do this alone.

After another excruciating few seconds, Dani nodded. The

two of them crept down the hall toward the voices. They turned a corner and discovered a closed door. Cat snuck up to the door and put her ear against it. After a beat, Dani did the same.

". . . should be all of it . . ."

". . . good . . . one less crusader . . ."

". . . if there's nothing else . . ."

One of the voices, though muffled, was familiar. The gravel-voiced man. Cat would recognize those gruff, scratchy tones anywhere. But what was that buzzing sound in the background? An electric toothbrush? A buzz saw? A hive of angry bees?

Beside her, Dani began frantically digging through her backpack.

Realization clicked. "You didn't silence your phone?"

Dani found her cell and winced at the screen.

"Better be important," Cat snipped.

"I was supposed to be at the mall right now," Dani murmured. "I told my friends—"

The door opened, sending Cat and Dani careering backward. The tall, dark-skinned MIB glowered down at them. He quickly closed the door behind him.

But not before Cat glimpsed something that made her heart gallop in her chest.

"How did you kids get in here?" the man barked.

Dani looked helplessly at Cat.

Right, the *stupid kids* defense. "Sorry, sorry!" Cat blurted, trying to look embarrassed—instead of exhilarated, which was what she really was. "We got lost. We thought this was our floor . . ."

The man pulled them both to their feet and then quickly

ushered them to the exit. "Next time you can't find your parents, go to the lobby, not the penthouse."

He shoved them out the suite door and stationed himself in front of it while they waited for the elevator to arrive.

It felt like forever.

Dani's ears were burning red, and her face was as pale as snow. Cat couldn't tell if she was genuinely freaked out, or angry, or a little bit of both. When the elevator finally arrived and they got in, the Man in Black glared at them until the doors closed.

Cat let out a hoot. "Did you see that? I can't believe it!"

Dani shook her head. "That was close. *Too* close. I could have sworn that guy was going to call the authorities."

"Are you kidding? He *is* the authorities. Plus, I don't think those Men in Black want the police crawling around their suite. Not given what I just saw."

Dani narrowed her eyes. "What did you see?"

"It was only for a second," Cat said, lowering her voice, "but when that man opened the door, I saw a medical setup. There were tools and what looked like a makeshift operating table. A really small one. That must have been what the two we saw at the incinerator were cleaning up after!" She paused, trying not to let her partner's serious face make her doubt her own eyes. "You really didn't see any of that?"

Dani sighed. "No, I did. But—"

"There's only one explanation that makes sense," Cat said firmly.

"And that is?"

"It was an alien autopsy."

Dani burst out laughing. "Cat—"

"I'm not joking." Watching Dani giggle was making Cat's chest hurt. "I don't think the EMP that took out my equipment was intended for us. I think it was meant for the UFO. The Men in Black are here trying to capture the aliens."

31

DANI

"I DIDN'T MEAN TO laugh at Cat," Dani admitted to Ms. Blanks on Monday morning. "I know it hurt her feelings. But—I mean—an alien autopsy?" She threw both hands in the air.

Ms. Blanks gave her arm a sympathetic pat. "Danielle, the path to scientific enlightenment is rarely straight and predictable."

"I know, I know," Dani grumbled. She'd heard Ms. Blanks say that before, whenever one of her students totally botched an experiment—or discovered something unexpected. "But the science fair is less than two weeks away. Right now, we have nothing to present. *Nothing.*"

"Danielle—"

"The McMurray Award is really, really important to me," Dani said. "I have to go to ScienceU." She couldn't spend another summer at ArtistiKids, shriveling up inside. And she couldn't risk another Dance of Doom. All of a sudden, she was blinking away frustrated tears.

"It's great that you care so much, Danielle," Ms. Blanks said gently. "Catrina cares a lot, too, though. You see that, right?"

Reluctantly, Dani nodded. She certainly couldn't question Cat's commitment.

After leaving the Parisian Hotel on Saturday, she and Cat had swung by Cat's house to pick up their bikes and then had returned to Weston Farm. They'd found a circle that was relatively untrampled and had spent two hours clipping stalks and scooping soil. Then—before Dani could figure out how to tell her partner she'd been working against her all this time—Dani's mom had called and asked her to come home.

Cat had stayed at the farm, but not long enough to witness the circle appear that night. Consequently, she'd been in a *mood* yesterday morning when Dani had called to see about going over to work on their project. It didn't help that Cat's mom had been given a rare Sunday off from work and had wanted to take Cat on a mother-daughter day trip hiking Mattapan Peak.

According to Cat's pattern, there were four more circles due this week. They'd have four more chances to get the evidence they each needed. Still, talking to Ms. Blanks, all Dani could think about was the time she and Cat had lost.

"An alien autopsy," Ms. Blanks said with a chuckle. "I have to confess, I didn't envision Catrina going . . . there. What made her jump to that conclusion?"

Dani moaned in response. "I have no idea."

Of course, she knew exactly what had given Cat the idea, because they'd both seen *something* in that penthouse. She couldn't tell Ms. Blanks that. She'd decided not to share the breaking-and-entering portion of the weekend.

But Dani had a theory. At Weston Farm on Saturday morning, the female agent had talked about needing a medic. The medical setup at the hotel had to be because one of them had gotten injured. Which meant the thing the agents had brought down to the incinerator, wrapped in a sheet, was probably bloody bandages and gauze. The agents didn't want house-keeping to ask questions when they emptied the trash.

Not that Cat would believe a rational explanation like that.

"Where were you when Catrina came up with this theory?" Ms. Blanks asked, still smiling.

"At the farm. Cat saw something in the crowd that set her off."

"Well, perhaps it doesn't matter if Catrina goes off in one direction, while you focus on your own work," Ms. Blanks said. "After all, you're trying to prove different hypotheses. Speaking of which . . . what *is* your current hypothesis?"

"Oh!" Dani exclaimed, getting excited. "I think the circles have something to do with this new weed killer, Weed-Be-Gone, being manufactured at the Bug-Be-Gone factory near Weston Farm. I found evidence of iron deposits in the crop circle soil, and iron is an ingredient in some herbicides."

"Iron deposits!" her teacher repeated. "Well. That sounds like something worth studying."

Dani beamed. "I thought so, too."

"Remind me of Catrina's hypothesis?"

"Officially, her theory is that the first thirteen circles will be real, and any that come after number thirteen will be fakes," Dani said. "She's going to look for quantifiable differences between the real ones and the fakes."

"Ah," Ms. Blanks said.

"But unofficially . . . ," Dani went on, frowning, "she's investigating Men in Black and alien autopsies and strange bits of metal."

Ms. Blanks coughed. "Excuse me. Strange bits of metal?"

"Oh, yeah. Cat found this weird piece of metal on Saturday."

"What did it look like?"

"I don't know, a broken key chain or a computer part or something. We were going to analyze it yesterday, but Cat's mom took her hiking instead."

Which was why Dani had gone another day without telling Cat the truth.

But she was totally going to do it today. Later. After school.

"Where did Catrina find the metal fragment?" Ms. Blanks asked.

"Um." Dani was also not too eager to tell Ms. Blanks about digging through an incinerator. The fewer adults who knew about their trip to the hotel, the better. "She . . . picked it up . . . somewhere. Cat's like that."

The warning bell rang for first period. "It sounds like you've learned a lot, Danielle," her teacher said quickly.

"I guess. We still have so much work to do—"

"Everything will turn out the way it's meant to."

Dani nodded. "Thanks, Ms. Blanks."

She was going to salvage this project yet. Starting this afternoon. The colorimeter and potassium permanganate Cat's dad had ordered for them were supposed to arrive today. Dani could dive into those experiments using the soil samples they'd taken from the farm on Saturday.

She couldn't wait.

HER MOM HAD OTHER plans. After school, before Dani could even ask to be dropped off at Cat's house, Dani's mom turned the car in the opposite direction. "I have a surprise for you!" she chirped.

Dani barely held in her groan of dismay.

"We're going to buy your ballroom dance supplies!"

"Mom. I told you, I don't want to—"

"You'll need a ballroom skirt and low-heeled shoes. Probably a new leotard as well. I think you've grown a bit."

Dani sank into her seat. She could only dream of having parents who'd spend money on the things she actually wanted and needed. Like microscopes, and mapping software, and Bunsen burners, and—basically Cat's entire bedroom. Cat didn't know how good she had it.

32

CAT

CAT SAT AT HER desk, knees bouncing with anticipation. She couldn't *wait* to test the strange piece of metal from the incinerator. The only thing missing was . . . Dani.

Who was supposed to be here by now.

Cat grabbed her new phone. The second her partner picked up, she asked, "Where are you?"

"I've been taken hostage."

"What?" Cat screeched. "Where did the Men in Black pick you up? Were they waiting at school? Did you see where they took you? I'm coming! I'll be there soon!"

She was halfway down the attic stairs before Dani could get a word in edgewise.

"Cat! Calm down. I'm with my mom."

"Then why did you say you'd been taken hostage?" Cat yelped, pressing a hand to her chest.

"We're at a dance shop. She's making me try on leotards and ballroom shoes. I'm here against my will."

"Oh." Cat went back upstairs. "Can you come here afterward?"

"I'll try," Dani said. "Gotta go. Mom's back." She hung up.

Cat looked at the mass spectrometer. It was her prized

possession. Well, sort of her possession. It was actually her dad's, but he was letting her borrow it. He didn't need it in his current job, but there was always the possibility he'd swoop in someday to reclaim it. Cat had convinced him she needed it (or maybe she'd just worn him down), and now she finally had a real excuse to fire it up.

She'd used it only once before, when she did a test run with her dad last year. He'd explained that it broke stuff apart so it could analyze the tiny pieces (in this case, atoms) to determine what elements were in the sample. He'd demonstrated by letting the mass spec analyze water and ammonium. The two substances had similar overall molecular weight, but the individual elements in each had different mass, so the machine could tell them apart.

Surely Dani would understand if Cat got started without her. After all, Dani was the one who kept harping on how little time they had before the McMurray exhibition.

Cat turned the machine on and loaded a small sample of the metal from the incinerator into the testing chamber. She checked the notes she'd saved from when her dad had shown her how it worked and set it to run an analysis.

Then she pulled on her dad's old puffy coat and settled into her chair to wait.

Waiting was the *worst*, Cat decided after about ten seconds. She grabbed a Mountain Dew from her mini fridge and chugged it.

She was saved by the sound of her email pinging. She had a notification from the ufology forum she frequented. Cat grinned widely when she realized it was a response from the poster, username CoverUpsRUS, who'd also encountered the Man in Black with a gravelly voice.

> Hey, thanks for getting in touch. That's wild that you got Gravel, too. (That's what I call him, for lack of a real name . . .) He must be a key member in their division. I crossed paths with him out in the desert. My team and I were investigating strange lights over the city and tracked them out that way. The dirt was disturbed, and several big saguaros had been knocked flat. We were sure we were on to something, but then our equipment went on the fritz, and several men in suits informed us we had to leave. We objected, but they had weapons and all we had were fried cameras, so we didn't stick around.

> I went back a couple of weeks later, and there was no sign of any disturbance anymore. The fallen cacti were gone like they'd never existed, and the dunes looked like they'd been serene for ages. They found something out there, and we almost did, too.

> What was your encounter like?

Cat hesitated before responding. How much should she tell this stranger on the Internet? She believed him, but . . . she also felt certain the MIBs were watching her. After all, they'd stolen her research from this very room. What if this message was a setup? She sat back in her chair and bit her lip. It killed her not to share her story, but she knew she had to wait until she had proof if she wanted any chance of making it stick. She quickly sent off a thank-you and closed her email.

The mass spectrometer wasn't done with its analysis, so she

mentally listed off the Men in Black she and Dani had encountered. There was Gravel, obviously—thanks, CoverUpsRUS, for that nickname. Gravel's primary partner seemed to be the white guy with the glasses. Since Cat hadn't seen any of the others wearing glasses, she decided to call him Specs. The second pair of agents, the Black man and the Asian woman . . . well, he was incredibly tall and thin, so he could be Beanpole. And the woman honestly looked like a movie star, so . . . Hollywood.

Cat jotted down the nicknames to tell Dani later.

The mass spec was still working, so Cat opened a new document on her laptop and titled it "Suspects." Somehow, the MIBs knew about their investigation. That meant she and Dani had either a leak or a mole.

She wrote down the name of every person she could think of who might have the slightest inkling about their project: Dani, Ms. Blanks, Robbie Colton, Mr. Hepworth, Travis from the hardware store, Sam and David (maybe Travis had told them about her visit?), Mr. CoverUpsRUS from the ufology forum, Dani's parents, Dani's friends, and Cat's mom. Her fingers hesitated over the keyboard for a moment, and then she wrote the last name: her dad.

Cat tapped her chin while she considered her list. She couldn't imagine Dani would endanger her own science project by talking to the MIBs, so she crossed her off first.

She thought for a moment about the time Ms. Blanks had wept while telling them about newly discovered symbiotic insects. The lady knew her science, that was for sure, but between her soft spot for the previously undiscovered and the fact that she was their teacher, it seemed unlikely she would betray them.

At least . . . not on purpose.

Cat had been about to cross off Ms. Blanks's name, but now she hesitated. Ms. Blanks was very engaged with their project and seemed genuinely proud of them. That, combined with her enthusiasm for scientific discovery, made it possible that she might have talked to the wrong person—maybe *before* Dani had asked her to keep the details of their research quiet.

Or maybe her classroom was bugged? Cat would have to do some poking around the next time she had a chance, just to be safe.

Ms. Blanks would remain on the list for now. Cat added a note next to her name: *Who has she told?*

Next, Robbie Colton was easy to write off; he was far too suspicious to talk to the feds. Besides, he was all in on bringing to light Hilldale's alien visitors.

Now, Mr. Hepworth . . . he'd seemed friendly enough, but he was also a liar. He hadn't made those crop circles, even though he'd said on TV that he had. Cat hadn't told him too much about their project, but he knew her name, *and* he'd been willing to give her and Dani free rein of his property. What if the MIBs had asked Weston Farm's owner to give them information about anyone investigating the circles? She highlighted Mr. Hepworth's name in the document.

Hardware-store Travis didn't think much of Cat. In fact, by the time Sam and David had returned, he'd probably forgotten she'd even been there. Still, she kept him on the list, just in case. She never had trusted Travis.

The ufology forums might be an issue. The MIBs were bound to be monitoring activity there, maybe even using accounts to bait people like Cat. She'd create a new username tonight to throw them off.

Dani was certain her parents weren't the leak, but Cat wasn't convinced. Who knew who Mr. and Mrs. Williams might know? Dani's friends, on the other hand, probably weren't a problem.

Cat looked at the last two names on the list. Her dad did work for the government . . . but he was her dad. If he was the leak, it wasn't intentional. The same went for her mom, not that Cat thought her mom had any friends with top-level security clearance. She sighed and left their names on the list, making a mental note to tell her parents as little as possible about their project from now on. Just in case.

Cat began to close her laptop, then stopped and groaned. She'd forgotten Scott Crawley. When Dani had said his name the other day, Cat had dismissed the notion of him being the source of the leak, but for all she knew, he could have gone home to his government-employed parents and told them how some kids were asking him about aliens at Weston Farm. Worse, she and Dani had talked to him in front of an entire locker room of boys. Any one of them could be the leak! And she didn't know any of the other boys' names. She bit her lip and wrote "high school football team," then highlighted that in yellow, too.

Ugh. By that logic, she couldn't cross Dani's friends off the list. What if one of their parents—or aunts or uncles or family friends—worked for the government or knew someone who did? She begrudgingly highlighted "Dani's friends" and wrote, *Family in government?*

Her list was getting out of control.

She went to close her laptop again, only to have another thought: She should probably find out who at the McMurray Corporation was responsible for approving project proposals—

Her mass spec finally beeped.

Cat squeaked and bounced over to the machine to read the results.

Hmm. It couldn't identify the metal. She checked the cheat sheet her dad had made her. The machine was supposed to be able to pinpoint the elements making up any substance placed inside it.

That meant the readings she'd gotten from the scrap of metal should be impossible.

There must be a mistake. Maybe she'd set it up wrong.

Cat ran the test again, more carefully this time. She waited, perched in her chair, back ramrod straight, gulping Mountain Dew for what felt like an eternity, until the mass spec beeped again.

The results were exactly the same. Impossible.

What if this wasn't a mistake? What if this was the proof she'd been looking for?

With shaking hands, Cat ran the test a third time (experiments must be replicable, after all). When the results came up the same again—the metal couldn't be identified—she whooped with excitement and danced around her room.

"Cat?" her mom called. "Are you all right up there?"

"Yep! I'm fantastic, Mom!" Cat giggled to herself, unable to stop grinning.

She'd found an element that wasn't on the periodic table! The metal must be from an alien spaceship, and the MIBs were trying to cover it up! And she'd proven her case using verifiable science! Dani would have to believe her now. They'd win the science fair; and Cat's dad would come see her amazing, award-winning project; and she could show the world irrefutable proof of extraterrestrial life.

Short of seeing a real, live alien, this was everything Cat had ever hoped for.

She scrambled for her phone and dialed Dani.

"Hey, Cat, I'm still—"

"OmigodDaniit'sanunknownelement!"

33

DANI

"DANI!" JANE WAVED HER hand in front of Dani's face. "Where'd you go?"

Dani startled to find her three friends staring at her across the lunch table.

"Wow," Nora said, shaking her head. "You were totally somewhere else."

"Outer space," Laurel chimed in, giggling. "Isn't that where Cat hangs out?"

Dani had been thinking about the UE, which was what Cat had decided to call the unknown element. She was convinced that if she said the words *unknown element* out loud, the Men in Black would have even more ammo against her. Dani had rushed over to Cat's last night and watched the other girl run a sample of the metal through the mass spectrometer twice. The results had been the same both times. Which didn't make any sense. The equipment had to be malfunctioning.

"Sorry," Dani said. "What were you talking about?"

"Our group costume." Jane popped a potato chip into her mouth. "You're in, right?"

"Of course," Dani said automatically. "Wait. Group costume?" She looked around the table. Laurel was a butterfly, in a twirling multicolored dress with hand-painted wings tied to her wrists and waist. Nora was Megan Rapinoe, complete with pink streaks in her hair. Jane was Cookie Monster, in a blue hooded sweat suit with googly eyes stuck on top and a necklace of cardboard cookies.

Dani, meanwhile, had almost forgotten about Halloween. The holiday had never been her favorite—not since the year she'd gone as Marie Curie and no one, adult or kid, had guessed who she was. This morning, when she'd realized what day it was, she'd gone through her sister's discarded dance costumes and dug up a feather boa, fringe skirt, and sequined headband. She was a nineteen-twenties flapper. "We're already dressed up," she said to her friends, confused.

"Okay, let's try this again," Jane said. "Jess Lincoln's parents are letting her throw a Halloween pizza party in her basement this evening. It's totally last-minute."

"And we need new costumes because . . . ?" Dani asked.

"Everyone's already seen these," Laurel said, like that should be obvious.

"Nora had the brilliant idea for the four of us to be the elements: earth, fire, wind, and water," Jane explained. "You seriously didn't hear any of this?"

Dani winced. "I'm sorry."

"For not paying attention," Nora said, a slight edge to her voice, "you get to dress up as *dirt*."

"Whatever you guys want, I'm in," Dani said quickly.

"We're going to the thrift shop after school," Jane said. "My mom can take us."

"Then we'll go from there to the festival," Laurel said.

"The . . . festival?" Dani echoed weakly.

"At Weston Farm," Laurel told her with exaggerated patience. "The city finally got the permit thing worked out. The middle school orchestra's playing at 5:35."

"After the concert, we'll go back to my place to change for the party." Nora raised her eyebrows at Dani and cocked her head. "Got it this time?"

"Yes," Dani said, "but I'm supposed to—"

"Go over to Cat's," Jane finished for her. "We know."

"Give us one day," Nora said. "Your experiments will be fine."

Dani gnawed on her lip. She felt like she could squeeze in the thrift shop *or* the festival *or* the party—but not all three. Then again, the festival was at Weston Farm. Maybe Cat could meet her there. They could . . . listen to Laurel's solo while collecting samples nearby?

But Dani also really wanted to go to the lab this afternoon. She wanted to start running her active-carbon tests. And obviously, she wanted another look at Cat's mysterious metal shard—

"Danielle?"

Dani turned to see Ms. Blanks coming toward their lunch table. Her favorite teacher looked strangely frazzled. Her pumpkin-colored scarf was askew. Her khaki pants were rumpled. Her hair was in a ponytail, which Dani had never seen before, and she looked like she might be wearing two different earrings. "Hi, Ms. Blanks," she said. "Is everything okay?"

"Yes. Just a quick question for you." Ms. Blanks looked at the rest of the table. "You girls mind if I steal Danielle away for a few minutes?"

Jane, Nora, and Laurel shook their heads.

"What's going on?" Dani asked as her teacher steered her toward a corner of the cafeteria.

"I was wondering if . . ." Ms. Blanks paused, seeming to collect herself. "Do you know if Catrina has run any tests on that piece of metal you mentioned yesterday?"

"Yeah. She put it in her dad's mass spectrometer."

"And?"

"She thinks it's something unidentifiable. Which is ridiculous, because it's not like she randomly discovered a whole new element." Dani snorted. "*That* would totally win us the McMurray Award, right?"

Ms. Blanks didn't share her laughter. "Have you seen and verified Catrina's results?"

"I watched her analyze the piece twice last night. The result was inconclusive both times. Clearly the mass spec isn't working right."

"Will you be going over to Catrina's house this afternoon?"

Dani thought about her friends and their plans. "Probably not until tonight," she said. "Why?"

Ms. Blanks leaned in close, a conspiratorial smile playing on her lips. "To tell the truth, I've become quite invested in your project. You've exceeded my wildest expectations."

Dani beamed. "Really?"

"Really. Keep up the good work."

AT THE THRIFT SHOP, Dani fidgeted as Jane, Laurel, and Nora poked through rack after rack in search of the perfect outfits.

"Try this one," Jane said, thrusting a dark-brown sweater into Dani's hands.

"Oh, with those tan leggings!" Laurel added. "That will look *so* earthy."

Dani nodded, wishing she was at Cat's instead.

She watched her friends argue over which shade of red made Nora look most like a flame. Then she set the brown sweater and tan leggings on top of Laurel's messenger bag and texted Cat that she'd be over in twenty minutes. She'd explain her quick exit to her friends later, at the festival. She ran for the door, grabbed her bike from Jane's mom's car, and pedaled away at top speed.

She was gasping for air by the time she turned onto Cat's street. As she approached, she saw the other girl walking up her driveway, holding a bulging shopping bag. When she saw Dani coming, Cat changed course. "Hi! I just ran to the store for some snacks—"

Cat was cut off by a bright flash of light and an earth-shattering boom. Both girls screamed and looked up. Smoke was pouring from the open attic windows of Cat's old farmhouse.

The attic.

Aka Cat's bedroom.

Aka their lab.

Dani and Cat stared at the fire, horror-struck.

"Cat . . . ," Dani breathed, unable to take her eyes off the flames licking at the wooden window frames. "What did you do?"

34

CAT

"I DIDN'T DO ANYTHING!" Cat started to run toward the house.

Dani grabbed her and held her back. "Cat, you can't just run into a burning building!"

"But our work—"

"It's, like, a thousand degrees in there!" Dani shouted. "You can't. I'm sorry."

Cat sank to the grass. Tears burned her eyes, made worse by the thick black smoke billowing in their direction. Their research—her equipment—everything she cared about—*gone*.

Her parents were going to kill her. Like, really, *really* kill her this time.

"I'm dead," Cat muttered to Dani, who was kneeling next to her and rubbing her shoulder. She was also on the phone with someone. At first that irked Cat, until she realized Dani had called 911. Why hadn't Cat thought of that?

Within minutes, the fire trucks arrived, and the firefighters got to work.

Dani tapped Cat's shoulder. "Maybe you should call your mom?"

Cat winced.

"I know it sucks," Dani said, "but it's better she hears it from you than from the police."

Cat groaned and flopped back in the grass of her front lawn. "Can't I just run away and hide under a rock for the rest of my life instead?"

"Wouldn't that put a damper on your life's work?"

Cat sighed. Dani was right. She couldn't very well become a hermit *and* expose alien life to the rest of the world. She pulled out her new cheap flip phone and dialed.

"Hello?"

"Hey, Mom, it's Cat."

"What's all that noise in the background? Where are you?" Her mom sounded mad already. That didn't bode well. But Cat pressed on.

"I'm at home . . . The police and fire department are here."

"Catrina!" Her mom's voice shifted from anger to shock and panic. "Are you all right? What happened? Was anyone hurt?"

"No, Mom, no one was hurt. But . . . there was an explosion. In my lab. I only stepped out to the corner store for a minute. I didn't leave anything on; I'm positive. I wasn't even running any tests! I think it was sabotage—"

"Catrina, stop." Her mom's voice was now crisp and stony. "I don't want to hear your excuses. I let you keep that equipment your father gave you on one condition."

She paused long enough that Cat realized she was expected to reply. "Don't burn down the house," she muttered.

"I can't believe you allowed this to happen." Cat's mom let

out a frustrated groan. "I'm very glad you're not hurt. I'm leaving work now. I'll see you soon."

She hung up before Cat even had a chance to say goodbye.

THE FIREFIGHTERS SAID THEY were lucky, but Cat sure didn't feel lucky.

Granted, they'd been able to contain the fire to her room. And they'd put it out relatively quickly, since it originated by her desk and the really flammable stuff like her bed and clothes were on the other side of the room. The small, locked metal cabinet tucked away in her closet that was filled with lab chemicals had been carefully removed by the firefighters as a precaution. But her equipment was toast.

When the firefighters finally gave Cat and her mom the all clear, it was dark. Structurally, the house was still sound, and most of the water damage was in Cat's room, so it was safe to go in and retrieve things they needed. But they'd be living in a hotel while the damage upstairs was repaired.

Cat's mom stayed outside to talk to the authorities—and to get hugs from the various neighbors who'd gathered to watch the drama—but Cat didn't hesitate. She ran straight into the house, Dani hard on her heels.

The two lower levels appeared to be mostly unaffected, aside from the awful smell and water dripping everywhere. But the door at the bottom of the stairwell that led to Cat's room was hanging off its hinges. She'd locked it before she left—couldn't be too careful with research-stealing Men in Black around—so the firefighters must have had to kick it in to get up to the attic. Cat blew past the broken door, bolted up the stairs, and skidded to a stop.

Disaster. Nightmare. Ruin.

None of those words was strong enough. Water dripped from the ceiling onto the charred remains of her desk and computer. Damp ash floated through the air, making her cough. Her bed and dresser were soaked and coated in a thick layer of soot. All her equipment was twisted and melted beyond recognition.

Cat stumbled forward. She fell to her knees in front of the mass spectrometer that had belonged to her dad. It had been reduced to shards of metal and glass coated with melted plastic. Cat wanted to cry, but all she felt was a horrible numbness.

Until she remembered something.

She leaped up and launched herself at what was left of her desk.

"It *has* to be here," she mumbled, pawing frantically through the wreckage.

"What are you looking for?" Dani sounded choked up and a little scared.

Cat whirled. "The metal piece. I locked it in my desk drawer when I stepped out. I thought it would be safe there . . . I . . ."

Her stomach dry heaved. She clapped both hands over her mouth and tried to pull herself together. She was not going to throw up. Not now. Maybe later, but not when she absolutely had to locate that piece of evidence. She began digging even more furiously through the wreckage.

From behind her, Dani said very, very quietly, "This is pretty bad, Cat. There may not be anything left to find."

"If it could survive an incinerator, it could survive this!" Cat waved her hand at her room. "If it isn't here, it's because someone stole it."

The words had barely left Cat's mouth before she was utterly convinced of their truth. This was the MIBs' handiwork. She'd be willing to bet the fire marshal's report would show signs of an explosive of some kind, maybe even an accelerant.

"Dani, don't you see? The Men in Black must've gotten wind of the fact that we had that piece." Cat bit her lip. "But how?" She answered her own question. "The leak. Someone you or I talked to is blabbing to the Men in Black."

"Cat, I really don't think—"

"It's either that, or . . ."

"Or what?" Dani asked faintly.

"Or else *I'm* under surveillance," Cat said. A strange thrill went through her. If *they* were watching her, then she really was on to something important. "Either way, this was no accident."

A throat cleared, and both girls jumped. One of the firefighters stood at the top of the stairs. "We still need to conduct a thorough investigation, but I think you should hear our preliminary report," he said to Cat.

Cat and Dani exchanged a look. Dani went straight to the stairs, but Cat darted over to her bed first. Right where she'd left it, tossed carelessly across her pillow, was her dad's old olive-green coat. She put it on even though it smelled terrible, then followed Dani and the firefighter outside.

Cat's mother was waiting on the front lawn. Earlier, she'd watched in silent shock as the firefighters battled the blaze, arm around Cat's shoulders. Now she swept Cat up into a big bear hug. "I'm so glad you weren't in that room when it caught fire," she said through tears.

Cat choked out a sob. She hadn't even considered that possibility. But now the thought made her knees feel like jelly.

She held on to her mom a little tighter as terrible images raced through her brain. What if she'd left out the components of the experiment she'd been running the night before? What if she'd left the chemical cabinet open and it had caught fire? Her house could have filled with poisonous gas or made the explosion exponentially bigger. Or both.

And if she'd been at her desk at the time . . .

Cat shuddered. "Me too."

Her mom released her but kept her close as the firefighter and a police officer briefed them on what they'd found so far. Dani stood a few feet away, looking anxious.

"You're one lucky little lady," the officer said to Cat. "This could've been a tragedy, but I think it's safe to say we're all glad it wasn't."

Cat didn't say it, but *she* sure considered it a tragedy. All that lost equipment and research . . .

A police detective approached. "Ms. Mulvaney, I'm Detective Lewis." He held out his hand to shake. "Do you know of anyone who has a grudge against you? Anyone who might want to harm you or your daughter?"

"A g-grudge?" Cat's mom stuttered. "Of course not."

"How's your relationship with your ex-husband?"

"John? Our relationship is fine. We're cordial. Why do you ask?"

Cat's spine tingled with a strange mix of fear and vindication. She knew what Detective Lewis was going to say.

"Well, we still have to run some tests," the detective said grimly, "but this looks . . . intentional."

The firefighter took over. "We found residue of what appears to be C-4. You're lucky you've got a sprinkler system in your house and that you called us so quickly. This could have been much, much worse." He narrowed his eyes at Cat. "Now, I have to ask, young lady. Upstairs just now, you said you thought this wasn't an accident. What makes you think that?"

Cat's face flushed. "I just—well, um." She gave a sideways glance at her mom, whose face was drawn with stress and fear. "We're doing research for this big science fair." Cat motioned over her shoulder at Dani. "We found something big and . . . I think someone sabotaged our work."

The detective made a note in his little book. "Interesting theory, since the epicenter of the blast was your desk. Whoever did it knew what they were doing."

"Yeah, but—" Something occurred to Cat. "A homemade explosive . . . ," she murmured. "A homemade EMP . . ."

"EMP?" the detective repeated.

"Call the hardware store!" Cat blurted. "The one on Smith Street!"

The officer and the firefighter looked at each other.

"Listen," Cat said. "Someone set off an electromagnetic

pulse at Weston Farm last Thursday. They bought the supplies to make it at the hardware store downtown. Travis—he works there—he wouldn't tell me the name on the order, but I bet it's the same person who—"

"Okay," Detective Lewis said, holding up a hand. "We'll check on it. Now, back to your desk: Was anything missing?"

Cat nodded enthusiastically. "Yes. At least, I think so. We didn't get through all the wreckage yet, but it wasn't where I left it."

"What wasn't?"

Cat wanted to scream that she'd discovered something totally new, something that would change the scientific community forever—but she also wanted to be taken seriously.

And if she *was* under surveillance, well, she didn't want the MIBs to know she was on to them. Best not to mention the mysterious piece of metal.

"All my research. All my notes, my backup drives, everything." That was true, even if most of that stuff hadn't been stolen *today*.

The detective raised his eyebrows. "All of it missing? Not burned—but missing?"

"Yes, sir," Cat said firmly. "Even the samples we were testing were removed from my mini fridge. Our whole project is gone."

35

DANI

IN THE SECONDS AFTER the explosion, Dani had blamed her partner automatically. It hadn't even occurred to her that Cat might be innocent. Just like Dani hadn't initially believed that Cat's notebooks and their experiments had been taken. But if Cat was right that someone—maybe even someone from the government—wanted to destroy their research . . . *what else was she right about*?

Dani got a full-body shiver. She wrapped her arms around her middle and hugged tight.

To distract herself, she pulled out her phone. She had a ton of missed texts, as well as a few missed calls. Jane, Nora, Laurel, Nora, Laurel, Jane, Jane.

Quickly, Dani sent a text to the group chat:

DANI: OMG phone was off!! I'm so sorry!!! Emergency at Cat's. I'll fill you in tomorrow.

She switched her phone to "Do Not Disturb" and scanned the neighbors who'd gathered to gawk around the perimeter of the Mulvaneys' property. She was surprised to see a face she recognized in the crowd.

"Ms. Blanks?" Dani jogged across Cat's yard to where their science teacher was standing by the mailbox.

"Hi, Danielle. I was driving home from school when I saw the commotion. I parked to see what was going on and to find out if anyone needed help. Then I saw you girls." Ms. Blanks gave Dani a serious look. "Is Catrina okay? Are you okay?"

"We're fine. I mean . . ." Dani felt the prickle of oncoming tears. She didn't bother blinking them away. She didn't need to pretend in front of Ms. Blanks. "I was actually really scared? I tried to be strong for Cat, but . . ."

"It's okay to be scared, Danielle." Ms. Blanks paused. "I saw you two go inside. What's the damage like?"

"It's bad. Cat's bedroom is a mess. And—" Dani shuddered. "Her lab. Our project. It's toast." Dani snorted past the lump that had lodged itself in her throat. "Literally."

"I'm so sorry, Danielle, but the important thing is that neither of you was hurt—"

"Ms. Blanks!" Cat popped up between Dani and their teacher. She had soot smeared across her face, which was framed with flyaways from her ponytail. Her oversize green coat was wet and reeked of smoke. "What are you doing here?"

"I was passing by . . ." Ms. Blanks put a hand on Cat's shoulder. "Are you all right?"

"I'm fine," Cat said, "but my bedroom sure isn't." She gave the teacher a considering look. "It's actually a good thing you're here. Dani and I need to borrow some equipment for our new lab."

"New lab?" Dani and Ms. Blanks said at the same time.

Their teacher cleared her throat. "Catrina, it's okay to take a moment to breathe. What happened here was traumatic—"

"I'm okay. Dani's okay. In fact, we're itching to get back to our research. Aren't we, Dani?" Cat poked Dani hard in the ribs.

"Ow," Dani said. "I guess so? But how—"

"We're moving our base of operations," Cat said.

"To the school science lab?" Ms. Blanks asked.

"No." Cat scoffed. "We're only going to rent what we need from the school."

"And take it . . . ?"

"I'm sorry, Ms. Blanks, but I can't tell you that. *They* could be listening."

Ms. Blanks looked like she'd swallowed something that didn't taste at all like she'd expected. "You mean the other teams competing for the McMurray Award?"

"Yep, that's what she means!" Dani blurted. When Cat glanced at her, she mouthed, *Later.*

"I can help you sign out some equipment in the morning," their teacher said after a beat of silence. "Meet me before first period."

"Great!" Cat shrieked. "Dani, let's go!"

"Go where?" Dani asked, following Cat as she beelined to their bikes.

Cat didn't answer until they were alone. "Your place."

"What's at my place?"

"Your garage." Cat smiled. "Aka our new lab."

Dani balked. "We have a ton of junk stored in the garage."

"We'll clear a space."

"But—" Dani took a deep breath. "I wanted to keep my parents out of this. At least until the whole project is done."

Cat gave her a curious look. "Why?"

"I want them to take me seriously," Dani muttered.

Her partner was quiet for a moment. "Is that why you didn't want me to talk about crop circles in front of your mom that night I came over?"

Dani nodded.

"But they have to find out sometime," Cat insisted. She squinted at Dani and then said, knowingly, "*Oooooooh*. The award. If we win . . ."

"If we win, they can't deny that this is what I'm supposed to be doing," Dani said softly. She didn't like how desperate her plan sounded when she said it out loud. "But my parents aren't the only part that makes me nervous."

Cat raised her eyebrows.

"If someone was willing to burn down your lab . . . I mean . . ." Dani gulped. "I don't want anyone to burn down *my* house."

Her partner's expression grew serious. "That's why we have to keep things hush-hush. The Men in Black won't be able to bug our lab if they don't know where it is."

"You think our lab was bugged?"

"Either that or someone we told told someone else . . ." Cat waved a hand. "I made a list of suspects yesterday."

"Can I see the list?"

Cat flinched. "It was in my room."

"Oh."

"I'll make it again after we set up our new lab. And I promise, we won't fill your parents in. We won't fill anyone in. Not unless we have to." Cat held out her hand. "So what do you say? You and me against the world?"

Dani took it . . . and her stomach flip-flopped inside her.

She *still* hadn't told Cat that she was doing her own research, trying to prove her own hypothesis. She certainly couldn't tell her tonight—not when Cat's lab was a pile of damp, smoking rubble. But she was running out of time.

She gulped and repeated what her partner had said: "You and me against the world."

IT WAS ALMOST EIGHT by the time they stood in front of Dani's garage, but the neighborhood was anything but quiet. There were trick-or-treaters all over the sidewalks. Dani watched a tiny ghost and an even tinier ninja fight a tug-of-war over a pumpkin-shaped bucket until their parents separated them. Before they could even stop crying, the kids were knocked to the ground by a sugar-fueled Captain America. Dani watched Cap race up to her own front door, ring the bell, and talk to her dad, who was in costume—just like every year—as a member of the band KISS.

Dani was supposed to be at Jess Lincoln's party right now. Before that, she was supposed to have been at Weston Farm for Laurel's concert. No wonder her friends had been blowing up her phone.

Beside her, Cat was bouncing with anticipation. "This is gonna be so perfect," she murmured. "I mean, it's not the same as . . ." The bouncing stopped. When she was standing still, it was obvious that Cat was hanging on to her optimism by a thread.

"Well," Dani said, extending her arm. "Here it is."

There was a reason their house looked like a home-goods catalog. The clutter was crammed in the garage instead. Out-of-season gear. Bins that held clothing and toys Dani and Mallory had outgrown, things their mom insisted she'd donate "one of these days." Their dad's collection of records and CDs, on top of an old sofa he called his "listening couch."

While Cat scanned the space, Dani held out her hand. "Coat."

"What? Why?" Cat pulled the puffy green coat tight around her body.

"I can put it in the wash. It'll be done when we are."

"I can't wash this." Cat looked away.

"Why not? It's just a coat."

"It's—it's my dad's."

"Oh." Dani suddenly realized she didn't know much about Cat's relationship with her dad, other than that he seemed to buy her any science thing she wanted. But maybe that wasn't what Cat really needed from him.

Cat picked at the zipper. "It's been more than a year since he's come to visit. He left this coat behind, and he said I could keep it. The inside still smells a little bit like him. It's . . . comforting. You know?"

Now wasn't the time to point out that the coat couldn't

possibly smell like anything other than smoke from the fire. Instead, Dani asked, "Is he coming to the McMurray exhibition?"

Her partner flinched. "He said he couldn't take off work. But maybe if we find something really incredible . . ." Cat trailed off, but Dani understood what she didn't say.

Dani held out her hand again. "I'll put the coat on the gentle cycle, I promise. Then we can get back to winning this award. Deal?"

Cat's eyes welled up. She took the coat off and handed it over. "All right. Thanks."

Dani went inside to the laundry room and started a load.

When she returned, Cat was inching the "listening couch" away from the wall. "Can you help me with this?"

"Shouldn't we come up with a plan first?" Dani asked.

"I already have one," Cat said through gritted teeth. "We'll set up here. The couch moves over there, with the camping stuff on top of it. Then we'll take those folding tables"—she indicated the ones the tents, sleeping bags, and backpacks were currently sitting on—"and put them here. With . . ." A quick scan. "Ooh, roll-y chairs!" She scampered over to the pair of mismatched desk chairs Dani's mom had tried before she found the perfect seat for her art studio.

"How did you figure that out so fast?" Dani asked.

"What do you think our attic looked like before I moved my bedroom up there?"

They turned on the security lights on the side of Dani's house and spread out into the driveway. They made good progress—

until they got to the corner Dani had been trying to ignore. Inside those six bins were all of Dani's failures. Dance shoes. Leotards and tights. Musical instruments. Charcoals and water-colors. Knitting needles and balls of yarn. Stage makeup.

"Is it stuff we can toss?" Cat asked hopefully.

"I wish."

"Should we go through it?"

"We should bury it," Dani grumbled.

"Oh. Artsy stuff?"

"Yeah. And my parents want to keep it. In case I change my mind. Like one day I'm going to wake up and want to finish that scarf I started knitting four years ago. Like I'm going to die if I don't master the time step, so we better keep those tap shoes. Like—"

"I get it," Cat said, holding up her hands. "We'll leave those boxes alone. But if you do ever want to clean it all out and you need a friend . . . just say the word."

"Thanks," Dani said, and this time her smile stuck around.

36

CAT

CAT HAD TRIED TO convince her mom to book them a room at the Parisian, but her mom wasn't having it. With repairs to pay for, the Holiday Inn would have to suffice.

Thankfully, the hotel wasn't too far from school. In fact, Cat could walk there and let her mom sleep in. She'd waited up for Cat last night and, while she wasn't as angry anymore, she'd made it clear that Cat would have to explain the loss of her dad's equipment to him—and soon.

That was a thing Cat dreaded.

On her way out on Wednesday morning, she swung by the continental breakfast and snagged a couple of muffins to munch on as she walked to school. Despite the unpleasantness ahead, Cat wasn't going to let it take the wind completely out of her sails. Their new, top secret lab was nearly set up in Dani's garage. Now she just had to get to school early to grab the equipment from Ms. Blanks.

But this morning, she'd realized a key flaw in her *Cat and Dani against the world* plan. She had an idea to fix the flaw. She just needed to convince Dani to go for it.

"ABSOLUTELY NOT." DANI CROSSED her arms over her chest while they waited for Ms. Blanks to find the key to the equipment locker. Their teacher rummaged around in her desk, muttering, while the two of them stood in the hall, arguing in whispers. "You promised me that—"

"I know I did, and I'm sorry. I wouldn't ask if I saw any other option."

Dani glared at her.

"You're the one who said your parents have zero interest in science and won't ask us a ton of questions or brag to their friends about your work—right?"

Dani winced. "First, thanks for the reminder. And second—"

"We need a ride, Dani," Cat said. "We need someone we trust to get us and the equipment to your place."

"I thought you didn't trust anyone," Dani grumbled.

"Of all the people I don't trust," Cat said, trying to keep her voice light, "I trust your parents the most. Plus, your mom works from home."

"What about your mom?"

"She's got work today, and later, she's going over to our house to assess the damage." Cat paused. "Also, she's, um . . . not my biggest fan at the moment. Which means your mom is the perfect solution."

"I guess."

"So you'll call her?"

"I'll call her," Dani said. "But you owe me."

"Here it is!" Ms. Blanks approached with the key. "Don't get many requests for the spare lab equipment. It got good and buried in there." Their teacher went to the back closet in the science room, and Cat and Dani followed. "Now, how are you getting this equipment to your off-site lab? Do you need help?"

Dani's face lifted. "Oh, that would be—"

"Totally unnecessary," Cat said, cutting her off. "But nice of you to offer. Dani's mom is going to help us."

"Oh, all right." Ms. Blanks almost seemed disappointed.

"Can we take this stuff back to our lab during science class, Ms. Blanks?" Cat asked. "We're just watching a film today, right?"

Ms. Blanks nodded. "Yes, I suppose that would be all right. Here, let's pull this all out so it's ready to go, and I'll write you both a pass."

"Thanks," Cat and Dani said in unison.

Once they had their pass, Dani dragged Cat into the hall by her elbow. "What was that about?" she demanded.

Cat played innocent. "What was what?"

"Ms. Blanks could've helped us! Then I wouldn't have to call my mom." Dani's cheeks had gone red and blotchy.

"Someone is watching us. They're trying to derail our investigation. The explosion is proof of that. No one can know where our new lab is. Not even Ms. Blanks."

"Stop being so paranoid! I don't think our *science teacher* is out to get us—"

"Neither do I," Cat said, "but she could have talked to someone who is. Plus, she's our adviser. No one knows more about our project right now, other than the two of us. What if they come after her, too?"

Dani went pale. "I didn't think of that."

"Why did you tell Ms. Blanks I'm worried about sabotage from other teams?"

"Because you told me to keep the details of our investigation quiet. And because . . . I didn't want to tell her you believe in Men in Black."

Cat gritted her teeth. "They *are* Men in Black, whether you believe in them or not. But I was going to say, you have good instincts. It's better that she doesn't know the whole truth."

Dani was silent for a second. Then she said, "Fine. I'll call my mom."

She turned away from Cat as she made the call. Cat couldn't help but listen in, even though she felt a little bit guilty doing so.

"Mom? Hey, what are you doing around twelve forty-five today?" Dani paused. "My lab partner and I need to borrow some lab equipment from school—just for a few days—to work on our big project." Another pause. "Yeah, the McMurray thing." From the way Dani said "thing," Cat could tell that her mom had used that exact word. "Could you pick us up?" Dani went on. "Our teacher wrote us a pass, since it counts as working on our project." Yet another pause. "Um. Our garage. Cat and I started clearing a workspace last night."

The next pause was a long one. Dani's mom was talking . . . and talking . . . and talking.

Finally, Dani interrupted her. "It's only temporary. The science fair is in a week and a half, remember?" Dani turned, and Cat could see the moment her deep frown turned to relief. "Of course. Thanks, Mom."

Just as Cat was about to do a celebration dance, Dani's mom said something else. In an instant, Dani's relieved grin was replaced by a weary grimace. "Yeah. Sure. Sounds great," Dani said and hung up.

"We're good?" Cat asked.

"Good enough." Dani spotted her friends rounding a corner and shouted, "Laurel, Jane, Nora! Wait up!" The three girls didn't pause, so Dani chased after them, leaving Cat standing alone.

AT THE START OF fifth period, Cat and Dani waited outside the school for Dani's mom, holding cardboard boxes of equipment. "Once we get this all set up," Cat said to fill the silence, "we should take stock of what we need to do to get back on track."

"I've already made a list." Dani gestured to her backpack, resting on the ground beside her.

"Perfect!" Cat grinned. "We'll review that together, and then we need to go back to Weston Farm. Since we've had one new formation every night since the start of the phenomenon, circle number twelve should show up tonight! Tomorrow will be lucky prime number thirteen!"

And my birthday, she added silently. She still hadn't mentioned that detail to Dani. She wasn't sure why, except . . . it was feeling more and more like a big deal. Not just because of the crop circles. Cat hadn't had a friend to spend her birthday with in years. Maybe she didn't want to jinx it.

"These will be our last two chances to collect uncontaminated samples from the real deal," she said aloud. "Any circles that appear after we hit thirteen will be the fakes the MIBs are using to confuse things."

Thirteen years between the formations. Thirteen circles spread out over thirteen days. And Cat, born during the last occurrence, would turn thirteen on the final night of this one. None of this was a coincidence. What if this was the year the aliens made contact?

What if that contact was meant to be with *Cat*?

A hatchback SUV pulled up to the curb, and Dani's mom waved. Dani let out a big sigh, then smiled back. The trunk popped open, and Cat and Dani deposited their equipment, then got in the car.

"Thanks so much for helping us out, Mrs. Williams," Cat said in her cheeriest voice. "We super appreciate it. We really want to do well on this project."

"Oh, of course. Now, Dani, what exactly will you be doing in the garage with all this stuff?"

Dani squirmed. "Just experiments. Looking at stuff under microscopes, that sort of thing."

"You can't do this at school?" Dani's mom frowned.

"Nope!" Cat interjected. "We don't have time during class. The project is highly competitive, so we need to work around the clock."

"Well, as long as it's only for a few days, I suppose it's all right,"

Dani's mom said, though she was clearly still perplexed. "And, Dani, you'll ask Mr. Linch about helping out with costumes for the winter musical like we talked about?"

Dani tried to smile, but it looked more like a grimace. "Can't wait."

"There's a production meeting next week," Dani's mom said, "but the real work won't start until after your little science project is done."

Cat caught Dani's eye. *Little science project?* she mouthed.

Dani gave a microscopic shrug.

They spent the rest of fifth period unloading and talking through Dani's list. When they plugged in the last extension cord, Cat surveyed their work. Beakers and pipettes, a Bunsen burner, two microscopes, petri dishes, test tubes, a thermometer, a scale, gloves, goggles, and two aprons. Her chest twinged. It wasn't the same as her lab back at home, but it would do—and most importantly, no one knew where it was.

The truth was still out there—and Cat was going to find it.

37

DANI

TONIGHT, DANI WAS DETERMINED to uncover the truth. As she walked away from Weston Farm's crowded entrance alone—she and Cat had decided to split up, to cover more ground—she talked herself through her hypothesis yet again.

1. The circles were not extraterrestrial in origin.
2. Weed-Be-Gone was to blame, along with
3. the application of a heat source to the sprayed soil. Because she couldn't figure out a natural explanation for the complex fractal patterns, she was still assuming that
4. human beings were involved.

Of course, there were missing variables. Weed-Be-Gone was a new product, while the Weston Farm Circles went back to 1984. Obviously, the previous years' circles had no connection to this particular herbicide. But one thing at a time. Dani just needed to keep following her lead.

The Men in Black were a distraction. So was the piece of mysterious metal. The doubts that were gnawing at Dani didn't matter. She had to present *something* to the McMurray judges, something that demonstrated her commitment to the scientific process.

The farther away Dani walked from the entrance, the quieter—and creepier—Weston Farm got. The crops whispered in the breeze. The bluegrass fiddle in the festival tent sounded like a mournful animal wailing into the night. Dani's flashlight cast odd shadows on the ground. She shivered, hoping she and Cat wouldn't be apart for too long.

But she was on a mission. Every piece of evidence they'd collected was gone. They needed more stalks. More soil. (Sadly, the incinerator ash Dani had sampled was a lost cause.) She'd meet up with her partner later—hopefully when the twelfth circle appeared. Without her fancy mapping software, Cat hadn't been able to pinpoint an exact location, but she'd made an educated guess.

Using her compass to orient herself, Dani reached the circle Cat had assigned her. She crouched and began to scoop dirt into the baggies she'd brought, marking each sample's location on a makeshift map—

Footsteps crashed toward her. Dani dove into the standing wheat stalks, heart pounding. She tucked herself into the shadows and waited, not entirely sure what she was waiting for.

Two men stepped into the circle. They pointed their flashlights back into the field.

"Over here." The voice sounded familiar, but it wasn't until the other man shifted his light, illuminating the speaker's face, that Dani realized who they were. It was Cat's Men in Black.

Another man came out of the wheat after them, carrying a long plank of wood with a thick piece of rope draped over his shoulder. "I'm coming, I'm coming," he grumbled. With a grunt, he dumped the board onto the flattened grain.

"We don't have all night," said the agent Cat had taken to calling Specs.

"You could've hauled me to any of these dang circles," the older man griped. "Why'd we have to come all the way over here?"

"The other side of the farm is rather busy tonight," pointed out the agent Cat called Gravel.

"The least you could've done was carried ol' Betsy for me."

The name "Betsy" clued Dani in. It was Mr. Hepworth, the farmer! What was he doing here with two government agents?

"Get in position," Gravel commanded, pointing at the center of the circle. In the flashlight's beam, Dani couldn't help but notice the bandage on his hand. That hadn't been there the last time they'd seen him. So much for Cat's alien-autopsy theory.

Mr. Hepworth situated himself so his feet were on the wood. He held the rope taut.

Specs was fussing with a camera. "Okay. Look surprised."

The farmer widened his eyes. He opened his mouth. When the flash went off, it showed a convincingly startled crop circle hoaxer.

Specs looked at the digital photo. "That'll do."

"The money you promised," Mr. Hepworth grumbled. "It hasn't come through."

"You'll get what you're owed," Specs said.

"I mean the extra," the farmer insisted.

Gravel placed a heavy hand on Mr. Hepworth's shoulder. "When this is all over."

Mr. Hepworth nodded. "Tonight's the last night?"

"No. Tomorrow," Gravel said.

"How many of these things am I supposed to say we made?"

"There will be sixteen in total," Specs said.

Sixteen, Dani mouthed to herself. Cat had said there would be thirteen real circles, plus a few extra fake ones to throw off the pattern. Hmm.

"And what do I say if someone asks why I kept doing the hoax?" Mr. Hepworth asked.

"Perhaps your boys were disappointed you came forward last week. They wanted to see the project through to the end." Gravel leaned in. "You're the one who decided to claim responsibility. You can come up with a story. Make it a good one."

Hidden in the stalks, Dani frowned. She and Cat had been sure Mr. Hepworth was lying, and now she knew that for certain. The farmer was being paid off . . . by the government.

But coming forward had been his idea? To get *more* money from them?

What was the original payment for, if not for taking credit for the hoax?

And what were the MIBs covering up anyway?

Dani felt like the truth was flitting around in the air above her head, just out of reach.

"Mr. Hepworth," Gravel said, his voice low and serious. "No more surprises. Are we clear?"

"Yes, sir," the farmer said.

"Then shall we go?" Gravel started to walk toward the edge of the circle. "We'd be happy to drop you off at home."

"No, thank you." The farmer backed away from the agents. "I'll walk." He left quickly, passing so close to Dani that she could've reached out and grabbed the hem of his pants.

She expected the agents to leave, too. But they lingered. Specs appeared to be studying the ground. "The soil's disturbed over here. Someone else visited this site, and recently." He paused, tapping his chin. "Do you think it was those girls? The ones we're supposed to be watching out for?" Specs looked in all directions.

"Does it matter?" his partner asked. "They're children. We have bigger fish to fry."

"I guess you're right," Specs said, still examining the area where Dani had scooped up her first sample. "After all, it's just a kids' science fair."

Just a kids' science fair? Dani couldn't hold in her gasp. The McMurray Award wasn't *just* anything. Not to Dani.

Still, she shouldn't have gasped.

At the noise, both agents swiveled in her direction. Dani flattened herself to the ground, facedown. She tried not to make a sound or move a muscle—but she was shaking all over.

The wait was agonizing. The men stepped closer. Their lights shone brighter.

"Must've been the wind," Specs finally said. "Let's get out of here."

All his partner said was, "Hmm."

After they left, Dani didn't get up for a long time. Her body went numb against the cold, hard earth. Her brain felt numb, too.

Those men—what they knew—and the farmer—the hoax inside the hoax—

She needed to talk to Cat.

But . . . should she talk to Cat?

Because they were working in opposition, anything that called Cat's theories into question—like, say, a picture of Mr. Hepworth, caught in the act of creating a crop circle—would only help Dani's case. The worse Cat looked on science fair day, the better Dani would look by comparison.

She could keep her mouth shut about what she'd seen and heard here tonight. It was awfully tempting. No one would ever know for sure that Mr. Hepworth was lying about being the hoaxer or that the government was paying him off to cover up . . . *something*.

No. Dani couldn't keep this to herself. She didn't need to lie or cheat to win the McMurray Award. The science would prove her right. And, well, her partner—her friend—deserved better.

Dani took a deep breath and let go of the easy way out. She grabbed her phone and dialed her partner's number. "Cat?" she said. "It's Dani. Where are you? There's something I have to tell you."

38

CAT

"ARE YOU SURE?" CAT asked her mom. "You're absolutely, one hundred percent positive?"

"Well, I didn't run any experiments in our hotel room, if that's what you're wondering," her mom said, sounding tired. She'd been at their house, going through the destruction. "But the box doesn't look damaged."

"It's just that—" Cat spotted Dani approaching. She waved at her partner and then pointed at the phone held to her ear. "The tiniest bit of smoke or soot could mess with the calibration. These are finely tuned instruments, you know?"

"Well, you can check when you get back here," her mom answered. "Which will be . . . ?"

"No idea!" Cat said cheerfully. "Depends on when the crop circle shows up!"

Her mother sighed. "Sweetie . . . ," she began.

Cat didn't let her finish the thought. "Dani's here. There are lots of grown-ups here, too. We're safe." She couldn't help checking over her shoulder for sinister Men in Black as she said that last bit. "I'll text you, okay?"

Another sigh. "Okay," her mom said. "I love you, Cat."

"Love you, too, Mom." Cat hung up and turned to Dani, raising her arms in triumph. "I have great news!"

"I have . . . news, too," Dani replied.

"I'll go first! The package my dad sent, with the colorimeter and stuff: It wasn't in my room!"

"Where was it?"

"In the kitchen! I could've sworn I took it upstairs, but I guess I didn't. Anyway, my mom says the box seems fine, so you can still do those soil experiments you were so excited about!"

"Yay," Dani cheered weakly.

Cat's enthusiasm faltered. Her partner had sounded so serious when she'd called, but Dani often sounded serious, so Cat hadn't thought anything of it. "What's your news?" she asked, suddenly not so sure she wanted to know. Unless . . . okay, what if what Dani had to tell her was something that *Dani* wouldn't want to say but that she knew *Cat* would be excited to hear? Like, what if Dani had seen proof of alien life?

Cat almost staggered as the full impact of what she was about to learn hit her.

Dani had seen something big. That had to be it. Cat felt like she was glowing.

Dani's arms were folded across her chest. She chewed on her lip. "You were right—"

"Yes!" Cat fist-pumped the air.

"Whoa, hold on," Dani said. "You were right about the Men in Black. There really is a cover-up. I . . . I saw Gravel and Specs in the field where I was collecting samples. They had Mr. Hepworth with them. They staged a photo to make it look like they caught him in the act of creating the circle. They're paying him to lie."

Cat gasped. "They said that? Out loud?"

"Yeah. He mentioned wanting the money they promised, and they said he'll get paid when this is all over. Tomorrow."

"After the thirteenth circle?" Cat asked.

"Well, they said there will be *sixteen* formations."

Cat blinked. "Sixteen?"

Dani nodded.

"There's our confirmation!" Cat hiss-shrieked. "Thirteen real circles and—"

"Three fake ones," Dani finished. "But there's more. Mr. Hepworth surprised them when he went on TV. Apparently, him claiming to be the hoaxer wasn't part of the original plan."

Cat tilted her head. "Huh. That doesn't make sense. Why were they paying him *before* he came forward?" She answered her own question. "Maybe to keep quiet about any proof of extraterrestrial life he found on his property—"

"They mentioned us!" Dani cut in loudly. "The Men in Black are looking for girls doing a science fair project."

Cat gasped. "Of course! The surveillance! They must've been paying Mr. Hepworth to let them know if anyone was digging around in the circles. The MIBs could have easily discovered where I live if he told them my name. I bet we're not the only people they've been keeping tabs on. But I haven't heard about any other explosions like the one in our lab, which means we're definitely on the right track—"

"Hold on, Cat." Dani held up her hands. Her face had

gone . . . strange. "That's not all I wanted to tell you. I—I haven't been completely honest with you."

A chill settled over Cat's shoulders. "About what?" she asked in a small voice.

"I haven't been a very good partner." Dani stared at the ground. "I've . . . I've actually been working on my own theory this whole time."

Cat felt like she'd been dunked in an ice bath. "What? But how? Why? We've been working together to collect samples and do the experiments and everything." She'd known Dani wasn't excited about their project at first. She'd assumed her partner was going along with it, believer or not. She'd assumed they were becoming . . . *friends*. "We're a team, right?"

There was a crash of drums and cymbals in the distance. The screech of an electric guitar. The wild howl of a rock singer and the earsplitting squeal of mic feedback. The festival tent had gone heavy metal.

But between Cat and Dani, there was nothing but a thick, painful silence.

"I found iron microspheres in the crop circle soil samples."

"Iron microspheres?" Cat squealed. There were *iron microspheres* in the soil? As in, the magnetic particles often found inside crop circles, believed to be caused by UFO radiation? Cat hadn't even noticed. How on earth had she not noticed a smoking gun like that? Oh, wait . . . because Dani had taken charge of the soil testing, and she *hadn't bothered to show Cat what she'd found*. "Why didn't you tell me?"

"I was trying to prove they were from the Bug-Be-Gone factory.

Their new weed killer has iron in it, and if it was being tested at Weston Farm, that could account for . . . um . . ." Dani cleared her throat. "I thought, if we studied the phenomenon from different angles, it would make our project stand out."

"Different angles," Cat repeated, voice flat.

"I would work on figuring out how the circles *weren't* extraterrestrial, while you tried to figure out how they *were*." Dani paused. "I thought it would help us win."

"Because that's what you want. To win the McMurray Award."

Dani flinched. "I also want to figure out the truth, just like you."

"No, not just like me," Cat hissed. "You're the exact opposite of me."

"I should have told you sooner—"

"You were pretending to be my friend!" Cat's legs began to wobble, along with her chin. "You were using me to get what you wanted."

"No, I—"

"Dani, they blew up my bedroom!" Cat's voice reached a new octave.

"I know, and I—"

A horrible thought occurred to Cat. "Maybe it wasn't Mr. Hepworth who told the MIBs about our investigation. Maybe it was you!" She pointed her finger at her partner.

Dani gaped. "You can't be serious."

"You're the only one who knew everything. Where we'd be, what we'd found . . . who else could have kept the MIBs in the loop this whole time?"

"Cat, I would never—"

"How better to sabotage my part of the project so you could advance your own theory? You've been working for *them*." Cat's mouth was running full steam ahead, and her brain was only beginning to catch up. "You wanted to win the award more than anything. And that meant making my experiments fail."

Cat's skin felt strange and itchy. She'd never had a lot of friends her age. She'd always been content to do her own thing, to follow her own interests and imagination. This was the first time in a long time that she'd thought, maybe, just maybe, someone else understood. Maybe she didn't always have to be alone, the odd one out. Dani had seemed like a kindred spirit.

And now she'd betrayed her.

It was hard to tell in the darkness, but it looked like Dani was blinking away tears. "I'm sorry, Cat. I just—I just—"

Cat's expression hardened. "You just didn't believe in me. Like everyone else."

39

DANI

"IT'S NOT THAT...," Dani insisted, but her partner turned away. "Cat, listen to me. I'm saying that you were right! Maybe not about the aliens. But the Men in Black! They're definitely up to something, and we can work together to figure out what it is—"

"Clearly, we can't." Cat looked over her shoulder at Dani. Her angry gaze seemed to bore right through Dani's head. "You know what? You care about this award so much, it's all yours. If this project matters so much to you, finish it by yourself."

"I can't do it alone," Dani said desperately.

Cat had started walking away, but now she paused. "Why's that?"

"I—the competition—" Dani stammered. "We have to work in pairs—" Even as it came out of her mouth, she knew it was the wrong thing to say.

Cat nodded sharply, once, and left.

DANI RODE AWAY FROM Weston Farm as fast as she could, crying so hard that she could barely see where she was going.

The look on Cat's face when Dani had admitted she'd been working to prove her own hypothesis—and that she'd withheld evidence—it was the worst thing Dani had ever seen. She'd felt that look like a punch in the ribs. She could still feel it.

Sure, Dani hadn't asked for this partner or this project topic. But she'd agreed to make it work.

She'd had *so many opportunities* to tell Cat the truth.

She'd been a coward.

The thing was, Cat had become more than a colleague. She and Dani were . . . friends.

Well, not anymore.

Dani rode up Jane's cul-de-sac and skidded to a stop outside the garage. She arrived at the front door breathless and sweating, despite the cold.

Jane's brother, Hayden, answered the door. "Oh. It's you."

Dani wiped at her wet eyes. "Hi. Is Jane home?"

Hayden turned and yelled up the stairs, "Jane! Four's here!"

"Four?"

"Yeah. My sister is One, because she's related to me. The sporty one is Two. Fashion Girl is Three. And you're Four." He smirked.

"You could learn our actual names," Dani said, freshly bruised to discover that she came in fourth place out of four people.

Hayden shrugged. "Jane! I'm closing the door in Four's face unless you come down right now!"

Jane appeared at the top of the stairs. "Dani!" she said, eyes wide. "What are you doing here?"

Dani hesitated in the doorway. Her BFFs had been a little frosty at school today, after she'd missed Laurel's performance and the Halloween party, but she'd apologized. "Is this a bad time?"

"No, of course not. What's up?"

"I've had a really bad night," Dani said, slipping out of her shoes and shrugging off her coat. "Can I come upstairs? This might take a while."

"Oh. Um." Jane glanced over her shoulder, toward her room. "Stay there. I'll be right down." She disappeared for a second and then returned with some dishes. "Figured I might as well drop these off in the kitchen," she explained at Dani's curious look.

"Hoarding much?" Dani asked. Her friend was holding three mugs coated in what looked like hot chocolate residue, as well as three small crumb-covered plates.

"Ha. Yes. Hoarding. That's me!"

It wasn't. Jane hated clutter and mess. She was the only middle schooler Dani knew who vacuumed her own room every evening before bed. She said it made her sleep better.

Suspicion bloomed in Dani's stomach. Not like a flower. Like mold in a petri dish.

"You know," she said slowly, "I'd really rather talk to you in private. Like, in your bedroom. Is that okay?"

Jane's smile looked forced. "We can use the living room? We can make Hayden leave?"

"Not a chance!" Hayden called out from the couch. He was playing a video game where a guy in medieval armor was battling an ogre. "I called dibs."

"We won't touch your precious game," Jane informed him. "Just give us five minutes—no, ten," she corrected herself after a glance at Dani. "Ten minutes of girl time."

"Nope," Hayden answered.

Dani's stomach-mold feeling was getting worse. "Is something going on?"

"No!" her friend squeaked. "Nothing's going on!"

Instead of pushing the issue, Dani went up the stairs. And despite her earlier protests, Jane didn't stop her. All she did was sigh sadly as Dani nudged open her door.

Nora and Laurel were sitting cross-legged on the bed. There was a giant bowl of popcorn between them. The TV was paused. Dani could see that it was a movie the four of them had talked about seeing together.

Jane, Nora, and Laurel were watching it without her.

"Oh," Dani said.

"Hi, Dani." Laurel waved sheepishly.

"Join us?" Jane asked, pink-cheeked.

"Um." Dani gulped past the lump that had formed in her throat. "It doesn't really seem like you want me here."

"Of course we want you here!" Jane took Dani by both hands and tugged her into the room. "We'll make space. I'll get you a brownie."

Dani pulled her hands back and tucked them into her pants pockets. "I don't get it. If you want me here, why didn't you invite me in the first place?"

Laurel winced. "It started as a homework thing. We have this presentation, for social studies . . . But we finished prepping that earlier than we thought, so we—"

"You would've said no," Nora interrupted. "That's all you do these days. You bail on us. Like last night."

"I texted! There was a fire at Cat's house, and—"

"You left us at the thrift shop *before* the fire," Nora said.

"That was for *school*! For our *project*!" Dani said. "You're my best friends."

"Are we?" Nora's voice was cool.

"It's just that you've been somewhere else lately," Jane said. "It's been, like, all crop circles all the time. You missed Friday's sleepover. You promised you'd come to the mall on Saturday, but you skipped that, too. And then yesterday . . ."

"We were there for you," Laurel said, "after everything over the summer."

Dani's friends had supported her after the Dance of Doom. It wasn't their fault that Dani's self-esteem had been circling the drain. It also wasn't their fault that this project with Cat had been helping her find her confidence again. But tonight, leaving her out—that was on them.

"We would've invited you," Jane insisted, "if we'd thought you would've come."

Dani looked around the room. There were three glasses of water on the nightstand. Three schoolbags on the floor. Jane had held three hot cocoa mugs and three brownie plates. There were three jars of nail polish on Jane's dresser, and three phones set out for selfie taking, and three pairs of eyes staring expectantly at her.

Hayden's nickname suddenly felt like a mocking sign some-one had taped on her back. Dani was Four. There was no space for her here.

"It doesn't look like you guys miss me," she said, blinking away a new round of tears.

"We do." Jane patted the bed. "Stay."

"You wanted to keep me downstairs. You didn't want me to come up here and see you guys hanging out."

"I didn't want to hurt your feelings! Even though you hurt our feelings." Jane gave Dani a reproachful look.

Dani stepped backward into the hallway. "I'm gonna go." Her friends called to her, but she didn't listen. If they really cared, this whole evening wouldn't have happened. Not like this.

She'd been waiting for this moment. She'd known that Jane, Nora, and Laurel would dump her sooner or later. She just wished it hadn't had to happen on the same day she'd also lost Cat.

40

CAT

WITH MR. HEPWORTH AND his supposed hoax back in the news, Cat was experiencing some highly unpleasant déjà vu. This morning, she'd tried to convince her mom that there was no birthday present Cat wanted more than to be allowed to stay home from school. All she wanted to do was go to Weston Farm and wait for the final crop circle to appear and the aliens to arrive. It was the thirteenth night! But her mom had made it clear that wasn't going to fly. And Cat still felt a bit guilty about the day she *had* cut classes. So instead, Cat's day passed in a blur of ridicule and laughter—except for the crystal clear moments she spent ignoring Dani.

Now that she'd calmed down a little, Cat didn't really think Dani had been reporting their findings to the Men in Black . . . but she still couldn't wrap her head around the fact that Dani had been lying to her for weeks. Working against the hypothesis of their project. Hiding evidence. Trying to prove Cat wrong. So much for teamwork. The lone reason Dani had even tolerated being teamed up with Cat was because the only way to enter the science fair was in pairs.

Dani had been prepared to humiliate Cat in front of everyone.

She kicked a rock as she walked toward the bike rack after school. Would Dani have pretended to work on the project and poster-board presentation with Cat and then—surprise!—set up her own next to it the day of the fair? How had she thought that was going to work?

It was clear to Cat that all Dani had been thinking about was herself.

Cat's feelings didn't matter. Cat's need to win the science fair, too, didn't matter.

Dani was no better than the rest of the kids at school.

Which meant Cat was alone. Again.

She was used to being alone. It didn't usually bother her too much. She had her research to keep her occupied—who needed to go to the mall and paint each other's nails when there were aliens and conspiracies to uncover? But for a little while, she thought she'd found a real partner. Sure, they had plenty of differences. But Cat and Dani were a lot alike, too.

Except, of course, Cat would never have done what Dani did. Not to anyone, but especially not to a friend.

This time, the loneliness really stung.

For the first time, Cat was actually relieved her dad wasn't going to be able to make it to the exhibition. She glanced at her phone for what felt like the hundredth time that day. No birthday texts or messages yet. Only her mom had wished her a happy birthday this morning, when she reminded Cat that they had a reservation at Luigi's. When she was little, Luigi's had been a birthday tradition. Ever since her dad left, it had felt like an empty ritual. But they did have pretty amazing chocolate cake.

"Hey, Strange!"

Cat whirled around to see Joseph Sims, an eighth grader and one of the stars of their school's basketball team, waving at her from the bus stop. "Hi," she said warily.

"Where's your sidekick?" Joseph asked.

The question was an ice pick to the chest. "I don't have a side-kick," Cat growled.

"Sure you do. The nerdy girl, the one who hangs out with Jane Benson. What's her name? I know it's not 'Science.'"

Cat sighed. "Dani Williams."

"Right, that's her. Anyway—"

"What do you want, Joseph?" Cat asked. Joseph Sims had never spoken to her. She couldn't imagine he had a good reason to now. Honestly, she wasn't in the mood to shrug off even one more mean joke. "I have somewhere to be," she lied, gesturing at her bike.

"Sorry. It's just that . . ." Joseph's mouth twisted, and he looked in all directions before blurting, "Do you two investigate weird creatures?"

"Um." Cat had done plenty of research on cryptozoology, but her field experience was sorely lacking. "Why do you— Never mind." She cut herself off, realizing he was making fun of her. Of course he was. "I'm leaving now."

"Wait!" Joseph said as Cat climbed onto her bike. "I'm serious—"

She left him, and whatever punch line he had planned, behind.

Halfway to the hotel, where she was supposed to change

into the only nice dress she owned for her birthday dinner, she pulled over to catch her breath—and check her phone. Not so much as a birthday cake or party-popper emoji from her dad. *There're still a few hours left*, Cat reminded herself as she swallowed the lump in her throat. Of all the years she'd hoped he'd remember, this was the one when she needed it most.

Cat closed her eyes and took a deep breath. She needed a distraction. Something productive.

But their new lab was safely tucked away in Dani's garage, and there was no way Cat was going there. She could head back to Weston Farm and gather more samples—she was willing to visit the farm as many times as it took—but today, she didn't feel like going alone. Somewhere along the way, she'd gotten used to having a partner in crime-slash-science. It wasn't just about having someone to share the workload. It was also that she couldn't cut a single corner. With Dani around, Cat had to follow every lead, rule out every red herring, and run every experiment with military precision. Dani's skepticism was forcing Cat to be the best version of herself.

Well, now she would need to be the best version of herself, by herself.

Was it too much to ask to have someone who shared her enthusiasm? Someone who actually believed her?

Realization struck Cat like a bolt of lightning: She *did* know someone who'd believe her. And he'd be just as excited about the triple thirteens as she was. She changed direction and headed toward the outskirts of town instead.

When the dilapidated garage and dirt road came into view,

Cat turned and parked her bike. An old beat-up pickup truck was in the driveway, which gave her hope Robbie Colton was home. Cat was so desperate for a lead right now, she'd happily follow any harebrained idea he might've gotten from a recent dream.

She felt like she could hear Dani grumbling in her ear: *Dreams? Seriously?* She waved the thought away like it was a gnat flying around her head. Robbie's dreams had led him to the crop circles as they formed thirteen years ago. If he dreamed something that came true again, that could count as a replicable result.

Robbie opened the door at her knock. "You again!" He shook his head and held the door wide. "Come on in—you're right on time."

Cat went inside. "What do you mean, 'right on time'?"

He chuckled, then groaned as he settled back down into his broken-in armchair. "Well, you've been in my dreams. I knew in my bones you'd be back sooner or later. Must mean the time is right."

A chill swept over Cat, leaving her adrenaline pumping in its wake. "The time is right for what?" She answered her own question: "The last crop circle is supposed to appear tonight. Are you saying . . . ? Are we going to . . . you know, make contact?"

Robbie took a swig from his soda can. "Maybe, maybe not. But I did dream of you and me and aliens in a cornfield . . ."

"You actually saw the aliens in your dream? What did they look like?"

"I wouldn't say I *saw* them. More like I got a very strong sense that they were there. But they could see me." He nodded sagely.

The chill transformed into a thrill. This might not be strictly scientific evidence, but it was still a lead. "I believe you. Tonight is going to be special; I can feel it. There are thirteen years between the circles, and this year, thirteen circles were spread out over thirteen nights!"

Robbie looked delighted. "Triple thirteens!"

"Also, um . . ." Cat ducked her head and added, "Today is my thirteenth birthday."

"What?" Robbie sprang from his armchair, tossing his can over his shoulder. It landed with a clatter in a pile of empty cans and takeout containers in the corner. "That settles it. We're going to Weston Farm. I can drive us—"

Cat grimaced. "I can't go now. I have . . . somewhere to be." Her mom would be waiting for her at Luigi's. Cat couldn't ditch her. "Can we meet at the farm after dinner? Say, seven?"

Robbie nodded. "I suppose I could use a couple of hours to gather all my gear. You promise you'll be there?"

Cat held out her hand for a solemn handshake. "I promise."

41

DANI

DANI HAD NEVER FELT so lonely. She'd spent the entire school day hiding from her three best friends, while Cat had spent the whole day avoiding Dani. One situation or the other, Dani could've handled, but both? She didn't just feel twice as bad. Her doom-and-gloom mood was *exponentially* worse.

Plus, Ms. Blanks had called out sick. The substitute had put on a documentary about ocean wildlife, which Dani would normally have loved . . . except that she'd really, really wanted to talk to her teacher. If there was a way to salvage her project, Ms. Blanks would know what it was.

Back when Mr. Hepworth had first come forward as the hoaxer, Dani had told Cat she didn't believe in karma. Now she wasn't so sure. Dani had screwed up—badly—and because of that, everything was falling apart.

All she could think of to do was to keep pushing forward with her experiments on the teeny, tiny chance that she'd still be at the science fair next Saturday. After school, she sat at the lab table in her garage, trying to pretend there wasn't a second roll-y chair sitting empty beside her. She spread out the soil samples she'd managed to gather before Gravel, Specs, and Mr. Hepworth had crashed into that circle last night. It was nothing compared to the bounty of stalks and soil she and Cat had gathered before the theft and the explosion, but it would have to do.

Dani divided each soil sample out into several separate specimen containers. She prepared slides from each sample to examine under the microscope. She designated two samples from each batch of dirt for active-carbon testing, in case Cat ever spoke to her again and brought over the potassium permanganate and colorimeter her dad had sent. Two more samples from each baggie were set aside for pH testing. That, Dani could do now; they'd borrowed a pH kit from the school lab. All the remaining dirt, she put away for later.

She buried herself in the methodical work of pH testing. She added distilled water to each soil sample and stirred. She let the solutions rest before filtering out the soil to leave the water behind. She dipped a pH strip into each canister of water and logged the numbers in her notebook.

She worked for hours. When she finally stood up, massaging the crick in her neck, she looked at how much she'd accomplished and thought, *This should feel good.*

But it didn't.

Not without Cat.

Plus, she was missing a crucial component of her experiment: If her hypothesis was that Weed-Be-Gone was the source of the extra iron in the crop circle soil and that heat transformed chelated iron into iron microspheres, she needed to get her hands on some herbicide. She did a quick Google search and then dialed Bug-Be-Gone's customer service line.

A bored-sounding woman answered. "You've reached Bug-Be-Gone. My name is Leslie. How can I help you?"

"Hi, my name is Dani Williams and I'm a student at Hilldale Middle. I'm doing a science project studying how herbicide interacts with soil. I was wondering if I could get a sample of Weed-Be-Gone to study."

"The product goes on sale November sixteenth."

"I know," Dani said, staring at the promotional page on Bug-Be-Gone's website. "But the science fair is actually on the eleventh, so I was hoping to request a sample in advance."

"I'm afraid we aren't able to give out samples," Leslie replied. "Especially not to children."

"But my experiment—"

"Sorry, dear."

Dani sighed heavily. "Can I at least ask you some questions about the product?"

Leslie launched into a peppy sales pitch. "Weed-Be-Gone is the newest innovation from Bug-Be-Gone, the company trusted by farmers and gardeners since 1977! Using a proprietary system of effective weed-killing ingredients—"

"Like what?" Dani asked quickly. "Can you give me an ingredient list?"

"It's proprietary," Leslie said, back to her normal voice, "which means it's owned exclusively by Bug-Be-Gone. So, no."

"How about the chelated iron? Can you tell me how that works, exactly?"

"I'm afraid not."

"What would happen if someone applied heat to the Weed-Be-Gone after it was sprayed? Would there be any, um, residue in the soil?"

"I really can't help you," Leslie said, sounding annoyed. "The product hits shelves in two weeks. Thank you for your interest in Bug-Be-Gone and its subsidiaries."

"Wait, I just need to—"

Click.

"Now what?" Dani asked the silent phone.

And just like that, she knew.

42

CAT

CAT SAT ACROSS THE table from her mom, munching on one of Luigi's famous breadsticks. It was delicious—hot and garlicky—but her thoughts kept wandering. Unfortunately, her mom could tell something was up.

"Don't worry about the house, Cat," her mom said. "The insurance will cover the damage. Hopefully we won't be stuck in that hotel for more than a few weeks. A couple of months, tops."

Cat sighed. While that wasn't what she was worrying about, it wasn't exactly lifting her spirits.

"I hope they catch whoever did that to us." Cat's mom shook her head and frowned. "I'll feel safer once they have someone in custody."

"Yeah, me too." Though in truth, Cat was sure the culprit would never be apprehended. The MIBs had done it. No way they'd get caught.

The waiter returned with Cat's usual order, chicken Parmesan with spaghetti. It was amazing—but still not quite amazing enough to get her mind off her project . . . and Dani's betrayal . . . and Robbie's dreams . . . and her dad forgetting her birthday . . . and, and, and . . .

"Cat?" her mom said after the cake arrived and the staff sang "Happy Birthday" and Cat cracked only the slightest of smiles. "Is something else wrong, aside from the house stuff?"

Cat stabbed at her cake with her fork. "Kind of," she admitted.

Her mom set her own fork down. "I know I haven't been around as much lately because I've been working the second shift. But once I've saved up enough for us to have a security cushion financially, I'll go back to the day shift. It'll be like it was before. Until then, you know you can come to me when you need someone to talk to, right?"

"Yeah, I know."

"Then spill." Cat's mom picked up her fork again and dug into her cake.

"It's the McMurray project. It's just . . . gotten really complicated."

"What happened?"

Cat gave her mom the highlights version, leaving out the MIBs—she definitely didn't need her mom freaking out and deciding she was grounded for her own good—and focusing more on Dani working against her this whole time.

Cat's mom frowned deeply. "Dani seemed like a nice girl. Do you really think she did this just to humiliate you?"

"Yes. No. I don't know." Cat let out a frustrated growl.

Her mom took her hand. "Between Dani's behavior and losing all the work you put into the project, you must be feeling a little desperate to get more data, huh."

Cat looked at her mom with surprise. "That's exactly it."

"You don't really want to be here tonight, do you, hon?"

At first, Cat was nervous about answering truthfully, but her mom was smiling, so . . . "No, not really. And it's not personal! I love spending time with you. But I got a new lead this afternoon, and I'm dying to chase it."

"Honestly, honey, there's only one thing you love more than Luigi's chicken Parmesan and death by chocolate cake." She gave Cat a significant look. "Aliens."

Cat squirmed. "Guilty."

"I'll have them pack up your cake to go. You can enjoy it later, after you've gotten this bee out of your bonnet."

"Really?"

Cat's mom laughed. "Yes, really. Just don't stay out too late, all right?"

"Thanks, Mom. You're the best!" Cat hugged her mom and ran out the door.

43

DANI

DANI PARKED HER BIKE by the tall metal fence that ran around the Bug-Be-Gone property. She checked her phone to see if Cat had responded to the text she'd sent, inviting her along on this mission. She hadn't. Okay, so Dani was on her own. That was fine.

Totally fine.

There were also no messages from Dani's three best friends. Ex–best friends? Whatever they were now, they'd probably started a new group text without Dani. Actually, they probably already *had* one—

No. She couldn't think about Jane, Laurel, and Nora. She had to stay focused.

Because on the ride here, she'd realized two flaws in her plan:

1. She'd told Customer Service Leslie her full name *and* that she was a student at Hilldale Middle. If Dani got caught sneaking around, someone would probably make the connection, and she'd be in loads of trouble.

2. There was no good reason for her to be visiting this factory. She didn't know anyone who worked here. This wasn't a school field trip destination—and even if it were, she was

alone. Also, it was the end of the workday. Dani didn't exactly look like she was ready to pull a night shift.

How was she going to get them to let her inside?

She heard Cat's voice in her head: *stupid kids defense*.

Dani looked at her bike and got an idea. She picked it up, took a deep breath, and hurled it to the ground. She picked it up and threw it again. Then she tore out two handfuls of grass and began smearing the juices into her jeans and muddying her hands. She grabbed some gravel and squeezed her fists until it hurt, so that the rocks would leave red imprints in her palms.

She pushed her bike toward the factory entrance, limping as soon as the security guard came into view. When he spotted her, he shouted, "Hey! Kid! You can't be here!"

Cry, Dani commanded herself. She pinched her arm with her fingernails. Not a drop. She'd never been able to produce tears on cue, no matter how many acting lessons she'd taken.

She was going to have to sell this without tears. She was probably doomed.

She approached the guard. "I crashed my bike."

"I can see that," he said. "You still can't be here."

"My phone died," Dani said, putting a hitch in her voice. "I need to call my mom."

The guard appraised her. "Your bike doesn't look that beat up. Find another phone."

"I think I sprained my ankle." Dani pretended to try putting weight on her right foot and then gasped in fake pain. The guard seemed unmoved, and Dani had a moment of panic. Could he tell she was faking? Had she been limping on the other foot before? "My parents don't know where I am," she babbled, "and it's getting dark, and they're going to be so worried! It'll only take a second for me to make the call—"

"How old are you, kid?"

"Ten," Dani said, hoping the guard wasn't good at guessing ages.

The guard's face finally softened. "I got a niece that age. My sister wouldn't want Amie riding her bike in the dark by herself." He looked at the factory. "One phone call. That's it."

Dani nodded, keeping her face serious even though she wanted to do one of Cat's happy dances. She followed the guard to the building's main entrance, where he swiped his ID card and held the door open for her.

"Bike stays out here," he said.

She propped it up against a wall.

The guard led Dani past a reception desk and down a long corridor. "Don't touch anything. There're hazardous chemicals here, kid. Stuff that could really mess you up."

"Good to know. Thank you." Dani slowed down her limping walk so she could get a good look at her surroundings. White walls, white tile, white fluorescent lights in the ceiling. Even the doors that dotted the hall were painted white. The signs over each door weren't any help for Dani's mission. The rooms were numbered, but there weren't any details about what was inside. A few of the doors had windows, but Dani was too short to see through them without rising onto her tiptoes—which she shouldn't be able to do anyway, with her "sprained" ankle.

The guard turned a couple of corners. "Almost there," he said.

"Where are you taking me?"

"Employee lounge. Safest place for a kid in here." He paused, looking back at Dani's tortured limp. "Sorry it's all the way across the building."

"That's okay." She wince-smiled, like she was bravely pushing past her pain.

"Might be some ice in there, too," the guy said. "That'll help the ankle."

He was putty in Dani's hands. She decided to take a risk. "Is there a bathroom in the lounge?"

"Yeah. You gotta go?"

"Mm-hmm." Dani faked embarrassment, ducking her head.

He opened one of those white doors—"Room 42"—and pointed to the restroom. "Go on. I'll wait here." He plopped onto a threadbare couch and picked up a magazine from the coffee table.

Dani ducked into the bathroom and . . .

Eureka! The bathroom had two exits! She squealed out loud and then clapped her hand over her mouth.

"Everything okay in there?" the guard called.

"Took a bad step!" Dani said, pulling out her phone as she hurried over to the door at the opposite end of the room. She sent Cat a quick text:

DANI: I got into BBG! Just wanted someone to know where I am . . .

Then she opened the second door. She was back in the hallway. Or was it another hallway entirely? She had no idea.

It didn't matter where she was, as long as she found her way to the Weed-Be-Gone and nabbed a couple of samples before the guard caught up with her. She looked in both directions. She picked one.

She ran.

44

CAT

AS CAT ARRIVED AT her prearranged meeting spot with Robbie, her phone buzzed. Her heart leaped. She hoped it was her dad, finally, wishing her a happy birthday . . . but no. It was *another* text from Dani.

All Cat wanted for her birthday was to forget about everything that was bringing her down. That included her former partner. She cleared the text notification without reading it and hunkered down in the bushes to watch the road.

While she waited, she mused about where the final real circle would show up and where the MIBs were planning to make their three fakes. Without her mapping software, all she had to rely on was her memory—which was really good, admittedly, but not perfect.

And what time would everything go down? The authentic circle would form in minutes, while the MIBs' fakes might take most of the night. Plus, there was always the risk of witnesses. How did the MIBs expect to pull off such a hoax? Did they have special tools? Were they already out in the fields, hard at work?

Cat wasn't sure if she wanted to catch Gravel and his colleagues in the act or if she wanted to steer as clear of them as she could.

She supposed it depended on where Robbie's dreams would lead them. Cat pulled out the disposable camera she'd picked up at the drugstore earlier and made sure it was open and ready. She sighed, trying not to think about how light her bag felt without all her state-of-the-art equipment.

Cat heard a snap behind her. She whirled, and came face-to-face with Robbie, and almost screamed. She'd heard people joke about alien hunters wearing tinfoil hats before, but she'd thought it was just that—a joke. There was no science behind the tinfoil theory, so she'd never believed any *real* alien aficionados would do it.

Apparently, she'd been mistaken.

Robbie's tinfoil hat was more of a cap. It covered his whole head and was so shiny, the moonlight glinted off it. A tiny bit of concern twinged in Cat's stomach. "What are you wearing?" she asked carefully.

"This?" Robbie grinned. "I brought one for you, too." He pulled from his bag a shiny piece of aluminum that had been shaped into a second cap and held it out to her.

"I'm good, but thanks."

His face grew grim. "All right, but you're taking a big risk. They can see right into your brain without these things."

Cat was determined to be nice, so she played along. "What makes you so sure?"

He shrugged. "I mean, how else do you think I got the dreams? Someone had to put them in my head. Must've been them. Now, I appreciate the dreams and all, but I don't need them knowing everything I'm thinking. And I don't want to get abducted, either." He leaned closer and whispered, "They can read minds. It's how they find you."

It was a far-fetched idea, even for Cat, but she couldn't think of anything to say to refute it logically. So instead of arguing, she followed Robbie into the cornfields. He had a contraption slung over his shoulder—she was fairly certain it was a beat-up old metal detector. Her thoughts brightened. That could prove very useful. If there really were iron microspheres in the soil, Cat and Robbie could use the metal detector to distinguish the fake circles from the real ones.

He stopped in a circle Cat hadn't been in before. It had the same distinctive atmosphere as the rest. The moon was high above them in a cloudless sky, lending the swaying corn a ghostly feel. Cat should love this . . . but after everything that had happened with Dani, she just felt hollow and sad.

Robbie, however, had no hesitations. "Let's set up base camp over there behind those trees." He pointed to the fence surrounding the field and the trees just beyond it. "Then we can scan this circle for anomalies until the aliens show up. We'll catch 'em this time; I can feel it." His round face beamed in the moonlight.

Cat tried to smile back. She really hoped his dreams were right.

45

DANI

DANI PUSHED THROUGH A set of heavy double doors and found herself on what had to be the factory floor. The room was filled with enormous metal vats covered in gauges and levers. There were signs posted everywhere listing rules and regulations. At the top of the list: VISITORS MUST WEAR PROTECTIVE GEAR AT ALL TIMES.

Dani grabbed a white coat, a hard hat, safety goggles, and rubber gloves from a shelf by the door. She wouldn't be subtle, dressed like this . . . but actually, if someone spotted her at a distance, maybe they'd think she was a particularly short employee, instead of a rogue seventh grader. She rolled up the coat sleeves, slung her backpack over her shoulders, and walked between the vats of poison with as much confidence as she could muster.

Then she heard angry voices, and her confidence failed her. She ducked into the shadows between two vats, heart pounding.

"The herbicide was supposed to be at Weston Farm *this morning*," a man said. Dani recognized his voice: It was Gravel, one of the Men in Black. "We paid for rush delivery."

"We told you we'd do our best but the time wasn't guaranteed," another man shot back.

"Do you know who you're dealing with?" Gravel growled.

"I don't care if you're the king of England. We couldn't get the new shipment together until this afternoon."

Dani peered around the metal vat, careful not to touch any of the gurgling pipes or blinking buttons. She pushed her safety goggles up to her forehead. Gravel was talking to a Bug-Be-Gone employee who was wearing an outfit much like Dani's but holding an official-looking clipboard.

"Your first order nearly cleared out what we had on-site," the employee went on, setting his clipboard on a table with a computer and a pile of paperwork. "Plus, my counterpart on the morning shift initially thought this was another drone job."

"We requested canisters this time," Gravel said crisply, "for manual application."

Dani's mind was spinning. The herbicide Gravel wanted— that had to be Weed-Be-Gone. But why was the government ordering it in bulk? Why did they need it at Weston Farm *tonight*?

And what was that about . . . drones?

The agent and the Bug-Be-Gone guy had their backs to Dani, so she crept closer.

She could see the clipboard the employee had put down. There was a typed page on top that kind of looked like the invoices Dani's mom sent after completing one of her corporate art murals. Dani silently got out her phone and opened the camera. She zoomed in, snaked her arm out from her hiding place, and took a burst of photos.

"Can I at least drive the truck to the farm myself?" Gravel asked.

"Be my guest. But if you don't return it within twenty-four hours, you lose your deposit."

Dani pulled her arm back and scrolled until she found a clear shot of the paper on the clipboard. It *was* an invoice, and it showed two orders. Both were labeled "U.S. GOVT—WFC 2023." The first order was dated October 1, and in the notes section, someone had written, "For drones." The second had yesterday's date, November 1, and the note said, "Hand spray."

So the government was purchasing Weed-Be-Gone and taking it to Weston Farm.

The government had also been paying Mr. Hepworth, the farm's owner, for . . . something.

Those two facts had to be connected, but Dani couldn't figure out *how*.

"I'm leaving," Gravel announced. "You will forfeit the rush fee, seeing as your product was not delivered on time."

"Take it up with my boss." The employee sighed as the Man in Black walked away.

Dani darted around to the opposite side of the giant vat just in time to see Gravel turn a corner. She picked up her pace, leaping over pipes and wires, grateful that her sneakers barely made a sound on the concrete floor. She followed the agent into a loading bay. A truck was idling by the exit.

Gravel swung open the driver's-side door. He held his phone to his ear, and Dani heard him say, "I'm on my way. Tell the boss—" The door slammed closed.

Dani had only a few seconds to decide what to do. She was pretty sure that this freight exit was nowhere near the factory's main entrance, where she'd left her bike. She was also pretty sure that she'd never be able to ride fast enough to keep Gravel in her sights anyway.

As the truck's engine roared to life, Dani sprinted across the floor, throwing aside her borrowed gloves and hard hat. She didn't have time to shed the coat or the goggles. She scrambled up onto the truck's wide metal bumper and pressed her body flat against the rear doors. She gripped the door handles with white knuckles as the truck bumped off the Bug-Be-Gone property and accelerated onto the open road.

46

CAT

CAT AND ROBBIE SET up behind the tree break, which mostly meant emptying their bags of the very little equipment they had: trowels and sample bags for Cat and an entire grocery store aisle's worth of tinfoil for Robbie. "You can never be too careful," he said. Then Robbie unshouldered his metal detector. "Have you tried one of these before?"

Cat almost laughed. Tried? The one she'd had before the MIBs got to it was a high-tech model that would sync its readings with her laptop. "A couple of times, yeah."

"Wanna do the honors?" He held it out, and she took it gratefully. She shouldered the strap and gripped the stem to make panning the ground in front of her easy as she walked around the circle. She and Dani hadn't collected samples from this circle yet, but she was confident it was a real one. Sure enough, it wasn't long before she got a hit, then another and another. They were small hits, signified by the soft, short beep, but she and Robbie dug up the earth to check them even so.

Just as she'd suspected: iron microspheres.

"My research partner found lots of these in the circles we sampled," Cat said, as irritated to be thinking about Dani again as she was happy to see the magnetic particles in the soil. They confirmed this circle was very real. She doubted Mr. Hepworth and the Men in Black kept iron microspheres in their pockets to sprinkle in the dirt. But what if there was even more here to find? "I'll keep going until I get a bigger hit." *If I get a bigger hit*, Cat reminded herself.

While Robbie puzzled over the microspheres, Cat methodically worked her way around the outer edge of the circle, moving toward the center. All the while, she kept her ears open for anyone else approaching. With any luck, the MIBs would bypass this circle tonight and leave them be.

Cat was so lost in her work that when the metal detector screamed a hit, she nearly jumped out of her skin. Pulse pounding, she confirmed the location and began to dig.

"That sounds like a good one," Robbie said, hovering over her shoulder.

Cat's trowel hit something solid. She scrabbled at the soil to dig it all the way out. She gasped, holding it up with shaking fingers. It was a small, rectangular piece of metal, lightweight and cool to the touch. Not much to look at, but Cat still felt dizzy staring at it.

This metal shard was just like the one she'd found in the hotel incinerator.

47

DANI

DANI HELD ON FOR dear life, white lab coat flapping in the wind behind her, as the truck passed the festival tent and turned down the narrow dirt road that led into Weston Farm. Before long, the truck slowed and dimmed its headlights. When they came to a complete stop, Dani peeled herself off the back door, massaging her aching hands. Her fingers felt like claws. She'd broken two nails, and one was bleeding.

The driver's door opened. Dani heard footsteps coming in her direction. She jumped off the bumper so fast that she stumbled and fell. She rolled into the cornfield a moment before Gravel rounded the corner and unlocked the truck's rear doors.

"Sure, I'll bring it over," he said into his phone. "Send my partner back for the next load." He leaned into the bed of the truck and emerged with two portable canisters labeled "Weed-Be-Gone." He started walking in Dani's direction.

Dani scuttled backward, crab-style, on hands and feet, keeping her eyes glued to the Man in Black, until—

"Gotcha!" A hand clamped down on her shoulder. Another hand clapped over her mouth, muffling her shriek. "I knew I'd catch you tonight!" a man crowed.

Dani aimed a hard kick at the man's shin. When he cried out, she jumped to her feet and shoved him away. She was surprised to see that he wasn't wearing a black suit. In fact, he seemed to have a piece of tinfoil stuck to the top of his head.

He lunged at her. "I've waited thirteen years for this!"

Dani dodged and ran—and then skidded to a stop as she entered a crop circle. A girl in a dress and an oversize olive-green coat crouched near the center, digging in the dirt. "Cat!" Dani shouted. "There's a maniac! He grabbed me! We've got to get out of here!"

Cat stood, gaping at Dani. "What are *you* doing here? And what are you wearing?"

Dani peeled off the safety goggles and shrugged out of her lab coat. "I hitched a ride on a Bug-Be-Gone truck. Come on!" She tugged on Cat's arm.

"A Bug-Be-Gone truck?" Cat said. "Why?"

"I'll tell you later! Listen, there's a scary guy out there; he tried to kidnap me—and the Men in Black are here somewhere, too; one of them was driving the truck I rode on—and—"

"The Men in Black are here?"

"Come *on*!" Dani dragged Cat out of the circle. They made it into the tall corn just in time. Gravel, Specs, Beanpole, and Holly-wood entered the crop circle from the other side. Beanpole was holding on to the man who had attacked Dani. "That's the guy!" Dani hissed.

"Robbie?" Cat whispered. "He said he was going back to his truck for more tinfoil."

"You know that weirdo?" Dani whispered back.

"Right." Cat's voice was stiff. "You think anyone who believes in the paranormal is a weirdo."

"Cat. He said he knew he'd catch me tonight—that he'd waited *years* to catch me." Dani shuddered. "I barely got away! I know I hurt your feelings, and I'm so sorry. But now we have to—"

"He thought you were an alien." Cat looked exasperated.

"He . . . what?"

"That's Robbie Colton. He's the one who witnessed a crop circle forming here thirteen years ago. I'm pretty sure he's harmless." Cat cleared her throat. "He had a dream that we would see aliens tonight. That's why we're here."

"He had a dream?"

Cat nodded.

"And you were in it?"

"Yes," Cat said, staring intently into the circle.

Dani followed her friend's gaze. Gravel was back on his phone. Beanpole was patting Robbie down. Specs and Hollywood were carrying Weed-Be-Gone canisters out of the circle, into the surrounding fields.

"I'm still mad at you," Cat whispered.

"I know," Dani whispered back.

"But can you explain . . . this?" Cat waved a hand at the scene in front of them.

"I went to Bug-Be-Gone to get a sample of their weed killer to test against my—I mean, *our* soil samples. At the factory, I overheard Gravel saying he'd ordered a shipment to be delivered to Weston Farm today. This was actually the second shipment of herbicide the government ordered. The first batch was fitted for drones."

"Drones?" Cat repeated. "They were using drones to spray the herbicide? Why?"

"I don't know. I took a picture of the invoice." Dani showed Cat the image on her phone. "Anyway, Gravel said he was coming here next, so I hitched a ride."

Cat was frowning. "I don't understand. Why are the Men in Black buying Weed-Be-Gone? Is it part of the cover-up?"

"Well, my hypothesis did have to do with herbicide," Dani said slowly. "Maybe they're planting evidence to push us toward a certain conclusion."

"Yeah, but . . ." Cat's frown deepened. "How would they know about your hypothesis? *I* didn't even know about it until yesterday. It wasn't in any of the research they stole from my lab, was it?"

"No. I took my notebook home with me every night."

Cat gasped. "They must have been surveilling your house, too!"

"Are you sure I didn't tell them everything?" Dani couldn't help snapping back. It turned out, having been accused of spilling all their secrets still stung.

"I never really believed that," Cat said quietly. "I was just upset."

"Which was my fault." Dani sighed. "I'm really sorry."

"Thanks." Cat cleared her throat like she wanted to say something else, but before she could, Gravel ended his phone call and beckoned his colleagues over.

"Spread out," he ordered. "The whole farm needs to be covered before sunrise—everything except the three circles in sector fifteen. Hope you all had an extra cup of coffee with dinner."

"I'm not getting paid enough for this," Hollywood said as she walked away.

"I found another piece of UE," Cat murmured. She held out a small shard in her open palm. Dani picked it up, turning it over in her hands. "It was in this circle. Robbie brought a metal detector. If we—" Cat broke off and snatched back the piece of metal. "Never mind."

Dani's chest clenched. "Cat."

"You made it pretty clear you don't want to work with me. I won't make you." Cat wouldn't meet Dani's eyes. "You can go home now."

"I think . . ." Dani blew out a long breath. "I think I'd like to stay."

Cat's eyes flickered toward Dani. "Really?"

"Really."

"Why?"

"What are the odds of us ending up in the same exact field—me riding up on a truck full of weed killer, driven by a Man in Black, and you chasing some tinfoil-hat guy's dream? There's something going on here. Something I . . . can't explain." Dani leaned toward Cat. "I want to know what it is. And I want to figure it out with you."

Cat smiled. "Good answer. Now, let's go trap some Men in Black."

48

CAT

CAT AND DANI HURRIED toward the tree line where she and Robbie had set up their "base camp." Some of Robbie's things were still there, and they might come in handy. They ducked behind the trees so that the MIBs couldn't see them. They needed to hurry. Of that Cat was certain.

Thank goodness for the oldies music currently blaring from the festival tent. Even from all the way across the farm, it was loud enough to muffle their passage through the corn. The MIBs probably wouldn't hear Dani and Cat unless they were right on top of them. And right now, they weren't.

Cat crouched to dig through Robbie's backpack. He had a compass, some chewing gum, nail clippers, six cans of Red Bull, and a ton of tinfoil. She groaned.

"What's wrong?" Dani asked.

"I was hoping he'd have a video camera. I don't have one anymore—not since that stupid EMP." Cat scowled. That night in the fields had done so much damage to . . . everything, really.

Dani held up her smartphone. "We can use this."

Cat smacked her forehead. "You're right. Thanks."

"Of course," Dani said. "We're a team, remember?"

A warm feeling washed over Cat, but she tried not to let it slow her down. "We need to get it on camera: the Men in Black planting evidence and making the three fake crop circles. We'll live stream it, too, in case they confiscate your phone. Then everyone will believe us."

"But . . . how do we prove they stole our research and blew up your lab?" Dani asked.

"Well, they're determined to end our investigation, right?"

Dani nodded.

"Let's let them know we're here—that we're still investigating, even after everything they've done to us. They'll try to stop us from getting any new samples, especially before they can pour Weed-Be-Gone all over everything. We'll record them interfering with our research. That's how we'll prove they're the bad guys!"

"That might work," Dani said thoughtfully. "We can leave clues in the fields, like a trail for them to follow."

"Yes!" Renewed energy flowed through Cat's limbs. "Then we'll catch them in the act."

A surprisingly devious look came over Dani's face. "I'm so in."

They got to work, sticking as close to the MIBs as they dared. Dani's backpack was stuffed full of project-related items, so it didn't take long for them to lay the trap. A torn latex glove on one cornstalk, a broken pipette at the edge of a crop circle, a plastic evidence baggie smooshed into the mud.

"All right," Cat said after they'd dropped all their bread crumbs. "The MIBs should have found at least a couple of the clues we've left by now."

"They probably think they're on to us."

Cat nodded vigorously. "Exactly. So let's give them something to chase."

Dani swallowed hard but smiled bravely.

Cat held out her hand to Dani. "Ready?"

"As I'll ever be."

Cat screamed at the top of her lungs: "This is so cool; you have to see it!" Then she and Dani took off at a run. Behind them, shouts rang out. The Men in Black had taken the bait.

They hadn't gone far when a familiar trilling began from somewhere over their heads. Cat's eyes shot up, and she squealed.

"Look! Dani!"

Her partner was standing stock-still a few steps behind her. "What *is* that?" she asked.

"An orb!" Cat jumped up and down and then pointed. A glowing light danced in the distance. "Look! There's another! We have to follow them! And get the live stream going!" She threw herself forward and then skidded to a stop, jogged back, and grabbed Dani's hand. Cat wasn't going to leave Dani behind. Not this time.

Together, they chased the floating balls of light. The crop stalks were tall, but the orbs zipped around at just the right height to be seen. Damp air whispered across Cat's cheeks. A wet, white fog rolled toward them. Within minutes, it was so thick that they were forced to stop running.

"Are you getting this, Dani?" Cat said excitedly.

Dani was frantically pressing buttons on her phone. "Shoot, I got logged out of my account. Hang on!"

By then, the fog had enveloped them so thoroughly that they couldn't even see the sky, just the smudgy glow of the swirling orbs. All they could hear was the trilling sound, getting louder with every second that passed. Then, without warning, the noise rose to a higher pitch, and the fog glowed with a brilliant light. Cat let out a delighted squeal.

Dani grabbed her arm. "What. Is. Happening?"

"A crop circle is happening!" Cat hollered back. She was dying to dive headfirst into the corn, but she was determined to witness this alongside Dani. Also, she wasn't sure what would happen if a person was in a crop circle at the time it was created. Given what happened to the corn and wheat, it was probably better to remain on the sidelines.

But oh, how Cat would love to be a fly on a cornstalk right about now . . .

The lights went out, leaving Cat and Dani blinking, adjusting to the sudden darkness. The fog receded as quickly as it had appeared, and the trilling noise stopped abruptly.

Another noise quickly took its place: human feet tramping through a field of corn.

The girls exchanged a glance, then whispered at the same time, "Hide!"

49

DANI

"WHERE ARE THE GIRLS?"

"They must be nearby, ma'am. We'll find them."

"See that you do."

Dani recognized both voices. One was the MIB Cat called Gravel. And the other . . .

Her world tilted on its axis.

The other voice belonged to Ms. Blanks.

As the cornstalks parted on the opposite side of the freshly formed thirteenth crop circle and two figures stepped into view, scenes flashed across Dani's mind's eye. Ms. Blanks, approving this decidedly unscientific project for a prestigious science fair. Ms. Blanks, wanting weekly check-ins with Dani to discuss what experiments she'd run. Ms. Blanks, hanging on Dani's every word as she described Cat's methods and findings. Ms. Blanks, standing outside Cat's house in the aftermath of the explosion.

Cat was the first to say it: "She's . . . one of them."

"I think," Dani croaked, watching Ms. Blanks order Gravel around, "she's their boss."

You trusted her.

You told her everything.

"Establish a perimeter," Ms. Blanks said as Beanpole, Hollywood, and Specs entered the circle. "Don't let them get past you. And for goodness' sake—don't hurt them."

"Are we filming now?" Cat whispered.

Dani fumbled with her phone, checking that they were both live and recording. "Yeah, we're on."

Cat took Dani's phone. She began to narrate: "This is Cat Mulvaney, coming to you live from the latest crop circle formation at Weston Farm. My partner and I"—she scanned the camera over to Dani and then back to the circle—"have set a trap for the Men in Black monitoring this year's phenomenon. During this live stream, we hope to prove beyond the shadow of a doubt that these agents have been working to deny the extraterrestrial origins of these circles, to hide the truth—"

Dani tuned Cat out. She focused on their teacher. Ms. Blanks had played Dani like a fiddle.

That realization took Dani past shock and into anger. She pushed to her feet.

Cat looked up at her, startled. "Dani, what are you—"

"Don't leave this hiding spot, and don't stop filming." Dani waited until the four Men in Black were gone and then stomped out of the tall crops onto the flattened stalks of the circle.

With a final cymbal crash, the music from the festival tent cut out. The field echoed with silence. Then cheers and applause.

Ms. Blanks turned at the sound of Dani's footsteps. "Hello, Danielle," she said.

"Is your name even Ms. Blanks?" Dani demanded.

"You're a smart girl. Think about that."

"Oh. 'Blanks.' I get it." Dani scanned her teacher from head to toe. Even out here, in the dark in a cornfield, she was wearing her pastel blouse and khaki pants, although her grayish-brownish hair was pulled into a casual ponytail. "You're supposed to be forgettable."

"Yes."

Dani hoped Cat was getting all of this. Just in case, she took a step back toward her partner. "You were . . . what? Assigned to come here? To do what?"

Ms. Blanks sighed. "To run the operation."

"You mean, the hoax?"

"I mean precisely what I said."

Dani squinted as all the things she'd learned about the Weston Farm Circles over the last two weeks swirled around in her brain. "The government is hiding something here at Weston Farm. It's . . . not aliens?" She wished she'd been able to say that as a statement, not a question—especially when her teacher smirked in response.

"No," Ms. Blanks said. "It's not aliens."

"Then . . . what—and why—how—"

"What has your research told you?" For a moment, Ms. Blanks sounded like the encouraging science nerd Dani had respected so much. Then she smirked again, and the illusion was shattered.

"The government," Dani began slowly, "has been doing experiments here. Weston Farm is a testing site." A puzzle piece clicked into place in her mind. "That's why you were paying the farmer: for the use of his fields and for the damage to his crops."

Ms. Blanks nodded. "Go on."

"The tests have something to do with Weed-Be-Gone . . . and drones."

Ms. Blanks nodded again.

"The glowing orbs," Dani said, eyes widening. "Those were drones. And the piece of metal Cat found—was it a part of one? Was that why you blew up Cat's lab?"

Ms. Blanks just looked at her.

Dani's brain did another zigzag. "The herbicide . . . the crop-duster pilot said he got outbid this year. You used the drones to spray the fields instead of a human and a plane. But . . . that still doesn't explain the *crop circles*!" Her voice rose in frustration.

"Think, Danielle."

Dani closed her eyes and thought.

"The Weed-Be-Gone by itself can't be what's flattening the field. Other farms use Bug-Be-Gone products, and this hasn't happened to them," she said. "And anyway, the first Weston Farm Circles were in 1984. If you've been running experiments since then, and you didn't want crop circles to form, you would have fixed the problem. Or else, your scientists aren't very good at their jobs." She opened her eyes and looked at her teacher.

Ms. Blanks cracked a smile. "I assure you, our team knows what they're doing."

"Which means," Dani said, "the crop circle is part of the experiment. Or it's, um, a by-product." She crouched, touching the soil with fingers that were going numb from the cold. "What if . . . what if . . ." *Oh.* "The iron microspheres."

"You got there," Ms. Blanks said. "Would you like me to connect the dots?"

"Yes!" Dani said loudly, praying Cat was still recording.

"In 1984," Ms. Blanks began, "the government was running an array of drone tests at various locations across the country. The Weston Farm project was about aerosol dispersal. We collaborated with Bug-Be-Gone, using our drones to deploy their product. In each of the first five tests, the crop was . . . damaged. The team went back to the drawing board and made adjustments. When the sixth test also flattened the crop, the project was scrapped."

"Five real crop circles and one fake one," Dani murmured, remembering the pattern Cat had insisted she'd found.

"In the postmortems for the Weston Farm tests, something interesting was discovered," Ms. Blanks continued. "The soil beneath the flattened corn and wheat had been altered. The pesticide was heated up by the drones' mild levels of radiation, and when it hit the soil, iron microspheres formed."

"My hypothesis!" Dani yelped. "Heat plus Weed-Be-Gone equals iron microspheres!"

"Yes, yes, well done," Ms. Blanks said, now sounding slightly annoyed.

"But . . . can drones actually—"

"Ours can," Ms. Blanks said crisply. "Do you want to hear the rest of the story or not?"

Dani nodded quickly. "I definitely do."

"The microspheres were found to have useful properties."

"Like what?"

Her teacher narrowed her eyes. "That is classified information. As is the recipe that produces it. Suffice it to say, further testing revealed that the microspheres' creation requires *this* soil, along with Bug-Be-Gone's proprietary formula, along with precise drone deployment."

"If they're so valuable, why only make microspheres every thirteen years?" Dani asked.

"That was how long it took the soil to recover from the first tests."

"Okay, but . . . why pretend it was crop circles? That's what this is, right?" Dani could suddenly see it so clearly. "The supernatural stuff is the cover-up. The aliens are the real hoax."

"The lore that grew around the Weston Farm Circles was . . . a happy accident."

"What do you mean?"

"The six tests in 1984 resulted in rudimentary crop circles. The day before the first test, the facility charging the drones had an electrical surge that resulted in a brief power outage. Appliances and electronics within a certain radius were affected. Meanwhile, someone reported seeing 'floating lights' over the mountains—which were, of course, our drones. By 1997, when we were ready to replicate the initial experiment, the local legend was already in place. The director of the 1997 project took those details and embellished them."

"The prime-number sequence," Dani said. "The map, with all the circles creating one giant fractal. The sounds and the fog and the orbs . . ."

"All by design," Ms. Blanks confirmed. "Advances in drone

technology over the past few decades certainly helped us flesh out the hoax."

"Were you there in 1984?" Dani asked. "Were you part of the first experiment?"

Her teacher looked a little insulted. "Danielle, how old do you think I am? Don't answer that. I was in high school in 1984. I was an entry-level drone technician in 1997. In 2010, I assisted the project director. This year, I took over as lead."

"But . . . why were you also our science teacher?"

"The middle-school-teacher disguise has worked in the past," Ms. Blanks said with a shrug. "But there were . . . complications this time."

"Cat," Dani said knowingly, and her teacher nodded.

"When Catrina submitted her proposal to make these circles her project for the McMurray Competition, I had to improvise. It would have been suspicious to deny a student of her caliber an opportunity to compete. But then I thought . . ." Ms. Blanks's lips twitched with amusement. "I could *use* her. Her genuine conviction . . . it was valuable."

"Because you needed to keep people believing in the hoax."

"Precisely. Her project—*your* project—was sure to garner attention. That attention would keep people from seeing what was really going on here. But then . . ." Ms. Blanks shook her head. "You refused to cooperate. You're a bright student, and a match for Catrina in so many ways. If you'd just done what you were supposed to do—well, you wouldn't have won the science fair, but . . ." The teacher waved her hand at the stalks of corn. "We also wouldn't have ended up here."

"You're blaming all of this on me?" Dani squeaked, indignant. "You lied to us! You stole our research! You—you blew up Cat's bedroom!"

"I did everything I could to keep the two of you safe."

"You—*wh-what*?" Dani sputtered. "Safe?"

"I didn't trigger the explosion until I knew the house was empty," Ms. Blanks said matter-of-factly. "I called 911 before the two of you even realized what had happened, hoping to confine the damage to a relatively small area."

"That doesn't make it okay—"

"Despite the mess you and Catrina have made of things, I can still save this operation. Your proof—it's gone."

Dani scoffed. "You just told me the whole story! I'll go public!"

Ms. Blanks stepped forward, pulling something out of her pocket.

"No," she said. "You won't."

50

CAT

CAT SAT FROZEN, LIKE she was caught in a tractor beam.

To her great disappointment, that wasn't the case.

There were no aliens in Hilldale. No spaceships overhead, no orbs with laser beams.

No, there was just . . . Ms. Blanks.

Who was walking toward Dani holding . . . something.

Dani backed away, toward Cat. Cat kept filming, even though the air around her felt thin.

All of Cat's evidence had just gone up in smoke, perfectly dismantled by Ms. Blanks and her drones. There was no way NASA would send her dad back to Hilldale now. Tears burned behind her eyes. That twinge of pain brought her back to the moment—and the risk Dani was taking, confronting their treacherous teacher.

Ms. Blanks hadn't just faked the crop circles. She'd blown up Cat's lab to cover up her own cover-up.

She wasn't merely a bad teacher; that was forgivable. What she'd done was—literally—criminal.

A rush of adrenaline filled Cat's limbs as she flipped open her own phone and quickly dialed 911. When the operator answered, she didn't waste a moment.

"Hi, this is Cat Mulvaney," she whispered. "My friend Dani Williams and I are at Weston Farm, being threatened by our science teacher, Ms. Blanks. Tell Detective Lewis she's the arsonist! And send help, please!"

"Stay calm," said the woman on the other end. "Can you tell me exactly where you are?"

"In the eastern cornfields, right beside the thirteenth crop circle. I've been doing a live stream, so you can—" Cat gasped as she got a clear look at what Ms. Blanks was brandishing at her partner: a syringe.

"Is everything all right?" the 911 operator asked.

"I can't stay on the line! Just—hurry!" Cat hung up.

A few feet away, Ms. Blanks's syringe glistened in the moonlight. "Tomorrow, you won't remember any of this," she said with a strange gleam in her eyes. "Don't worry. It's painless—"

Cat leaped up from her hiding spot and tackled Ms. Blanks. The teacher tumbled to the ground, the syringe rolling off into the corn.

Cat scrambled to her feet. "Dani! Run!"

"Cat!" Dani yelped. "The recording—"

"I got it! I— Ah!" Cat shrieked in surprise as Ms. Blanks grabbed her ankle and pulled her down. As she hit the ground, she reared back and threw Dani's phone. "Catch!"

Dani squinted as the phone arced through the night sky, trying to get herself into position. She held out her hands. When the phone dropped into them, she turned and ran.

Ms. Blanks was already up, ready to chase her.

"Throw it back to me!" Cat yelled, feeling like they were

playing the world's most dangerous game of monkey in the middle. She pushed to her feet.

Dani tossed the phone. Cat fumbled the catch but managed to hold on. Ms. Blanks abruptly changed direction, coming for Cat.

"Incoming!" Cat shouted, throwing the phone again.

This time, the device sailed over Dani's head, landing in the nearby corn. Dani dove to the ground, groping around frantically. "I can't see it, Cat! I can't see it!"

Just then, a bright light exploded over the cornfield.

The bottom dropped out of Cat's stomach. This was it. The Men in Black, or whoever they really were, had finally caught them.

Game over.

Except Ms. Blanks seemed just as surprised as Cat.

"Police! Nobody move!"

Ms. Blanks ran headlong into the corn. Two figures broke off from behind the light and chased her. Meanwhile, the familiar form of Detective Lewis approached Cat and Dani.

"Miss Williams and Miss Mulvaney?" he asked. "Are you all right?"

"Yes." Cat's voice sounded an octave higher than usual. "How did you get here so fast?"

"We'd been made aware of your live stream. When you called 911, we already had a few cars on the way to check things out. You told the 911 dispatcher that your teacher was the arsonist?"

"She confessed!" Even with the video, Cat was suddenly terrified he wouldn't believe them.

"And she was going to hurt us tonight, too!" Dani added. "There's a syringe around here . . . somewhere." She gestured at the crop circle.

"Your phone, Dani!" Cat began to hunt around in the dark. Dani joined her, and soon they found the device.

Cat frowned when she turned it on. "The live stream cut out. It must have ended when it hit the ground. Shoot."

Dani leaned over her shoulder. "What did we get on film?" Together they rewatched the video with the detective. The audio was crystal clear. Hearing it again was a painful reminder for Cat as to how wrong she'd been about the Weston Farm Circles. Cat felt deflated. Her whole life, she'd believed they were the real deal, and all along, it had just been a government science experiment. The only thing keeping Cat from wallowing was the fact that Ms. Blanks was still out there.

One of the other officers pulled Detective Lewis aside. Cat was dying to know what they were saying, but the two men kept their voices too low for her to make out.

"Do you think they found Ms. Blanks?" Dani whispered to Cat.

"I hope so. Though there is a lot of grain to get lost in here . . ." Cat bit her lip.

The detective returned, clearing his throat. "We don't usually get to tie up a case with a neat bow like this. But the video you took tonight is pretty incriminating, especially because we'd already been following a different lead in connection with your teacher."

"Really?" Cat leaned forward. "What else did she do?"

The detective shook his head to indicate that he wasn't going to answer. "We've located her car on the outskirts of the farm. We're combing the surrounding area, as well as the house she was renting, for clues. Do you have any idea where she might go to hide out?"

The girls exchanged a wary look. "We only saw her at school. We don't even know where she lived," Cat said.

"Maybe she went back to the Bug-Be-Gone factory?" Dani suggested. "Or the Parisian Hotel?"

Cat smacked her forehead. "That's right! The other agents were staying there. Oh! Detective Lewis! There are four government agents here somewhere! They were working for Ms. Blanks. You have to find them!"

The detective nodded and made a note. "Officer Adams here is going to take you back to the station to ensure you remain out of harm's way. Your parents can pick you up there."

Cat and Dani packed their things as quickly as they could. Then they piled into the back seat of the police car. Officer Adams, a short, stocky man of few words but with a kindly demeanor, swung by the Bug-Be-Gone factory to pick up Dani's bike and then drove them to the police station.

On the road, Cat called her mom. She told her about Ms. Blanks and everything they'd learned. At first, Cat's mom thought Cat was making up stories, but when Cat said she and Dani were on their way to the police station, her mom began to come around. "I'll be there as soon as I can, honey," she said.

When they reached the station and got settled in a waiting area, Dani immediately turned to Cat. "Are you okay?"

Cat shrugged. "I mean, my life's work just went down the tubes, so no, not really?" She slunk down in the seat. "I was so sure we were going to make contact tonight. Everything pointed to it! Thirteen years, thirteen circles, thirteen days. And the thirteenth circle even fell on my thirteenth birthday! Now, *that* would have been the best birthday present ever."

"It's . . . your birthday?" Dani asked haltingly. "Why didn't you tell me?"

"I guess . . . I guess I just didn't want to jinx it." Cat sighed heavily. "Not that it matters now."

Dani shook her head. "Well, you may not have gotten the aliens, but you did get a government conspiracy, if that's any consolation."

That was true. And kind of cool, actually, now that the scary part was over.

"We uncovered a real cover-up," Cat said.

"Happy birthday, Cat," Dani said. Then she began to laugh. Cat started laughing, too. They laughed until tears ran from their eyes and the other people in the waiting area gave them strange looks, including a rather stern one from an officer.

Cat's birthday might not have been everything she'd hoped for, but it would have to be enough. For now, anyway.

51

DANI

NINE DAYS LATER

THE DOORS TO THE college gymnasium swung open, and the McMurray Youth Science Competition was officially underway. Dani looked over at Cat and mustered a nervous smile. "Good luck."

Cat scoffed at her. "We don't need luck," she said. "We've got this." But her confident voice wavered just a little. Dani clearly wasn't the only one feeling anxious about today's results.

Dani looked around the room at the other displays. Their competitors' projects all seemed to be well researched and carefully explained. None of them had a giant green alien head peering down from the top of the poster board, either.

Well, Ms. Blanks *had* said it would be important for their project to stand out.

Not that Dani wanted to think about her evil former science teacher right now.

The local police had nabbed Ms. Blanks in the basement of the Parisian, where she'd been incinerating evidence. After her arrest, she'd been transferred into federal custody. She hadn't been seen or heard from since. Cat said it was because Ms. Blanks had been "disappeared."

As for the Weston Farm Circles . . . the government had admitted to running a "completely safe" operation on the property but had insisted the details of that operation remain classified. They'd disavowed Ms. Blanks's actions as those of a "rogue employee" and had refused to comment on Dani and Cat's findings.

They could say "no comment" all they wanted, but since the live stream, the story had taken on a life of its own. Dani and Cat had been interviewed on the news. So had representatives from Bug-Be-Gone. So had faculty and grad students from the university's Agricultural Sciences program. Even Robbie Colton had gotten his moment in the spotlight.

Judging by the dirty looks Dani and Cat were getting from some of the other kids in the gymnasium, their fifteen minutes of fame hadn't gone unnoticed. But Dani knew the truth: Fame wouldn't get them the McMurray Award. Today, only their work mattered.

"Dani!"

Dani looked over to see Jane, Nora, and Laurel approaching.

"Hi!" she squeaked. "You came!"

"Of course we did," Jane said immediately. "We wouldn't miss it, right, guys?"

Behind her, Laurel nodded hesitantly, and Nora gave a tight-lipped smile.

Dani and her friends had been walking on eggshells since that awful night at Jane's house. Everyone had apologized, but things still didn't feel the way they used to. Nora, in particular, seemed to be holding on tightly to her hurt feelings.

But they'd shown up.

"I'm glad you're here," Dani said. Then she realized what they were wearing. "And you made . . . T-shirts?"

Jane looked down at her top, which was bright pink with a hashtag printed on the front: #SCIENCEANDSTRANGE. "It was Laurel's idea."

"We made you both shirts, too," Laurel said, holding them out.

"It's a peace offering!" Jane chirped a bit too brightly.

"Thanks." Dani took the folded garments and handed one to Cat.

"This is great!" Cat said, holding her shirt up to admire it. "Thank you!"

"We're proud of you, Dani," Jane said.

"This is really cool," Laurel added.

Both of them looked pointedly at Nora until she begrudgingly said, "Congrats."

Dani felt a wave of affection for her BFFs—even grouchy Nora. "Do you guys want to hang out tomorrow?" she blurted.

"Sure," Jane said, glancing at the others for confirmation. "What did you have in mind?"

"Well, we could—"

"Dani!" Dani's mom walked up, gaping at the green alien head. "Rourke, look at this!"

Dani's dad glanced up from the ScienceU brochure he'd been reading. "Good job, sweetie."

"Hi, girls," Dani's mom said to her friends.

"Hi, Mrs. Williams," Jane said. "Dani, we're going to . . . walk around a little."

"Okay. I'll text you all about tomorrow?"

Jane nodded. "Good luck with the judges."

"Yeah, good luck," Laurel echoed. Nora gave another tight-lipped smile. Then the three of them headed off.

Dani's mom scanned the charts and graphs Dani and Cat had painstakingly drawn and then picked up a jar of soil from their table and squinted at the black specks. "Are those . . . ?"

"The iron microspheres, yeah," Dani said.

"This is what the government was making at Weston Farm?" Her mom frowned. "All that trouble for something so tiny. What are they even for?"

"My theory," Cat jumped in, "is that they're ball bearings for devices that use nanotech. The future is now!"

"Oh?" Dani's dad said, a beat too late.

Dani's mom cleared her throat. "Where do the aliens fit in?"

"Well, crop circles *are* an extraterrestrial phenomenon," Cat said. "I mean, these weren't. But the truth is still out there!"

"Did this whole thing start as . . . the two of you researching aliens . . . for a science award?" Dani's mom gave Dani an odd look. Then her face brightened. "I understand now."

"You do?" Dani asked.

Her mom beamed at her dad. "Rourke, she's found her discipline."

Dani shot a look at Cat, who shrugged, equally confused.

"Performance art," Dani's mom said. "This is genius, sweetie.

You're subverting the expectations for a science competition. Asking viewers to question their ideas of what is real. Using scientific language to describe the imaginary, the fantastical."

"But—this wasn't aliens," Dani protested. "And it isn't a performance. We used *real* scientific methods to determine that—"

Her mom clapped her hands. "Next you should do a project on unicorns."

For a moment, all Dani could do was gape at her mother. Then she blurted, "I'm not doing costumes for the winter musical! And I'm not taking ballroom dance lessons!"

"That's fine. Focus your energy on your next art piece." Her mom patted the alien head on their display. "Well done, Dani. We are so proud." Beside her, Dani's dad nodded his encouragement.

"Dani!" Cat motioned with her head. Three people were approaching their table, McMurray Corporation badges on their lapels.

"Ooh, break a leg!" Dani's mom kissed her on the head and dragged her dad away.

When the judges reached them, Cat held out her hand. "Hi! I'm Catrina Mulvaney, and this is Danielle Williams. This is our research project: 'Crop Circles: Science Fiction or Science Fact?'"

"Seems like you girls are a little famous," said the shorter of the two men, whose badge read, JEFFERSON HAWES, PHD, EVOLUTIONARY BIOLOGIST.

Dani let out a shaky laugh. "I guess so, Dr. Hawes. We definitely weren't expecting that."

The other man—a PhD in biomedical engineering named Teo Morales—picked up a canister of soil and shook it, much like

Dani's mom had. "We had a chance to walk through here last night. At first glance, your research seems solid."

"We'd be happy to tell you more about our methodology, Dr. Morales," Dani said, heart fluttering. "Do you have any questions for us?"

The third judge, an organic chemist named Alicia Anderson, stepped forward. "Quite a few, actually. You mentioned in your written report that you began the month pursuing opposing theories. Can you tell us about that?"

Dani glanced at Cat. "That was my idea. To be honest, I don't think it was the right move."

Dr. Morales tilted his head. "It led you to the correct conclusion, did it not?"

"Well, yes," Dani said, "but we would have gotten there faster if we'd been working together."

At that, Cat flashed Dani a smile.

"We also want to hear more about your experiments," Dr. Anderson said. "You focused your research on the damage to the wheat and cornstalks, as well as the impact on the soil?"

"Yes, but before we talk about that . . ." Dani pointed to Cat, who launched into an explanation of the prime number and fractal patterns that had helped her predict when and where each circle would form. Then she talked about microwave radiation and stalk-node damage. As they'd rehearsed, Dani took it from there. She shared how she'd spotted the black specks in the soil and tried to figure out what they might be. Then she dove into the pH and colorimeter tests she and Cat had run to assess the health of the soil. Finally, she shared how Weed-Be-Gone fit into all of it.

"Of course," Dani said, "Ms. Blanks's confession—"

"On the live stream," Dr. Hawes said, nodding. "My son made me watch the recording."

"Right, that's what put the final pieces together for us. We did do some tests this past week to try to confirm what she'd told me. We acquired a canister of Weed-Be-Gone"—actually, they'd snuck it home from Weston Farm, but Dani wasn't about to admit that part—"and gathered soil samples from the control fields."

"Because we didn't have the drone tech they were using for the Weston Farm tests," Cat said, "we weren't able to replicate the iron microspheres. They were obviously using something more advanced than what's available to the general public. But you can see our results here." She pointed to that section of the poster board.

"The piece of metal you found and tested in the mass spectrometer," Dr. Anderson said. "Do you have a theory as to what it was?"

Dani crossed her fingers and toes that Cat wouldn't mention spaceships. She was relieved when her partner said, "We believe it was probably part of one of the drones." Cat looked like she wanted to say something else, but to Dani's relief, she held it in.

"It was taken when your other research was stolen?" Dr. Hawes asked.

"I actually found two pieces of metal," Cat clarified. "The first piece disappeared after the explosion in my lab. The second one was taken by the Men in—I mean, the government."

Two unfamiliar agents had shown up at Dani's house the morning after their confrontation with Ms. Blanks at Weston Farm. Dani and Cat had been awake most of the night, frantically typing up everything they'd seen and experienced, fueled by Mountain Dew and Cat's chocolate birthday cake. Dani's parents had still been in their pajamas when the doorbell rang.

"About that. Why didn't they take all of your research?" Dr. Morales asked. "Why only retrieve the metal shard and let you keep the rest?"

"We asked the same thing," Dani said. "One of the agents said we might as well finish our project. The cat was already out of the bag."

"It sure was," Dr. Anderson said, shaking her head in apparent amusement. She looked at her colleagues. "Have you heard enough?"

Both men nodded.

"Then it is my honor to award you first prize in the Grades Seven to Nine category." Dr. Anderson reached into her satchel and pulled out an enormous blue ribbon. After a moment's consideration, she pinned it onto the giant alien head like a fancy bow.

"Thank you!" Dani squeaked. "Thank you so much!"

Dr. Anderson smiled as she continued. "You demonstrated a breadth of knowledge, admirable attention to detail, an ability to think outside the box, and persistence and adaptability in the face of numerous challenges—all qualities that will benefit you, should you choose to pursue a career in the sciences. Congratulations. I look forward to seeing you both next summer in my lab at ScienceU."

52

CAT

DR. ANDERSON POINTED TO the alien-head pins Cat had set out for visitors to their table. "May I?"

"Of course!" Cat yelped. "Take as many as you want!"

The judge attached a pin to her McMurray Corporation badge and handed pins to her colleagues, who did the same. Then they all shook Dani's and Cat's hands and walked away to present more awards.

Cat couldn't hold it in any longer. She jumped up and down and let out a squeal. "Omigoshomigoshomigosh! Dani! We did it!"

Now that the judges were out of earshot, Dani began hyperventilating.

"We're actually going to ScienceU!" she cried. "And I don't have to learn ballroom dancing!"

Cat grinned and held out a fist to bump. "Sisters in science for the win!"

Dani laughed and bumped Cat's fist in return. "Sisters in science."

Cat couldn't seem to stand still. Not only had their project won the McMurray Award, but now she had a real partner. Cat was sure this wouldn't be their last adventure.

And oh, did she ever have some ideas on what Science and Strange could investigate next . . .

"Cat?" Her mom's voice brought her back down to earth.

"Hi, Mom."

"This looks great," her mom said, taking in their poster board with a big smile. She touched the first-place ribbon. "Congratulations to both of you."

Dani's smile was wide and genuine. "Thanks for coming, Mrs. Mulvaney."

"I wouldn't have missed it. Cat, I'm so glad you found a partner to work with. I'm just sorry you two got dragged into your teacher's terrible antics."

Cat had told her mom everything about what had happened with Ms. Blanks, down to the last detail. When Detective Lewis had confirmed that Ms. Blanks was their primary suspect in the lab explosion and the EMP deployment, any remaining disbelief had vanished.

"Oh, Cat," her mom said. "Your father should be calling any minute. He wanted to see your presentation on FaceTime, since he can't be here in person."

Her dad's reaction to their adventure had been a little different from her mom's. He'd been solemn when he'd called after viewing the recorded live stream. "Be careful, Cat," he'd said. "The truth scares people. Some will go to great lengths to hide it, especially when people come uncomfortably close to it."

Then he'd agreed to replace some of her equipment as an early Christmas present. It wasn't only that Cat had been exonerated from carelessly ruining her tech. She might have laid on the guilt over him forgetting to call on her birthday a *little* thick. But the guilt trip was for a good cause: scientific advancement. So . . . worth it.

Right on cue, Cat's new iPhone—*thanks, Dad*—began to ring. She answered it and said, "Hi, Dad," waving at the screen. "Can you see me okay?"

"Hey, honey. Yep, the picture's great."

Cat held up the phone to Dani. "This is my partner, Dani!"

Dani waved. "Hi, Mr. Mulvaney. Thanks so much for the potassium permanganate and the colorimeter. They were really helpful."

"Glad to hear it," Cat's dad said.

Cat panned the phone slowly over their poster board, taking the time to explain each test they'd run and the results they'd found. "The judges loved it! We won first place in our division!" Cat squealed again. "The best part is, we get to go to ScienceU next summer!"

"This looks quite thorough, sweetheart. I'm very proud of you."

Cat grinned, feeling warm and fuzzy inside. Her dad might not be here in person, but this was the next best thing.

"Well, I've got to go," her dad said, "but I'm glad I got to see your project. Love you, kiddo."

"Love you, too. Bye, Dad," Cat said and then slid the phone back in her pocket.

"Really great work, girls." Her mom gave her a hug and a kiss on the forehead. "Dani, if your parents are here, I'd love to say hello."

"Yeah, they're here somewhere . . . ," Dani said, rising up onto her toes to peer across the room.

Cat's mom nodded and walked away, and then it was just Dani and Cat.

Science and Strange.

That really did have such a nice ring to it.

As the afternoon wore on, their display got lots of visitors. Many were curious about the conspiracy they'd uncovered, but plenty asked questions about their science and methodology, too. The judges had almost finished putting ribbons on all the winning projects when a boy with messy blond hair and dirty Converse sneakers walked up.

"Hey," he said. "I'm Johnny Lee. I heard some other kids talking about your project." He leaned forward. "Was your teacher really a Man in Black?"

Cat cleared her throat as Dani raised an eyebrow at her. Even though they'd decided to leave that phrase out of their final presentation, Cat might have mentioned the whole Men in Black thing and government conspiracy once or twice . . . in the past hour.

"She was." Cat certainly wasn't going to deny it when asked outright. "And," she said, speaking faster, "we don't know where they got the drone technology they were testing. Maybe they were trying to replicate something from the Roswell crash! Or—"

"Cat." Dani cut her off, laughing. "Really?"

"Aliens are real, Dani. Maybe they weren't responsible this time, but even the government admits there are UFOs. The evidence they've released proves it, and who knows what else they're still keeping top secret?"

Dani rolled her eyes, but Cat could tell she was more amused than annoyed. "There may have been some unidentified flying objects caught on film," she said, "but that doesn't mean every advanced piece of technology out there is extraterrestrial."

Now it was Cat's turn to shake her head. "Someday, Dani, you'll see I'm right."

"You guys should visit our town sometime," Johnny cut in. "We may not have crop circles, but we do have a lake monster."

Dani, who'd been taking a sip of one of the many Mountain Dews Cat had brought, nearly spit out her soda. "Lake monster?"

"Yeah, kind of like Nessie, but in Springfield. Lots of people have reported sightings. If you guys like weird science, maybe you'll want to check it out."

Cat's gears began to turn. "We would totally—"

"Cool, sounds fun." Dani was already ushering the boy away. "Thanks for stopping by!"

"I'll be in touch!" he called over his shoulder as he left.

"Dani, we have to go to Springfield!" Cat bounced on her toes. "It can be our next project!"

"I was hoping that next year's McMurray proposal would be something more earthbound," Dani said wryly.

"A lake monster is totally earthbound!"

"Technically, a lake monster would be water-bound," Dani countered. "And you know that's not what I meant."

"Okay, then not for the McMurray Competition. We could investigate stuff just for fun! I can see it now: Science and Strange, Paranormal Investigators! We could make a logo and everything."

Dani mulled it over. "You said your dad is going to replace some of your lab equipment?"

Cat nodded excitedly. "Pretty much everything but the mass spectrometer. He's still upset about that one."

"I bet there are lots of people who have strange things happening in their hometowns," Dani said. "We could work together to rule out any paranormal elements."

"Or . . . rule them *in*," Cat threw back.

Dani snorted. "Do you promise there will be just as much science as strange?"

"More, even!"

"Then I guess we'll have to plan a trip to Springfield."

Cat threw her arms around Dani, surprising both of them. "This is going to be awesome!"

"I think you're right," Dani said. She pulled one of the T-shirts her friends had made over her head. "Turns out, you and I make a pretty good team."

Cat smiled so wide, her face hurt. "So we're doing this?"

"Is the goliath birdeater the largest known species of spider?"

Cat laughed. "I'm assuming that's a yes?" At Dani's nod, she held out her hand to shake. When Dani took it, Cat felt a shiver of anticipation run up her spine. "Now," she said. "Why don't I tell you everything I know about lake monsters?"

ACKNOWLEDGMENTS

First and foremost, we want to thank each other! Since Kathryn first asked MarcyKate if she would consider trying to write a book together back in fall 2017, this collaboration has been pure joy.

Thanks to our editor, Holly West, who responded to our initial submission with the most insightful revision letter. Although at the time, it was a pass, you inspired us and helped *The Thirteenth Circle* dig deeper and soar higher. We are infinitely grateful to have you on our team. And to the rest of the crew at Feiwel & Friends: We are so lucky to be working with you. Thanks for everything you do.

Thanks also to agents Suzie Townsend and Alyssa Eisner Henkin for their shrewd notes on the early drafts and for working together to find this book the right home. Additional thanks to Sophia Ramos, Dani Segelbaum, and Alice Fugate for their work on this project over the years.

Thanks to artist Brittney Bond for creating the cover illustration of our dreams.

Writing this book involved a *lot* of research. In particular, Kathryn would like to thank Robert R. Schindelbeck, Extension Associate and Director of the Soil Health Lab at Cornell University's School of Integrative Plant Science, for sharing his extensive knowledge and for being willing to brainstorm how a UFO might impact soil health. Kathryn also thanks Brooklyn-based educator Nancy Landau-Gahres for her advice on middle school science curriculum and experiment design.

MarcyKate would be remiss if she did not give a shout-out to the unidentified flying object that flew over her neighbor's house in late fall 1989 and launched her own lifelong obsession with UFOs. Over the years, many books, movies, and TV shows have prepared her to write a book like this one, but she would particularly like to thank the TV show *Expedition Unknown* and host Josh Gates for providing a wealth of inspiration regarding UFOs and demonstrating how to take a scientific approach to investigating the weird and wonderful. And just about every UFO-related documentary, show, and special that's been on the Discovery Channel in the last several years. Also, the wonderful people from Lull Farms and Brookdale Farms in Hollis, New Hampshire, who were kind enough to sell us individual stalks of corn so we could test some of the experiments described in the book.

Thanks as well to Emily Deibert, PhD, a working scientist and middle grade writer, for the scientific authenticity read. We are so grateful for your feedback.

To our families: Jason, Logan, and Xavier; Justin and Evelyn. You're our "one in five billion."

And finally, to our readers. Thank you for going on this adventure with us. The truth is out there—and you have the power to find it.